HOT SHOT

A *HOSTILE OPERATIONS TEAM* Novel

USA TODAY BESTSELLING AUTHOR

LYNN RAYE HARRIS

Copyright © 2014 by Lynn Raye Harris
Cover Design © 2014 Croco Designs
Photo of male model © Jenn LeBlanc/Illustrated Romance.
Interior Design by JT Formatting

www.**lynnrayeharris**.com

Printed in the United States of America

First Edition: July 2014
Library of Congress Cataloging-in-Publication Data

Harris, Lynn Raye
        Hot Shot / Lynn Raye Harris. – 1st ed

        ISBN-13: 978-0-9894512-7-7

        1. Hot Shot—Fiction. 2. Fiction—Romance
        3. Fiction—Contemporary Romance

OTHER BOOKS IN
THE *HOSTILE OPERATIONS TEAM* SERIES

ONE

Three years ago…

JACK HUNTER RESISTED THE URGE to shrug. He'd been lying in this position for six hours now, waiting for Athenasios Metaxas to emerge from the safety of his private retreat on this remote stretch of beach in the Caribbean.

Nick Brandon lay beside him, eye to his spotter's scope, searching for signs of the target. Jack rolled his neck and squared his eye over the lens again. All he had in his crosshairs were a few windows. There were lights on inside, but the only movement he'd seen had been a maid.

"No sign of the target," he reported.

"Copy," came Kev MacDonald's voice over the earpiece.

Jack sighted down the scope again and dialed two mils to the right on Brandy's instruction. They were 750 yards away, which was closer than they liked to be, but the terrain was such that this was the best location. Nowhere else had a visual of the entire rear portion of the house.

It was a full moon. The light shone down on the gleaming stucco of the villa, illuminating the pool and patio area. At the end of a long dock, a sixty-foot yacht lay at anchor. The yacht was dark.

Metaxas had been sailing the Caribbean for the past week, but now he was here and scheduled to meet with several men—terrorists—who'd traveled from the Middle East and were due to arrive tonight via helicopter. The helipad was lit but empty.

Jack pulled in a breath, his finger resting beside the trigger. He was patient—you had to be patient to be a sniper—but this was one op where he couldn't wait to pull the trigger.

Because HOT wasn't going to let that meeting happen. Metaxas had been a thorn in their side for years, but he'd recently taken his dirty dealings up a notch. If this deal was allowed to take place, a whole lot of bad people would be getting shiny new weapons with which to kill innocent civilians.

Not happening.

"Movement," Nick said.

"I see it."

A moment later, the rear doors slid open and a woman walked outside. Waves of blond hair cascaded down her back, shining almost white in the moonlight. She was wearing a bikini that barely covered her tits and ass, and she had on high heels that made her legs look a mile long.

"Jesus," Nick breathed.

"Yeah." Jack didn't typically lose his head over a gorgeous woman, but even he had to admit that this one was put together in ways designed to make a man drool. Just another brainless bunny attracted to a rich man and doing everything she could to keep him interested.

"No. I mean, yes, she's hot—but that's not it. We got a problem here."

Jack took his eyes off the scope and turned to look at his spotter.

Brandy glanced at him. "You don't recognize her?"

"Should I?"

"Dude, that's just about the hottest fucking pop star in the world right now. Haven't you ever heard of Gina Domenico?"

Jack sighted down the scope again, focusing on the woman's face. Christ Almighty on a cracker, they so did not need this right now. If he dropped Metaxas and his guests tonight, even with the maid and other household servants present, it wouldn't be huge news. It would be a blip on the radar. An interesting tidbit mentioned on the evening news and quickly forgotten in most quarters.

If he dropped the bastard while a fucking American pop star was a guest, it'd be all over the news within hours—if it wasn't trending on Twitter sooner. And while no one would connect an arms dealer's death to HOT or the American government, the attention would be magnified a thousandfold if Gina Domenico was involved.

"I've heard of her," he bit out. He'd more than heard of her. His wife had loved Gina Domenico. Hayley had bought all her CDs and played them incessantly. His heart burned with thoughts of his wife. After her death, he'd never wanted to listen to another Gina Domenico song in his life. He'd shredded the CDs and smashed Hayley's iPod.

The woman on the patio pranced on her high heels toward the pool, hands on hips. Then she put a hand to her forehead and whirled around again. She marched over to the lounge chair where she'd set a bag and fished out a cell phone.

Double fuck.

"What's going on there, Hawk?" It was Kev "Big Mac" MacDonald's voice calling him by his team name. "Report."

"Complication. Gina fucking Domenico just walked out of Metaxas's house. She's standing by the pool right now."

"Goddammit," Kev said. "Stand down until I report this."

"Copy."

Nick continued to take readings of the wind speed and direction, and Jack continued watching Gina through the scope. He knew who she was, but he hadn't paid any attention to her before. Hayley hadn't been the sort of woman to buy celebrity magazines or watch tabloid television. Jack recognized the star now that he knew who she was, but until Nick had said so, he'd just thought she was the latest hot blonde fucking Metaxas.

And wasn't she? Didn't matter if she was a pop star or not. There was no other reason for her to be here.

"Shit," Nick groaned.

Jack didn't answer, but he heard it too—a helicopter slicing through the night and getting louder as it got closer.

The helicopter swooped in over the ocean and set down on the pad. The door to the house opened and Metaxas swaggered outside. He went over and sat at a table while the maid hurried out with a tray containing food and beer. Someone flipped a switch and more lights came on, illuminating the pool and the blonde. She put her phone back in her bag and sauntered over to where Metaxas sat. He dragged her onto his lap and kissed her.

She pushed him away, finally stumbling to her feet and tugging her bikini back into place while Metaxas laughed. She did *not* look happy as she marched back over to her bag and tugged out a robe, belting it around her waist with almost furious movements.

But Jack couldn't worry about her. The helicopter's rotors slowed as three men emerged from the craft.

"Seriously need some guidance here," Jack growled into the headset. "Tangos on scene."

Jack didn't think he was going to get an answer at first, but Kev's voice came over the earpiece. "You're cleared. Get it done and get out."

Thank God. Jack's heartbeat slowed to a crawl as he watched the three men walk toward the patio where Metaxas sat. He stood and held his arms out, saying something in welcome. Gina picked up her bag and started for the door. Jack wanted to wait until she went inside, but he couldn't take the chance that the men would follow her.

"One mil to the left," Nick said.

Jack turned the dial. The crosshairs lined up perfectly on Metaxas's head. Jack pulled in another breath—and then squeezed the trigger on the exhale when his body was perfectly still.

Metaxas dropped like a stone. Jack sighted and fired three more times, dropping the other tangos as they tried to run.

Gina Domenico screamed. And then she grappled with the door handle, yanking open the door just as two of Metaxas's bodyguards came rushing out. One of them grabbed her by the arm and jerked her around when she tried to run past him.

"Shit," Jack said. And then he made a decision that shocked even him. He hadn't had any feelings since the moment he'd gotten the news that Hayley had hydroplaned her car on the way to work and smashed into a tree.

Strike that. He hadn't had any feelings for anyone but her and their unborn baby since then. But this woman had meant something to Hayley, and he couldn't walk away from that. What would she think of him if he did? Hayley'd had a heart bigger than anyone he'd ever known. She would never leave anyone to suffer if she could help.

"Big Mac, we can't leave her with those people. Metaxas's men will think she was involved somehow."

"We can't help that."

Jack could hear her screaming, even at this distance. And then the man holding her slapped her so hard her head jerked to the side.

"They'll kill her. You know it as well as I do. And that will mean a media field day when the press gets hold of this."

"We can't go in," Kev said. "It's not authorized."

Beside him, Nick was still feeding him information. Because Brandy knew he was gonna take the shot. *Two shots.*

And his spotter was with him.

The man hit her again, knocking her head back the other way. Jack dropped him, and then he dropped the other one. Stupid sons of bitches. If they'd had any sense, they'd have gone inside and stayed away from the windows. Who walked outside, saw four dead bodies that had clearly been shot from long range, and then stayed out there while the unknown assailant was still around?

The helo pilot spun up the rotors. Jack took aim and placed a round in the engine. The helicopter sputtered and coughed. It wasn't going anywhere tonight.

"Goddammit, Hawk," Kev said over the headset. And then he huffed out a breath. "Get to the extraction point double-quick. We got company coming."

He sighted down to the patio again. Gina was gone. If there were more men inside, he didn't know, but he'd given her a chance at least.

"Copy," he said as he and Nick started to break down the gear.

Gina didn't bother with her suitcase. Everything important was in her beach bag anyway. She ran through the house until she hit the garage. The maid was screaming and crying somewhere behind her, but Gina wasn't hanging around to see what happened next. Athenasios had more men in his compound, and it would only be a matter of minutes before they arrived. And she didn't want to try to explain why she was still alive when their boss wasn't.

She'd heard the crack of a gun in the night, and then she'd turned around to see Athenasios on the ground with his head split like a melon and his guests dropping one by one in succession.

And then the bodyguards had come outside and one of them had grabbed her, shouting accusations and threats. Her face still hurt where he'd hit her. She had enough personal experience getting hit to know she'd be bruised tomorrow.

Gina hurried over to the closest car—a Mercedes of some sort—and yanked open the door. Athenasios kept the keys in his cars while they were garaged because he said no one would dare to steal from him.

And this wasn't stealing, she told herself firmly as she pressed the button to start the engine. This was borrowing from a dead man.

But she had to get out of here. She didn't know who had shot Athenasios or why, but she wasn't sticking around to find out. She'd discovered during her weeklong journey on his yacht that he wasn't quite the nice Greek industrialist he claimed to be. She'd wanted to escape before now, but there'd been nowhere to go when sailing across an ocean.

God, she'd been so stupid. She'd thought a man like Athenasios could protect her, that his power to keep the media away and give her a much-needed respite from the spotlight was a blessing.

Instead, it had been a curse. She'd been trapped, and now she would be dead if she didn't get away.

The garage door cranked up slowly and she jammed the gas before the door was all the way up, just sliding under it with enough clearance to get out. Gina whipped the car around and shoved the gearshift into drive. Then she was bolting down the driveway and out onto the road.

She had no idea where to go, but she hoped she'd stumble onto civilization if she drove far enough.

The full moon helped illuminate the road, but it was twisty and turny and her heart pounded as she navigated the hairpin curves. And then she caught a flash of headlights behind her and her stomach fell to her toes.

Athenasios's house was remote. While she supposed it was possible that someone was simply out for a drive, she wasn't betting on it. Either some of his men had come after her, or whoever had shot all those men was after her too.

Maybe it was a kidnapping attempt. Her blood froze at that thought. There had been threats against her, but that was pretty much expected when you were as high profile as she was. Tears pressed against the backs of her eyes, but she refused to let them fall. She'd just wanted to escape the fishbowl of her life for a while. Just a while, dammit.

Out of the frying pan and into the fire, Regina—that's what her mother would have said if she were still alive.

Gina stomped on the gas and whipped the Mercedes around corners like an IndyCar driver. Thank God her manager had made her take that defensive-driving course a few months ago. If she made it out of here alive, she'd kiss Barry for that.

Trees overhung the road, obscuring her vision. The headlights did their job, but it wasn't as good as when she'd had moonlight too. Behind her, headlights flashed through the trees from time to time. If the car wasn't following her, then she should have left it behind when she sped up.

But they were coming for her. Gina pressed the pedal down again, hoping she was better at navigating these curves than they were.

Up ahead, a dirt track led off the road and into the trees. Part of her said to keep going, but part of her said she had to get off the road and hide. At the last second, she whipped onto the track. The car bumped and thumped against the ground until she slowed down. Gina had to turn off the lights, even though it would mean she couldn't see. Slowing to a crawl, she tried to navigate her way farther off the road. Once she was out of sight, she rolled the window down, listening for the sounds of another car. It was screaming up the incline and she swallowed a knot of panic.

Gina stopped the car and waited. Finally, the other engine roared by and kept going down the road. She made herself breathe slowly, in and out and in and out, but her heart still pounded hard. She would have to wait here for quite some time before it would be safe to go.

Though maybe this track went somewhere. She turned on the parking lights and drove slowly down the road. And then the front wheels dropped from beneath her and she realized too late that she'd hit a ditch.

She put the car in reverse and tried to back out of the gully, but the wheels spun wildly.

Gina dropped her head to the steering wheel. Now what? Tears flowed freely, and that made her angry. She wasn't a quitter, dammit!

She sat up, determined to try again—and a bush with eyes appeared in front of her. A wave of fright washed over her, immobilizing her. And then she frantically grappled for the power button on the window.

But the bush moved toward her—and the window wasn't going up.

TWO

SHE DIDN'T SCREAM. JACK FOUND that intriguing because he would have bet his right nut that a woman as pampered as she was would scream. He had his hand on the door and she was frantically trying to lift the window.

Then she hit his hands with the heels of hers. He grabbed her wrists and held her hard.

"Miss Domenico, it's okay. I'm not here to hurt you."

She blinked those green eyes of hers. They were shimmery with tears. Silvery tracks streaked down her cheeks, and he knew she'd been crying. But she hadn't screamed when he'd materialized in front of her. The ghillie suit he wore was designed to make him disappear in terrain such as this. He could have stayed hidden, but she'd driven right toward him. And then she'd gotten stuck.

Maybe he should have left her, but he could hear Hayley's voice in his head, telling him he had to help. In spite of the fact he and Brandy had split up because they'd been taking fire, in spite of the fact he was late to the extraction point, in spite of it all. If her being here at this

11

moment wasn't a sign from the universe, he didn't know what was.

"Wh…who are you? If it's money you want, my manager will pay."

He blinked. And then he realized what she meant. Ransom. She thought he was here to kidnap her.

"Miss Domenico, I'm not interested in money. I'm here to help you."

"Y…you are? Who sent you?"

How to answer that one? "The United States Army, ma'am." It was close enough to the truth, and maybe if she thought he was one of the good guys, she'd calm down.

She didn't look too happy with the information, though. In fact, he'd swear she'd just cringed. He let her wrists go and she sank back into her seat.

"The car's stuck, ma'am. You'll have to come with me if you want to get out of here."

"I'm wearing a swimsuit and high heels." Her eyes widened. "Oh wait, I have flip-flops in my bag."

He had emergency gear in his rucksack, including a Mylar survival blanket. If he could get them somewhere hidden, he could take care of them both long enough for help to arrive.

"I'm afraid you have no choice, ma'am. If you stay here, they'll find you eventually. If you come with me, I'll get you out safely."

She chewed her lip as she looked at him. He knew he looked strange, like a bush with a face—though even his face was darkened with greasepaint. The only thing that made him look human would be his eyes and the flash of his teeth when he spoke.

"You still haven't told me your name."

"Jack Hunter." He cleared his throat. "My wife was a big fan."

"Was?"

And there it was, that twist in his heart that still caught him unaware sometimes. It'd only been eight months, so it wasn't unexpected—and yet it hurt.

"She died, ma'am."

Her breath hitched. "Oh, I'm sorry." She reached for the handle and opened the door. And then she stood and dragged her beach bag with her. Swiftly, she changed her shoes—but she didn't leave the old ones behind. He would have told her not to because it was positive ID she'd been in the car, but either she'd thought of that or she just loved her shoes.

She fixed him with a determined look. "All right, Jack Hunter. I'm ready. But you have to call me Gina, okay?"

"Yes, ma'am. I mean Gina." He pointed to the east. "That's the direction we're going. About six miles, and we'll come out on a beach with sea caves. We'll hide there until help arrives."

She swallowed. "Sounds fun."

He cocked his head as he stared at her, but then he decided she was making a joke. The word that kept swirling in his brain when he looked at her was *tough*. It was turning out to be a surprise. She was tougher than he'd thought she would be. Smarter too, he'd bet.

"Then let's go." He hadn't taken but a few steps when she called out.

"I can't see you. You disappear."

The ghillie suit. He turned back to her. "We can't turn on any lights, I'm afraid."

He thought about asking her to hold on to his suit, but it was possible pieces of the camouflage would tear away. There was only one solution he could think of.

"You'll have to hold my hand."

He stretched out his hand to her and she placed hers inside. He felt a jolt of awareness throttle through him. It was shocking to his system after all this time. He hadn't wanted a woman since Hayley died—and he still didn't, goddamn it—but for the first time since then, sexual awareness reared up and reminded him that he hadn't lost the ability to feel desire.

Jesus H. Christ.

He wanted to let her go, but a tremor passed through her and he knew he couldn't. He'd said he was here to help, and by God he was going to help. Even if he had to suffer from the things her touch was doing to him.

Gina did her best to keep up with Jack. When she stumbled, he slowed, and when they reached any obstacles, he helped her through. She'd lost count of how many times his hands had spanned her waist, but she hadn't lost sight of how sparks had zinged through her every time. She kept telling herself it was nothing when in fact it was terribly disconcerting.

She'd learned a long time ago that sex was a weapon people often used against each other. And she really should have remembered it when she'd made the decision to date Athenasios Metaxas. He'd come to one of her concerts in Greece a couple of months ago, and he'd been so handsome and suave—and he'd commanded such power over his domain that he'd made her feel safe.

Until this past week when he'd shown his true nature. He'd wooed her with such meticulous attention to detail that she'd thought he was a dream come true. His brother had given her the creeps, always staring at her, but Athenasios had seemed perfectly normal.

He'd flown to wherever she was staying, wined and dined her, and behaved like a perfect gentleman. He'd called her—not too often—and told her how lovely she was and how much he enjoyed her company. And then he'd asked her to go sailing in the Caribbean with him.

She'd agreed.

That's when she'd discovered he wasn't a dream at all. He was brutal and thoughtless and he believed women were his for the taking. Her included. He hadn't raped her—she couldn't call it that—but he'd forced the issue when she wasn't quite certain she was ready to take that step with him. Then he'd started making plans for her life as if he had every right to do so.

Gina shivered as she remembered how helpless she'd felt, how trapped.

"You okay?"

She looked up at the dark blur that was her companion. If he hadn't been holding her hand, she would have thought he wasn't there at all. He spoke quietly, and she pitched her voice low when she answered, remembering that he'd told her it was okay to talk so long as she was quiet.

"Fine. Just tired. And a mosquito bit me. Guess I

missed a spot with the bug spray."

He chuckled. The sound warmed her. He'd been amused when she'd pulled bug spray from her bag and doused herself.

"Sorry to laugh. It's not funny."

"No, I don't mind. You have to laugh at something, right?"

"You amaze me with how calm you are about all this."

She waved a hand. "Oh, I hike through the woods in a bikini and a robe all the time. It's especially fun when running away from madmen."

"Yeah."

She bit her lip. "I guess if you're with the Army, you must know something about what happened back there."

"I do. But I'm afraid I can't tell you about it."

"I was there. I saw it. Someone shot Athenasios and the men who arrived by helicopter. And then they shot the bodyguards."

"You really need to keep those details to yourself when you get home."

"Trust me, I don't want anyone knowing I was anywhere near there when it happened."

"Wasn't he your boyfriend?"

Her hand tightened on his, but she quickly made herself relax. She couldn't pretend Athenasios had been a good person when she knew better. In many ways, he'd been no different from the men her mother had dated who'd hit her when she was a teenager. "Not really. Our relationship, such as it was, was definitely ending just as soon as I got away from him."

"Too bad you didn't leave sooner."

"I tried. He wouldn't let me."

He didn't say anything for a long moment. "It's good you're out of there. He wasn't a nice man."

"No, I know it now. I suck at picking men, apparently. It's a family trait, passed down from mother to daughter."

"I'm sorry to hear that."

Gina sniffed. She liked the comforting feel of his hand on hers. Especially when he gave her a little squeeze of support.

"Would you tell me about your wife? Unless it's too painful."

He didn't say anything for a long while. She didn't know why she'd asked, except she'd wanted to think about something other than the fact she was currently on the run from Athenasios's men—and who knows who else.

"We were high school sweethearts," he began, his voice a little rusty. "I joined the Army after school and we ended it, but I found that I didn't like being without her. So I went back and married her a couple of years ago. She was a vet tech."

"She wasn't easy to forget."

"No." He pulled in a breath. "Still isn't. Hayley was on her way to work during a bad storm when her car hit a patch of water and hydroplaned out of control. Broke through a railing and landed upside down in a creek. The impact killed her, which was a good thing because the creek waters were rising. She was scared of drowning, so I'm glad she didn't go that way."

She squeezed his hand convulsively. "Oh Jack, I'm so sorry. I shouldn't have asked."

"No, it's fine. The counselor said I have to talk about

it. It was eight months ago. She'd have been in the hospital having our baby right now."

Oh God, this did not get any better, did it? Gina swallowed the lump in her throat. He spoke so calmly, but she knew it had to be killing him inside. She didn't know him at all, and yet she hurt for him.

"I'm sorry is so inadequate, but it's all I know to say."

"It's all anyone can say. What else is there?" He was quiet for a while as they trod through the woods. She noticed that he stopped and listened every so often. But there was nothing out here other than typical night sounds. She tried not to think about snakes or spiders—or heaven knows what else liked to hang out in tropical jungles.

When he spoke again, though he was always so quiet when he did, the sound startled her. "Hayley loved your music. Drove me crazy listening to your albums. I haven't listened to any of your songs since she died. Don't want to hear them."

"I understand."

Some of her songs came from a deep well of pain and insecurity inside, and she was especially proud of them. But others, the ones her manager always pushed her toward, were big splashy numbers with thumping beats and killer dance moves. Those were the ones that had made her popular. But she wouldn't ask which songs Hayley had liked more. Maybe it was best she didn't know.

She'd been wanting to make a change for a while now, but every time she tried to get her way, a phalanx of music company executives and flunkies came down on her hard. So did her manager.

"Star power sells, Gina." "The kids love the dance

numbers." "You're outselling Beyoncé now—do you want to fuck that up?"

Maybe she did. Hell, she didn't know what she wanted, but she knew that she wasn't satisfied lately. As someone who had everything she could ever want, she felt guilty for complaining.

So she mostly didn't. Except sometimes, dammit, she wished she could have something more. Something that couldn't be bought.

Up ahead, it seemed lighter out, and she realized they were approaching the edge of the woods. The sound of the ocean swelling against the beach reached her ears and her stomach twisted. What was waiting for them out there?

"Will we make it out of here alive?" she whispered.

"That's my plan. Don't worry, I've been in tougher spots than this and here I am. Metaxas's men are amateurs, and that's an advantage for us."

They skirted the edge of the woods for a while, until he determined they were where he wanted them to be. They emerged from the woods and hurried along a cliff face until he found the caves he was looking for. Gina hesitated in the entrance.

It wasn't a cave so much as a nook carved into the rock. Once she climbed in there with him, they'd have to stay close together until they were rescued.

He turned to look at her after he slung his rucksack down and stowed the rifle he was toting. And wow, it was some rifle. She hadn't realized everything he'd been carrying when they'd been in the woods. But now the moonlight illuminated more than she'd seen before.

"Why do you look like a bush?"

His teeth flashed white. "Camouflage. No one notices

another bush, right? Helps me get close enough to the target."

Target. Gina gulped as fresh understanding dawned. "Are you the one who shot those men?"

The light in his eyes dimmed a little. But then he nodded. "That's my job."

Her heart thudded. He'd shot four men in the blink of an eye. And then two more when that bodyguard had been slapping her around. She should be horrified, and yet...

"The last two... Were they part of the job too?"

His gaze was steady. "No."

She dropped her eyes from his, unable to look at him for the worry she'd let too much show in her face. Fear, gratitude. Awareness.

"Thank you." Her voice was soft, her throat tight.

"You have to get inside now, Gina. I know it's not a lot of room, but you're safe with me."

She looked up then, let him see what was in her eyes. She'd never trusted anyone so quickly in her life. But she knew, inherently, that she could trust him. "I know I am."

He held his hand out and she took it, her skin sizzling with the contact. They stared at each other for a long minute—and then they went inside and sank onto the sand together.

THREE

THEY SPENT THE HEAT OF the day in the small cave. It went back far enough that they could get out of the sun, but it was narrower at the rear and they had to sit side by side, bodies touching as they watched the ocean swells rolling in. They couldn't see the beach from where they were since they'd had to climb up a little bit to reach the cave.

Jack had removed the bush—aka ghillie suit—and sat beside her in a muscle-hugging black T-shirt, military camo pants, and boots. Gina was aware of him in ways she'd rather not be.

But he'd wiped the greasepaint from his face with a cloth, and her breath had caught at what was under there. A day's worth of stubble adorned a face that would have looked good on an action-film poster. His hair was blond, his eyes piercing blue, and the hint of a dimple in his cheek when he smiled was enough to make her heart thump.

Not that he smiled much. He'd opened up his pack and given her an energy bar and some water, which he'd told her to conserve. They'd sat in companionable silence for a long while, and then she'd dozed, waking when it was broad daylight to discover that she'd fallen asleep against him and that he'd put his arm around her so she would be more comfortable.

She'd apologized, but he'd shrugged and said it was no big deal. Though she hadn't intended to, she fell asleep again, and when she woke this time, it was dark. She blinked at her surroundings, but then it all came back to her, and she pushed away once more from the solid mountain that was Jack Hunter.

"You feeling okay?" he asked.

Gina sat up and stretched. Her face throbbed where Athenasios's thug had hit her, and she was a bit sore after hiking through the woods in flip-flops, but she was alive and that was something.

"I'm okay. A bit stiff."

"When the moon sets, we'll get out of here for a bit. Go for a swim. The saltwater will help."

Gina was doubtful, but on the other hand, she'd love to stand up for a while. A shaft of moonlight shone into the cave, and she turned her head this way and that, trying to relieve the stiffness in her neck.

Jack swore softly, and then she felt his hand on her chin. He was gentle, but she flinched anyway.

"I won't hurt you."

"I know." And she did know it, but he'd surprised her.

"You're starting to bruise. I've got a cold pack."

He turned to his rucksack, and she marveled at all the things he had in there. It wasn't huge, but it carried an arsenal of supplies, weaponry, and medicine. And condoms.

Her eyes widened as he set some of those aside for a moment.

"Wow, you really are prepared."

He glanced at her over his shoulder. "A bit of everything in here."

"Including condoms."

He grinned. "They're for keeping ammo dry. You'd be surprised."

"I guess I would."

He pulled out a bag that he squeezed and shook. When he handed it to her, it was cold.

Gina put it to her face, wincing a little as she did so. "Thanks."

He was putting stuff back in the pack. "I'm sorry I couldn't stop that from happening."

Her heart contracted at the regret in his voice. He cared and she liked that. No one cared much about her as a person so much as they did about her status and money.

Stop. That's pitiful, and you aren't pitiful.

Damn straight. She'd never been pitiful and she wasn't going to start now. Poor little rich girl. She was self-made, but money came with heartaches of its own. She'd learned that lesson only too well, but she still wasn't going to whine.

"You saved my life. I'd be pretty ungrateful if I was angry because someone hit me first. Wouldn't be the first time it happened."

He grew still. "What does that mean?"

She was embarrassed she'd said that much—and then she thought, *What the hell?* He was a stranger to her and it no longer mattered. Maybe they wouldn't make it out of here anyway, no matter what he said. Why keep pretending?

"It means I didn't have a dad. It means I had a mother who changed boyfriends like most people change socks. It means that some of them were angry, and some of them lashed out."

"Jesus," he said. "I'm sorry."

She shrugged. "It was a long time ago. I'm over it."

"If it helps, I'd shoot those men for you if I could."

She laughed, though maybe she shouldn't. "I almost wish you could." She pulled in a breath and shifted the Mylar blanket he'd given her earlier over her body. "The worst one was a guy named Randy. He was a soldier. He liked to drink and slap women around. Mom first, then me. And then one day he had a bulge in his pants when he was hitting me—and I just knew I had to go."

"Christ, Gina." He sounded horrified, and she liked him even more.

"Nothing happened. I ran away that night, and that was it. The end of Regina Robertson and the beginning of Gina Domenico, though it took a lot of years of hard work. I slept on streets sometimes, in bus stations and dodgy apartments…" She shook her head. "I don't know why I'm telling you this."

"I don't mind."

"No selling your story to the tabloids later, all right?"

It was his turn to laugh. "Sweetheart, my boss would hang my ass from the spire of the Capitol if I did such a thing. Even if it wasn't against my moral code, it'd be career suicide—and this is all I have now."

She hated how lonely he sounded. She reached out and put her hand on his. His skin was warm, and once more that sizzle of lightning flooded her. "I was kidding,

Jack. I know you won't go to the press."

He didn't move for a long moment, and then he turned his hand and ran his fingers against her palm, softly, sweetly. It was as if he'd touched the heart of her, because her entire body grew tight with anticipation.

"What made you choose the name Gina Domenico?" His voice was soft, and she knew he was deliberately moving on. Getting her away from the awkwardness of what she'd just told him.

"My mom always called me Gina, so that was easy. And then I saw a story about an Italian artist named Domenico something-or-other." She laughed. "I can't remember his last name, but I never forgot Domenico. It sounded foreign, classy, and I decided that would be my stage name."

"It worked for you."

"Definitely." She wanted to whimper when he dropped his hand away. "What about you, Jack? How did you end up here?"

"I joined the Army because I wanted adventure and a paycheck. Here I am."

She sensed it wasn't the whole story, but she had no right to push him. "Here you are. Good for me."

His gaze dropped to her mouth and sparks snapped in her belly. It shocked her that she wanted to lean into him, press her mouth to his, and feel his heat and strength. After the last week with Athenasios, it surprised her that she could want that kind of closeness with any man right now.

He pushed away from her and crawled toward the mouth of the cave. Then he shot her a look over his shoulder. "Moon's nearly gone. Want to get out of here for a bit?"

"Sure." She crawled out of the cave and stood up. Jack walked away from her as if he couldn't stand to be near her for a moment longer. She tried not to let it bother her as she strode down the beach and stopped at the edge of the water.

But it did.

Living in a tight cave with this woman wasn't exactly easy. Or comfortable. Jack shifted for the millionth time that day, trying to relieve the pressure of a hard-on. Last night he'd had to get out of the cave before he did something stupid. She'd been looking at him with wide, trusting eyes, and he'd found himself wanting to kiss her.

It pissed him off. And scared him too.

He hadn't wanted a woman since Hayley died, and now he was stuck in a tight spot with a woman who was miles out of his league by anyone's measure—and all he could think about was stripping her out of that damn bikini and burying his aching cock in her body.

Shit.

She stirred against him and he knew she was waking. It was almost dark out, and soon they could get outside again. He couldn't wait. Except, after they'd swam and exercised a bit last night, it had been chilly in the cave and they'd ended up huddling together for body heat since they couldn't have a fire. The Mylar blanket was meant for one, so if he didn't want to freeze, he had to get under it with her.

Her robe was pitiful protection against the cool night air, so he'd wrapped his arms around her and let her burrow.

They talked, but no matter how much they said or how many things they discussed, his body stayed in a perpetual state of arousal. He couldn't wait for HOT to find them. He'd sent a signal, but he had to be careful with the electronics in case Metaxas's men were also looking for them.

"Hey," she said.

He looked down to see her smiling up at him. He liked her smile. "Hey yourself."

She shifted away from him and he let out a small sigh of relief. When she touched him, his entire body lit up like a beacon. He'd been thinking about that for a while now, and he knew it had to be because it had been so long since *anyone* had touched him. His heart might be dead, but his dick wasn't, and this was the first time since his wife died that he'd actually been close to a woman.

A soft, sensual, lovely woman with a body that had no doubt fueled a million masturbatory fantasies. He had to remind himself who she was, because when he looked at her, all he saw was a beautiful, tough, somewhat insecure woman who hid a core of vulnerability beneath a worldly exterior.

"I guess the Lone Ranger hasn't arrived to save the day yet," she said.

"No, not yet."

"But the evil villain hasn't arrived either, so we're doing all right." She frowned. "How are we on food?"

The food was meant for one, not two, but he hadn't

told her that. He just kept dividing it up and telling her it was all right.

"We've got a couple of days yet."

"Will they find us? Your guys, I mean."

"Yes." He had no doubt HOT would come. If they weren't here yet, it was because there'd been some serious shit happening after they'd taken out Metaxas. The gun-runner basically owned this part of the island, and his people controlled access via the public road. As for the water approach, well, that was a bit trickier.

But Jack's guys would come.

She stretched her arms out in front of her. Her robe gaped open and the bikini top showed the swell of her breasts to perfection. Jack deliberately looked elsewhere while his dick throbbed a little more than before.

"I would love a shower and some coffee." She looked down at her body. "And some more clothes."

"Yeah, that would be nice."

Her robe slipped a little more and... *fuck*. Was that a belly-button ring? He hadn't noticed it before because she'd been covered up. And when he'd looked at her through the scope, it hadn't been her belly he'd been con-centrating on.

She looked up and caught him staring at her. His first instinct was to look away, but he didn't. He just... didn't.

"You're a good guy, Jack," she said softly.

"Not really." He sounded gruff.

She pulled her robe closed and sat with her arms wrapped around her middle, and that one gesture ripped through him.

"Shit," he said. "I'm sorry. You don't have to be un-comfortable with me."

"But I am." Her head was bowed. "And not for the reasons you think. That look you gave me just now... I think it causes you pain."

He blew out a breath. "Yeah. It's been... There's been no one since Hayley died."

She looked up, her eyes shiny. "I think that's sweet and sad and wonderful. And I'm really sorry, Jack. Really."

There was a lump in his throat. "I know." He shook himself and pushed up to crawl toward the opening. "I think it's safe to go for a swim now."

He stepped out of the cave and didn't look back. Right now he needed a dip in the ocean. It wouldn't be cold enough to douse this flame, but at least it was a start.

Gina slipped into the cool water and immersed herself. When she came up again, she could hear Jack swimming nearby. It was dark, but the moon was out and the stars were plentiful. After the first night, Jack had realized they were fine if they stayed in the shadow of the rock. The moon gave them light, but it didn't pick them out for anyone who might be looking.

Still, he'd warned her it was a risk. But it was a risk they had to take because staying in that cave certainly wasn't easy. Gina floated on her back and thought of the way he'd looked at her. A shiver drifted over her, but it wasn't due to being cold. She'd thought he wasn't interested in her at all—in fact, she'd felt terrible for being attracted to him—but then he'd looked at her with such an expression of raw hunger that she'd grown instantly wet.

She'd closed the robe because her nipples were hard, not because she'd been upset that he'd been looking. Now her nipples hardened again, spiking against the fabric of her top. She let a hand drift up and over her breasts. Another shiver rippled through her.

She sank beneath the water again, only this time she stayed down, forcing her mind to go blank, her thoughts to drift away. When she surfaced, she wasn't alone.

"Jesus, Gina," he said, his voice a hiss because his strictures about talking loud still applied. "I couldn't see you at all."

She slicked her hair back from her face. "Sorry."

"I thought something happened."

Her face grew warm. "Nothing happened. Clearly."

She was watching him so intently that when the next soft swell bumped into her, she didn't let it roll over her the way she should have. Instead, she let it carry her forward until she had to put out her hands to stop herself from crashing into him.

His skin was warm, hard, and slick beneath her touch. The muscles were defined… and suddenly tense. His hands went to her waist, steadying her.

"Sorry," she said again. It was such a small sound. A useless sound.

His fingers flexed against her waist. And then his hand slid up her ribcage, around to the tie of her bikini top. Her heart fluttered like a frantic moth. She wanted him to untie it so badly.

But he didn't. He simply traced his finger along the

line and she wanted to whimper.

"It's okay, Jack," she said. "Do it. I want you to do it."

"Do what, babe?"

"I want to be your first after..." Because there was something sweet about this man, something vulnerable, and she ached for him. "God, I'm sorry if that sounds insensitive—"

He dragged her against his body—his very hard, semi-naked body—and fused his mouth to hers before she could finish her sentence. His tongue met hers and her body shuddered as hot need washed through her.

He put his hands under her ass, and she wrapped her legs around his waist, moaning when his cock slid against the thin fabric of her bikini. He was big, hard, and she flexed her hips, sparks tingling deep inside her as the bundle of nerves in her clit rubbed against him.

Oh, she wanted him inside her. And yet she knew how difficult this must be for him, how emotional. She wanted to tell him she understood, and yet she was certain he wouldn't want to hear it. That she would sound like she was patronizing him.

She lost herself in the kiss, moving her body against his, her excitement rising, her pussy aching, the tension inside her spinning tighter and tighter.

He seemed to know what she wanted and he began to flex his hips, moving his body against hers. His hand moved, and then she felt a finger slide beneath her bikini. When he encountered the slick heat of her, he groaned.

"You're hot for me," he said against her cheek.

"I know. Please, Jack, do something about it. Or if you'd rather not, stop now and leave me here to cool off, okay?"

He pulled back to look at her, his eyes searching hers. "Leave you? Fuck no."

He started moving toward shore, still carrying her, and then he set her down and pulled her up the beach, grabbing his clothes on the way. He'd stripped down to his underwear to swim, a pair of black briefs that cupped his perfect ass.

When he got her inside the cave, he laid her down on the Mylar and stripped off her wet bikini. Then he warmed her with his mouth, licking her salt-drenched flesh until his hot mouth closed over one nipple and she clutched her fingers in his hair, gasping at the intensity of the pleasure.

"Please," she begged, her fingers twisting in his hair. "Please."

He reached for his pack and pulled out a condom package—thank God for those condoms—and ripped it open with his teeth. She helped him sheath his cock—and then he pushed into her slick folds, sliding deep inside her until they both let out a moan.

He held still for a long moment and she began to think he might be having second thoughts. But it was dark in the cave and she couldn't see his eyes. She reached for him, ran her fingers over his cheek, his lips, and then down over his chest.

He shuddered once, and tears sprang to her eyes as she wondered what that shudder was about. Was he regretting this? Angry with himself? With her? But he was still hard, still deep inside her, and when she shifted against him, arching her hips up to him, trying to increase the friction on her most sensitive places, he made a noise that might have been a groan or a protest.

But then he started to move, and everything else fell away…

FOUR

Present day…

"THAT'S RIGHT, FRIENDS, WE'RE GIVING away last-minute tickets to see Gina Domenico tonight at Wolf Trap. This is her first concert in the DC metro area in more than three and a half years—"

Jack flipped the radio dial to off, then glanced in the mirror at the guy tailgating him. He must have looked pretty pissed, even with his eyes hidden behind his Ray-Bans, because the dude backed off. Jack rested his arm on the windowsill of his 1969 classic Mustang, ready to give the guy the finger if he did it again. Not mature, but some days you just needed an outlet.

Today was definitely one of those days. The name he'd just heard on the radio was still pinging around inside his brain like a bullet fired into a rubber room. Jesus, Gina fucking Domenico. Her name managed to twist him up inside in more ways than one.

It wasn't a name you could forget, because she was constantly the subject of attention. And when she'd disappeared from sight for a few months after they'd gotten off the island, she'd become even more intriguing to the media.

He hadn't been surprised by her disappearing act. They'd spent three days together, waiting for rescue, sharing food and water—and body heat. God, had they shared body heat.

It shamed him every time he thought about it. It was like he'd betrayed Hayley when he'd had sex with Gina. But, goddamn, it had been a long three days and they'd talked about every fucking thing under the sun. She seemed like such a normal person under all the glamour and wealth. A lost, frightened soul you just wanted to take care of even though she wrapped herself in toughness like a turtle encased in a shell.

He'd told her after that last day when his body was sated and the guilt was eating him alive that it couldn't go anywhere. That he loved Hayley and always would.

But Gina had lifted her chin and said, "Don't get all excited, Jack. I was lonely and bored and you were here."

Her answer had stunned him in a way, though maybe it shouldn't have. She'd used him for comfort—hell, they'd used each other—but it was nothing more than a bit of hot sex between two people who weren't certain they would make it out alive. There'd been no deeper meaning, no bond. It was sex, pure and simple, and it was done.

When HOT had finally arrived, she'd taken Big Mac's hand when he'd tugged her onto the boat, and then she'd huddled against the wall until they'd reached their transport farther out to sea. There, she'd been debriefed and taken to the nearest island where they'd arranged for her to be flown back to the States anonymously.

Jack hadn't talked to her again. Hadn't seen her, other than on television or staring back at him from magazine covers in the checkout line. He hadn't wanted to see her, though every once in a while he caught himself thinking of that last day together on the island. Was she really the wounded soul she'd seemed or was the truth more nebulous than that?

He would never know. A few months after the island, she'd disappeared. Gone to a private retreat in Europe, according to her manager, where she was writing new songs and resting. Jack had thought she probably had PTSD after her ordeal, and he'd hated that it had happened to her. That he'd been at least a partial cause of it by shooting those men in her presence.

A year later, she'd emerged again, armed with new songs and ready to take on the world. She'd seemed healthy and happy, and he'd been glad for it. Six months after her comeback tour, she'd adopted a baby and gone into seclusion again. She performed when she wanted to perform, and when she didn't, she usually lived in a house somewhere in Europe and vigorously maintained her privacy.

Jack took a right onto the parkway and headed into the setting sun. He'd had her for a few hours once, and he could still remember how she felt when he slid inside her body that first time. He remembered the way her breath hitched in and how she cried his name when she came.

He'd violated way too many principles that day, and he'd lived with the guilt ever since. Worse, he'd dreamed of her when he should have only dreamed about Hayley.

Hayley was slowly fading now. It was normal, according to the psychologist, but it still felt wrong somehow. He would never forget Hayley, never forget how much he loved her. But he didn't wake up wondering where she was anymore. And he wasn't celibate either. After Gina, he'd remembered how good it felt to get lost in the physical and he'd rejoined that bandwagon a few weeks later when the urge had gotten too great to ignore.

His cell phone rang and he picked it up without taking his eyes off the road. Not many people had his number, and they were all people he wanted to talk to anyway.

"Hunter," he said.

"Jack." Her voice was soft and shaky, but he recognized it anyway.

"Gina? How did you get this number?" Anger shot through him that someone in his circle had betrayed his privacy. And then there was the curiosity. What could she possibly want? To see him? To reminisce about old times?

Fuck no. Even though his body went rock hard at the thought.

"My b...baby," she said. "S...someone took him."

His blood froze. "Jesus," he breathed. "Why are you calling me? You should be calling the police."

"No! They said not to. They said they'd kill him. Jack, please." She sobbed then and it twisted his stomach into knots. The Gina he knew didn't break down. She'd been so tough, even when she'd been scared beyond reason. She'd never broken down, not like this.

"Tell me what you need."

What did she need? She needed her baby back. Gina twisted her hands together and then dashed her fingers beneath her eyes for the thousandth time since she'd gotten the call. Why had she left little Eli in New York? She didn't like leaving him, but she'd flown down for this concert and then she was flying back immediately after, so it had seemed like the right thing to do. He had a nanny. The building was staffed by security. And she'd hired her own security once the new threats started coming.

She'd told herself it was simply a crazed fan. She was accustomed to that and she could deal with it. But someone had taken Eli from his nanny when she'd gone out for coffee that afternoon. Just snatched him up and then told her not to call the police. Instead, they'd given Cassie a note and told her to read it to Gina over the phone.

Call the police and your baby dies. Wait for instructions.

Gina shot up from her seat and paced the spacious living area of her suite. She'd thrown everyone out and told her manager to let Jack in the instant he arrived. He was the only person she could think to call since the police were out of the question. It hadn't been easy getting his number, but she'd persevered because she had to. And then he'd answered with that clipped "Hunter," and heat had flared in her belly at the sound of his growly voice.

She raked a hand through her hair and then pressed her fingers to her lips to stop a sob from escaping. She'd held it together pretty well up to now, but she was on the edge of her control. Eli was innocent, just a sweet little boy who was so happy and perfect. He didn't throw fits. Cassie had said he was the calmest baby she'd ever cared for.

And he was. Just so unflappable and calm.

But what must he be feeling now that he'd been ripped from the arms of the nanny he knew? What would those people do with him?

The door opened and her manager stood there. He'd been furious with her the past few weeks because she hadn't wanted to sign a new contract with the record label and their relationship had been strained. But now his eyes were red-rimmed and her heart dropped to her toes. Did he have news…?

"Barry?"

He stepped aside and Jack Hunter appeared in the door, all tall and golden and handsome. Oh dear God, she could see Eli in him. Her gut twisted into knots. She'd kept Eli a secret from him—from everyone except a few very trusted people who knew the baby she'd "adopted" was actually her own child—and the guilt of it tore at her.

But she hadn't known, when she'd given birth, whose child Eli was—Athenasios's or Jack's—and she hadn't known for months, not until he grew all that wheat-blond hair and his little face formed into a smaller version of Jack's. Softer and sweeter, but unmistakable to her.

She'd been so relieved that her baby was Jack's. But how could she tell him? How, when he'd told her he never wanted a child because he couldn't be there for one? He'd lost his wife and unborn child, and it had nearly killed him. He'd decided he couldn't have a normal family life like other men because he was a career soldier and his job required him to deploy at a moment's notice. How could he be a typical husband and father with a life like that?

He'd made her heart hurt when he said that, but who was she to tell him differently? They'd spent three days together, talking about everything, but they'd still been strangers.

Jack strode into the room like he owned it. His hair was cropped closer than the last time she'd seen him, but it was still darkly golden. His blue eyes lasered into her. He wore a faded red T-shirt that stretched across his muscled chest. His tattooed arms were bare and he wore a pair of faded Levi's with a hole in one knee. On his feet were flip-flops.

Gina broke at that moment. Whatever she'd been holding in escaped in a rough sob—and then she rushed into his arms and buried her head against his chest. If he was surprised, and she had no doubt he must be, he didn't let it show. He just wrapped those strong arms around her and held on tight while she tried to control her tears and failed miserably.

"He's just a baby, Jack. Just a baby."

Jack rubbed her back. "I know, sweetheart. I know."

The door quietly closed behind Barry and then they were alone. Jack continued to hold her, but she pushed away from him, determined to get herself together. She had to do it for Eli. She couldn't fall apart like this.

She turned away and swiped her eyes, her fingers trembling and her heart hammering. She hadn't seen Jack since she'd left the boat to head to the airport. He'd saved her life, taken care of her, and she'd walked away because she had to. Because he wanted her to.

She'd told herself in the weeks that followed, before she knew she was pregnant, that the feelings she'd had for him were simply the result of trauma. You couldn't fall for a man in three days just because he talked to you like you were an ordinary person. Or because he touched you so sweetly that it made your body sing.

She knew what she was, what people thought she was, but for a few days in Jack Hunter's presence, she'd felt fresh and clean. Like an unwritten slate. It had been a novel experience. She'd wanted more, but he hadn't.

And really, wasn't it best anyway? He was an Army sniper and she was a celebrity. How in the hell would that have worked out? He couldn't afford the media attention that went with her, and she couldn't ask him to leave his job just so they could date.

God, she was ridiculous. Always falling for the wrong guy and then finding out just how wrong he was.

Except, with Jack, she'd fallen harder than usual. It was just like her to want the unattainable.

"I'm sorry," she said, turning back to him and forcing a smile. "I know getting upset won't help."

"No one can blame you." His voice was full of sympathy and that quiet strength she'd gravitated to on the island. He made her feel safe. That's all there was to it.

She went over to the couch and sank down on it, willing the phone to ring as she did so. Of course it didn't. She put a hand over her eyes and tried to press the tears away. "I didn't know who else to call."

"Tell me what happened."

She told him about poor Cassie, about her trip for coffee, about the three men who'd cornered her and taken Eli from his stroller. "They told her if she screamed or called the police, they'd kill her. They gave her a note and told her to call me." Gina felt so helpless, so angry, as she thought of sweet Cassie enduring that. "They said they'd kill Eli if I called the police. They said to wait for instructions."

"Do you have any idea who did this? Has anyone been stalking you?"

She tugged a throw pillow onto her lap and absently played with the fringe. "I always have stalkers. There've been some notes over the last few months…" She sucked in a breath. "But I hired extra security just to be sure."

Jack's face was dark with anger. "What kind of notes?"

"Someone hates me, wants me to suffer, wants me dead. That kind of thing."

"I wish you would die, hateful bitch." "I'm going to cut off your arms and legs and feed them to sharks." "You should be raped repeatedly and thrown to a pack of hungry lions, deceitful whore."

Gina shivered.

"Who were they from?"

She shrugged. "I don't know. The postmark is often from Las Vegas, but that's as far as we got."

"Where was the security detail when your nanny went out?"

She looked up to find Jack still staring at her. "She didn't think she needed anyone just to go for coffee. It was broad daylight, and the coffee shop is only a block away."

Gina rubbed her temples. She was trying so hard not to be furious with Cassie. It wouldn't do any good and it wouldn't help find Eli, even if it would be satisfying to blame someone. Besides, Cassie was nearly inconsolable right now anyway.

In truth, the threats were always against Gina, not Eli. And since Gina was the visible one, the high-profile one, Cassie hadn't considered that an anonymous woman with a toddler would be identifiable to anyone. And she shouldn't have been. But someone had obviously been paying very close attention.

Jack came over and sank down in front of her. He took her hands in his and waited for her to look at him. "Gina, I'm sorry this happened. But I don't know what you want me to do. This is a job for the police or the FBI, not for a soldier. If you want me to make some calls, I'll see if I can't get the FBI involved discreetly—"

"No!" She gripped his hands tightly. "I was with you on that island. I know what you did, what your team did. You know all about covert ops, and you can find where Eli is and get him before they know you're coming. You did it with Athenasios and those men. You did what no one else had been capable of doing. *You* are the right man for the job."

FIVE

SHE WAS HOLDING HIS HANDS tightly and her face was white. Her green eyes were wide and liquid, and she looked at him like he was her savior. Like he was the only one who could fix this for her.

But how could he fix anything? He was one man, and this wasn't his area of expertise. His gut roiled with the idea that he had to tell her no, but he had to be honest with her. It was a blow seeing her again. He hadn't expected it. He'd seen her on magazine covers and television, so he'd gotten used to that little knot of tension in his gut each time.

But to see her again in the flesh? To touch her? His body vibrated like a guitar string pulled too tight. Any second and the string would snap.

"Gina, sweetheart, the military doesn't get involved in something like this. It's a domestic kidnapping case, not a terrorist plot. I want you to get your baby back, and I'll stay here with you if you need me to, but you have to let me call the FBI. This is their area of expertise, not mine. Or my team's."

Her expression fell—and then her face twisted in anger. Her cheeks flushed bright and her eyes were glassy. "If this was your child, would you be saying these things to me? Would you tell me that you couldn't help, but you could call someone? Would you leave your child's life in the hands of a bunch of strangers who might very well fuck the whole thing up?"

"I know you're upset, but you aren't being reasonable. The FBI isn't going to fuck it up."

"You don't know that!" She ripped her hands from his and shoved to her feet. Then she stalked past him and started to pace. Her long blond hair shimmered under the lights as it whipped around with her movements. She was wearing stiletto boots and a black miniskirt with a purple silk tank top tucked into it. A wide black belt cinched her small waist and emphasized the swell of her hips and breasts.

She was beautiful. Gut-wrenching, cock-hardening, ball-busting beautiful.

And she was angry. The hairs on the back of his neck stood at attention as she sizzled and sparked. But he had to calm her down. She'd called him, of all people, and he knew that meant something. But he wasn't a magician and he couldn't change the laws. The military did not handle domestic kidnapping cases.

"Babe, it's their job. They aren't incompetent."

She whirled again. And then she pounded her fist on her chest to punctuate her words. "He's *my* baby. I love him more than anyone else, and you're asking me to trust strangers who don't even know him with his life?"

He spread his hands. "I can't help you, Gina. I don't have any authority here."

She stopped her pacing and stared at him like he'd grown two heads. Her hands were on her hips and her chest heaved as if she were on the verge of something momentous.

"You have as much at stake in this as I do."

A bolt of unease shot through him. "I care that you're upset and that someone stole your child. I said I'd stay here with you. I'll call my boss and tell him I have to take leave. I'll be here for you."

She stalked toward him then, her breasts jiggling with every step of her booted feet. Her hands stayed on her hips. Her eyes spit fire at him.

"There's something you need to know, Jack. Eli is not adopted. He's my baby." She paused for a long moment, her gaze never leaving his, and his unease flared higher. "I gave birth to him nine months after you rescued me."

He couldn't breathe. Couldn't process what she was saying to him. His chest grew impossibly tight, like someone was wrapping him in steel bands and tugging with all their might. He thought of Hayley, of her car skidding out of control, and of their unborn baby in her womb. Sweat rose on his arms, his chest, his brow.

He couldn't seem to speak at first. His voice, when he found it again, was hoarse. "You were Metaxas's girlfriend."

Her eyes closed as if he'd hit her, and his gut clenched into a hard knot. He knew what she'd gone through with that rotten bastard. When she looked at him again, her gaze was soft and hard at the same time. How did she do that?

"Yes, I was his *girlfriend*, for what that's worth. And yes, I slept with him. I told you at the time. But I also slept with you, Jack. And Eli doesn't look like Athenasios. He looks like *you*."

Pain bloomed in his soul. It was as if someone had shot him through the heart and left him to writhe his last few seconds in agony. He was cold and hot and he wanted to sit. And maybe throw up.

But he stood there and faced her, clenching his hands into fists to keep from wrapping them around her neck. He was never emotional, never out of control. He was always cool and unflappable and patient. It's what made him the best damn sniper in HOT. Snipers had to possess extraordinary control, and he did.

Right this moment, however, he had no idea where that control was. He felt so many emotions whipping through him. Pain, fear, anger, loss. Denial. Oh, denial was huge. She could be lying.

But even if she wasn't lying now, she'd certainly lied before. For more than two years. He had a son, according to her, and he'd never even looked into his boy's eyes.

"If you're telling me the truth," he snarled, "you have no idea how much I want to strangle you right about now. You fucking lied, Gina. To the world. To *me*."

For the first time, she looked contrite. It didn't soften his anger, but he did feel a tiny pinch of sympathy for her. And that only pissed him off more.

"It's the truth," she said, her voice quavering once again. "I didn't know for sure until about a year ago. And I wasn't sure you would want to know. You told me you didn't want children."

"Jesus." He whirled away from her before he was sick. He was so fucking pissed he was shaking. He strode across the room and then back again. But he stopped where he couldn't reach her. "I was talking about choices. But when there is no choice, when the kid already exists—I think I have a fucking right to know."

Tears spilled down her cheeks again and his heart twisted. He wanted to hold her. And kill her, goddammit.

"You're right. I just didn't know how to tell you. But please, Jack, don't let your anger with me stop you from helping me now."

He blinked. "You really fucking think I'd refuse to help you because I despise you right now? That's my kid too, and I've never even met him. And now someone has him and I might never get to—"

A sob broke from her and she slapped her hand over her mouth to contain it. He felt like an asshole. What the fuck was he saying? His vision grew blurry and it took him a moment to realize what it was. Fucking tears? He never cried—except once.

And he wasn't about to do it again. He hadn't been able to save Hayley, but he could do something about finding his son. Eli wasn't lost to him yet.

"We'll find him, Gina. Somehow, we'll find him. I promise."

He hated her. Gina could see it in his blue eyes, in the tension of his muscles. His jaw was tight and he kept his hands clenched at his sides. She didn't blame him, not really. Guilt and fear twisted tighter in her belly. Eli was all that mattered. She didn't care if Jack hated her so long as he helped her get her son back.

Their son.

Right. Gina shoved a shaky hand through her hair to get it out of her eyes. She hated that she'd told him the truth like this, but she was desperate. He *had* to help her. She didn't trust anyone else. The FBI wouldn't care about Eli the way she did. She knew they were competent and that they would do their jobs—but it only took one person giving away their presence to alert the kidnappers. And Eli would be dead.

She couldn't take that chance. She needed someone who was just as invested as she was.

And Jack was. She could see it in his eyes, in the set of his jaw. She had to believe he could do this. That Jack and that magic military team of his could find Eli and rescue him before it was too late.

"I believe you." She *had* to believe him. To do anything else would destroy her.

He raked his fingers through his hair. Then he blew out a hard breath. His brows drew low as he concentrated on something. "I'll call my team leader, ask for time off. And I'll ask for the commanding officer to call his contacts. He knows people."

She sank onto the couch again as all the nervous energy went right out of her. She wished like hell she still smoked because she could damn sure use a cigarette right about now. But she'd given that up years ago when someone had suggested she was damaging her voice.

Still, the urge sometimes rolled through her and made her long for the days when a little bit of nicotine in her system could calm her frayed nerves.

"Then what?"

He shoved his hands into his pockets and stood there looking a bit lost. She recognized the expression as one that Eli sometimes wore. It made her heart twist.

"I don't know. We have to wait for them to call, right? When we know what they want, we'll figure out what to do."

She hunched over and rubbed her hands up her arms. She was chilled now, the anger and adrenaline of the previous few minutes draining away and leaving her empty.

"I have to cancel the concert. No way can I go on." Barry would understand. He would handle everything in his usual efficient way. He wouldn't be happy about it, because this was her big comeback tour and they'd been fighting about everything from the music to the costumes. But after years of doing what everyone else wanted her to do, she'd finally put her foot down after she had Eli and said she was going to do what she wanted. Fewer flashy dance numbers. Less style over substance.

She still gave people a show, but on her terms. And they were taking the changes pretty well even if Barry was upset with her over it.

"You might want to reconsider that," Jack said, and her head snapped up. "I know you're upset, but they seem to want you to behave as if everything in your life is the way it should be. If you don't go on, the speculation will be intense."

"I can be sick. It happens."

"And the media will camp outside your doorstep wondering what's wrong."

She hugged herself tighter. "I don't think I can do it, Jack. How can I go out there and sing for two hours when my baby is in danger?"

He almost smiled. "Do you know how many times I have to do things I think I can't do? It's my job to do those kinds of things. And I do. One thing I learned about you three years ago is that you're pretty damn tough. You can do it, Gina, because you're strong enough to do anything you have to do."

She bowed her head as fresh tears welled behind her eyelids. Damn him. When he said something like that, emotion flooded her. She didn't like to think that he was right, but what if he was? If she canceled now, with less than three hours to go, the media attention would swell. Awareness that something was wrong would increase dramatically. How would she keep it together with microphones shoved in her face everywhere she went? With people wanting to know if she was dying or when she would reschedule? This was the last concert for six weeks, so if she got through this one, she didn't have to think about it again for a while.

"All right," she said, head still bowed. "I'll do it."

"His name's Eli, huh?"

She looked up at the uncertainty in Jack's voice. Her heart flipped. He was so damn handsome. So rough and rugged and beautiful in a way no Hollywood pretty boy could ever be. He was poster material with those blue eyes and muscles. And he was tattooed. She remembered that well. Tattoos on his back, his arms, his chest. Winding tattoos of words, guns, snakes, animals, leaves, flowers. She could see the branches and scrolls of his tattoos peeking from beneath the sleeves of his T-shirt. He planned to get them all the way to his wrists someday, but he hadn't done it yet.

He was a beautiful canvas that she'd gotten to explore once. But he was also a man, and he was looking at her with a combination of anger and curiosity that made her heart hurt.

"Jackson Eli Robertson," she said, embarrassment heating her cheeks.

His gaze slewed away from her. And then he fumbled in his pocket and fished out his smartphone. "I'll make those calls now."

But he didn't stay there to do it. He walked into the bathroom and shut the door behind him. Shutting her out.

SIX

JACK STOOD IN THE MARBLE bath with its steam shower big enough to hold an elephant, its Jacuzzi tub and wall of mirrors, its granite counters and fancy sinks, and told himself to breathe. He set the phone on the counter and gripped the edge of the granite tight as he looked in the mirror.

Goddamn, he had a son. And she'd named the boy after him. *Jackson*. Why had she done that?

He pulled in air, willing himself to be calm. And then he turned on the sink faucet and splashed his face with cold water. He blotted his face with a towel and threw it on the counter.

A fucking rich-girl pop star. A media sensation. A woman who couldn't step outside without ten photographers showing up to document her every move.

Why had he lost his ever-loving mind and made love to a woman like that?

Because nothing about that situation had been normal, that's why. They'd just been two lonely people in that cave. People with a lot of baggage and a live-for-the-moment attitude because they could be discovered at any time. They'd snuck out at night to bathe in the ocean, but they'd spent the rest of their time in close quarters, talking for hours and then curling up together for heat. Hell, in retrospect, it was amazing he'd waited two days to get inside her.

Not that he'd had that many condoms. Apparently, though they were good at keeping things dry, they weren't particularly useful for the one thing they were designed for.

Jack straightened and gritted his teeth. Nothing for it now but to call Matt Girard or Kev MacDonald and tell them what was going on. No, he still couldn't use the team for this, but he'd use every last contact he had to get his kid back safe and sound.

And then what, asshole?

Was he going to sue her for custody? Demand his rights as a father?

"You don't fucking have a clue, do you?" he asked his reflection. An hour ago, he'd known who he was and what he was doing—now, he was as lost as if someone had stuck him on a raft in the middle of the ocean and left him adrift.

He picked the phone up and dialed. Matt answered on the third ring. "Hawk. What's up?"

"Got a situation, Richie."

He could hear the other man mentally brace himself. "All right. What is it?"

"Gina Domenico's in town."

"Yeah, saw that on the news. Evie's going to the concert with Georgie and Olivia."

It didn't surprise Jack that Lucky wasn't in that

group. She was a bit more reserved than the other three. And she was one of the team now, in spite of her recent marriage to Kev. Married soldiers didn't go into battle together, but HOT was able to bend the rules any way they wanted these days. A good thing, or Kev and Lucky would have both left.

"Her kid's been kidnapped."

"Holy shit. Are you sure?"

Jack gave him a rundown of everything that had happened up until now—with one important exception.

"All right, so she called you and you want to help her. I get that. But man, she needs to let the FBI get involved."

"I'll talk her into it. But I'm going to need a leave of absence."

"Hawk, I don't think—"

"There's something else." Jack's throat was closing. Was it fear? Desperation? Old wounds threatening to choke him? He didn't fucking know. Since he'd walked into this hotel room earlier, his whole life was upside down.

"Okay. Am I going to like it?"

"I doubt it."

"Let me have it then."

"The kid's mine."

There was silence on the other end for a long moment. "I'm not even going to ask how that happened." Matt blew out a breath. "But you aren't in this alone. We'll be there in an hour."

"You can't get the team involved—"

"Fuck that. Did you guys back out when I needed you to help me find Evie's sister? Did we let Georgie handle her problems on her own? Or Olivia? Did we walk away when she came to Billy for help? No fucking way, Hawk. We're brothers. And we aren't leaving you to deal with this alone, you copy?"

Jack pulled in a deep breath. "Yeah, copy."

"Be there in an hour."

Half an hour after Jack came out of her bathroom and started pacing the living room, asking her about her routines, about the threats she'd received, and about how many people knew her schedule, there was a knock on the door. He went over and looked out the peephole—and then he yanked the door open and a phalanx of tall, muscled men with serious expressions strode into her suite.

Gina's heart kicked up at the sight of all that muscle and might, but this wasn't the first time she'd seen these men. She didn't really remember them individually since she hadn't spent much time with them, but they were familiar in a way that made her heart jump. Jack had told her they were coming, but she hadn't really known what that would mean.

She still didn't, but already she felt as if her son's life was in better hands than if she'd gone to the FBI. A knot of tears pressed against her throat, but she held them back and concentrated on breathing.

The big surprise, however, was the four women who came into the room with the men. Three of them were dressed in heels and looked ready for an evening on the town. The fourth looked, oddly enough, like a soldier. She had a mane of dark blond hair and her arms were criss-crossed with fine scars. But it was her tough expression that put her into the column with the men. She didn't look like the sort of woman who would take any shit from any-one. In fact, she made Gina think of a blond Lara Croft.

Gina stood and wrapped her arms around her waist.

"Gina, you remember Matt?" Jack asked.

A tall man with dark hair and piercing gray eyes came over and took her hand. "Hey there, *chère*. Been a long time. I'm sorry we have to meet again in these circum-stances, but we're gonna do everything we can to take care of your boy, yeah?"

She sniffed and nodded, afraid to speak for fear the waterworks would start again. A black-haired woman sep-arated herself from the others and came forward when Matt shot her a look.

"Hi, sweetie," she said softly, taking Gina's hand. "I'm Evie Baker and I'm going to be with you for the rest of the evening, okay? Anything you need, you just ask."

"I need my baby," she said, her throat tight.

And then she felt like a bitch. She shouldn't have said that when the other woman was just being nice. She started to apologize, but Evie hugged her.

Ordinarily, Gina would shrink from the contact. But damn if it didn't feel nice to have someone wrap her up in a sisterly hug. And then Evie gave her a soft smile.

"My little sister was kidnapped last summer. These guys found her and busted up an organized crime ring while they were at it. So don't you worry, okay? It's just gonna take a little time, but they're on it."

Gina's cheeks felt hot with embarrassment—and gratitude. "Thanks."

"That's right," the tough blonde with the scars said. "These guys can do anything."

"And gals." It was the tall man standing next to her who'd spoken. He wrapped an arm around her and tugged her in close as she smiled up at him. Gina's heart twisted at the look they shared. Definitely in love. Definitely happy together.

Jack had been standing off to the side, looking anywhere but at her. But he glanced over at that precise moment and their gazes locked. Her pulse thumped even as his eyes hardened.

"So what's the plan?" she asked, forcing the pain from that look down deep. What right did she have to expect tenderness from him? She'd known for a year that Eli was his and she'd done nothing about it. It had seemed like the right thing at the time, but it was hard to hold on to that logic when he was standing here in front of her, wounded and angry.

As if sensing the undercurrents, Matt glanced at Jack. "You have a concert to give. The ladies are going with you and they'll run interference when necessary. Then you'll come straight back here when it's over. We'll set up a command post and wait for instructions from the kidnappers."

"What if they call my cell phone?"

One of the guys grinned as he held up a case that looked like it contained electronic equipment. "Not a problem," he said. "We'll catch everything."

Gina pulled in a breath and tried to keep calm. "What if they find out you're here? They'll think I called the police."

"They aren't going to find out," Jack said. "The team swept the area before they arrived. If anyone was watching, we'd know."

Matt nodded. "Yep, that's right. Whoever took your baby, they aren't watching you now. If they were, they'd call and tell you to get rid of us."

"They said they'd kill Eli—"

"They won't," Jack said. "They want something. They'll try to get it first. Killing him means they lose their bargaining power."

She nodded. It made sense, but it was hard to be logical when someone took your baby. All she wanted was Eli back. And she'd give the kidnappers anything they wanted to achieve that goal.

"We need to stay with you until you hear from them. We'll take the room next door," Matt said. He raised a hand, as if anticipating her question. "They aren't in New York anymore."

Her stomach dropped. "How do you know that?"

"Because we've been doing this kind of thing a long time," Jack replied. "It's not just a random grab, and you aren't an ordinary target."

Gina licked suddenly dry lips. "All right. But how can you get a room here? The hotel is fully booked, and this floor is reserved for VIPs."

"We can't," Jack said. And then he turned to Matt. "But the colonel can."

Matt grinned. "Damn straight. I'm calling Mendez."

"Who's Mendez?"

Evie gave her that sweet smile again. "A miracle worker, if you ask me. The colonel will get it done, don't you worry. Now let's get you ready for that concert."

Gina let the other woman hustle her into her bedroom. Two of the women—the ones dressed for an evening out—joined them. The other one stayed with the men.

"This is Olivia," Evie said, pointing at the woman with wheat-blond hair. "And this is Georgeanne."

"Call me Georgie," the brunette said.

"Who's the other one?" Gina asked, glancing at the closed door.

"That's Lucky," Olivia said with a smile. "She's part of the team."

Gina sank onto the edge of the bed and sucked in a breath. "Oh, God, I don't want to do this tonight. I really don't."

"I know, hon. But you have to." It was Georgie who'd spoken. "If the guys think you need to go on, then you really do."

Evie came over and squeezed her shoulder. "Matt told me you spent three days hiding in a cave before rescue and that you didn't fall apart once. I think you're strong enough for anything, Gina."

"Jack was with me." She swiped beneath her eyes as tears welled up again. "I wouldn't have made it without him."

"Jack's a good guy to have at your side. But who do you think told Matt you never fell apart?"

Warmth rolled through her at the thought of Jack saying something nice about her. But he didn't know that she *had* fallen apart. It was only after she'd gotten on the plane. Three days in a cave with a man and she'd felt things way out of proportion to the length of time she'd known him.

Because she was fucked up that way.

Gina stood and pressed the heels of her hands beneath her eyes. "All right then, I guess I better get over to the venue. Hair and makeup are there, as well as wardrobe." She nodded at the three of them. "I'm sorry if I've messed up your plans tonight."

Evie laughed. "You didn't. We were coming to see you."

Gina swallowed as a sudden awkwardness settled over her. She was two people living in this body. First there was little Regina Robertson who was shy and scared and afraid to talk to people because she didn't know what to say. Regina liked to write songs and play her guitar or piano. But Gina Domenico was different. She was the persona, the star. The one Gina trotted out for fans.

She was larger than life and always knew what to say or do. But she wasn't the one in charge at the moment.

"I, uh, wow, that's so nice of you," she said, running her hands down her skirt.

"Hey," Georgie said, and Gina met her sympathetic gaze. "It's okay. You aren't used to this kind of thing, and you must get crazed fans wanting a piece of you all the time." She shrugged. "We're just three friends who happen to like your songs. But I promise you we're all very normal. We know you aren't our new BFF, and we won't be selling our story when this is over."

Gina felt herself coloring again, but Olivia snickered. "Normal? Your man blows things up for a living. Mine could start World War Three with the tap of a computer key if he weren't so darned honest. And Evie's? I'm afraid of what he could do if he decided to be bad."

"I'm sorry," Gina said softly. "You've all been so nice. I didn't mean to suggest you weren't normal."

"Hon," Georgie said, waving a hand, "until we walk a mile in your shoes, we can't judge. So don't you worry about it another second. There are far more important things to take care of tonight."

"If you aren't comfortable with us there, it's okay," Evie said. "We'll figure something out."

Gina's heart thumped. "Oh please no, don't leave me. I was surprised, that's all. It's fine, really." She closed her eyes for a second and dug the strong Gina up from within. When she was *that* Gina, she felt like she could conquer anything. She felt a sense of calm confidence envelope her and she opened her eyes, giving them a dazzling smile. "Let's go, ladies."

She marched over to the door and swung it open. And collided with Jack, who was standing there with a hand up as if he were about to knock. Gina bounced off his hard body. Her stilettos caught in the rug and she started to tumble backward. But Jack shot forward and caught her before she hit the ground, scooping her against him and pulling her upright again.

Gina gulped in air as her heart rocketed into over-drive. She had her hands on his chest, her fingers curling into his T-shirt as she steadied herself. His hands spread around her waist, his fingers burning through the silk of her top.

"I'm sorry," she said breathlessly. "I didn't know you were there."

His gaze dropped to her mouth. And then his fingers tightened and he set her away from him. But he didn't let go, and for that she was grateful. She wasn't precisely steady on her feet yet.

"We've decided that I'm going with you. Just in

case."

"I…" She stared into his eyes and couldn't think of one damn thing to say. And then she shook herself. "Just in case of what?"

His eyes were hard. "In case this is something more than a simple kidnapping."

SEVEN

JACK STOOD OFFSTAGE WITH HIS arms crossed over his chest and watched Gina perform. Evie, Georgie, and Olivia were in the VIP section of the front row, dancing and singing along. Sam McKnight was on the opposite side of the stage, watching the crowd from there. Their eyes met across the distance and they nodded.

So far, there was nothing out of place. Nothing but Jack's thoughts. They'd decided, back at the hotel, that a couple of the guys should go along too, just in case there was more to this kidnapping case than it seemed. From there, they'd all piled into the limousine that was waiting out front for Gina, along with her manager, Barry, and headed out to Wolf Trap. Gina had disappeared into a dressing room along with the women, who had somehow become fast friends with her.

Or maybe she just kept them near so she wouldn't have to be alone with him. Whatever the case, she'd emerged from the dressing room an hour later looking like a goddess. Her blond hair hung over her shoulder in a cascade of golden curls. Her eye makeup was heavy and exotic.

And the dress she wore was fucking off the chain. He'd thought the stilettos and miniskirt was her performance outfit. He'd been wrong. She'd emerged from the dressing room in a skin-tight rubber minidress. Or at least it looked like rubber to him.

It was electric turquoise and it hugged every killer curve she had, dipped into every hollow, and made him instantly hard. Her legs were a mile long in platform heels that looked diamond-encrusted. He'd been incapable of looking at Sam because if he'd seen the same hungry look on Sam's face, he'd have wanted to deck him.

But Sam had been focused on Georgie—and now he was focused on the crowd. If he found Gina sexy, he was too cool to let it show.

And she was sexy. Too fucking sexy. Jack remembered the feel of her body beneath his, on top of his, but he'd convinced himself in the last three years that it hadn't been as spectacular as he'd thought. But, wow, she was built for sex and sin. She had the kind of proportions that often resulted from surgery—but there wasn't anything about her that was enhanced. No, it was all real. He knew it for a fact.

She sat at the piano now, in her rubber dress with her breasts ready to spill out at any moment, and rolled her fingers across the keys in a haunting melody that rose and fell along with her voice. Goddamn, she was good. Her voice was whiskey-smooth, husky and honeyed, and it took him back to those days when he'd come home and Hayley would have the music cranked up loud.

Had they made love to Gina's sexy voice? He was almost positive they had, but he didn't want to think about that right now.

Hell, he didn't want to think about anything to do with Gina. Or Hayley. No, what he really wanted to do was climb into his Mustang, point the nose west, and just keep driving as fast and far away from here as he could go.

Gina hit a high note, her voice powering through it while the crowd screamed. And then she trailed off soft and low, her fingers skimming the keys like they were a lover's body.

Her lashes dropped down, covering her green eyes, and her mouth pressed against the mic as she finished the song. And then she stood up and grabbed the mic from its holder. The number shot into overdrive then, pumping and thumping while she gyrated to the music.

Finally, the lights went down and the pyrotechnics exploded. Gina rushed off the stage while the dancers prepared for the next number. Her skin glistened with sweat as an assistant hurried over and blotted her face with a towel. Then the girl handed Gina a bottle of water, and Gina tipped it back and drained half of it.

She looked up and caught his gaze. For the barest of seconds, she smiled. And then she was gone again, back onto the stage and getting into position for the next song.

It went on like that for nearly two hours. Jack's heart thumped with the bass beat, his ears throbbed, and his body ached as he watched the woman on stage and tried to reconcile that somehow, in some alternate universe, he'd had a child with her. It didn't seem possible. She was so completely out of his orbit and nothing at all like the kind of woman he preferred. He'd grown up the only child of workaholic parents, but he'd had a best friend whose mother stayed home and baked cookies. He'd loved going to their house because Chris's mother was so welcoming and warm and made him feel like he was one of her own.

He'd wanted a wife like that, one who baked cookies and did crafts and got messy with the children. Hayley was that kind of wife. Hayley would have been surrounded by kids and pets, and Jack would have loved going home and seeing his happy little family.

He watched Gina finish her last encore song, a rocking dance number from her catalog that he remembered her telling him she was tired of. But she gave it her all. Flames and steam shot from the stage, the lights went down, and the crowd roared. Gina was not a woman who would ever bake cookies or get messy with a kid.

If she had been that sort of woman, maybe their child would still be here now instead of with strangers who had yet to make their demands.

Gina rushed off the stage and straight toward him, her retinue in tow. He gritted his teeth and resolved not to stare at the jiggling flesh of her breasts.

"Has there been anything?" she asked, her green eyes wide and fearful behind the heavy makeup. "Any calls or demands of any kind?"

A pinprick of guilt speared into him for the thoughts he'd been having about her unsuitability. She obviously loved the kid. "No."

"What's taking them so long?" Her eyes filled with tears, and he realized that she'd been holding back the edge of panic for the last two hours while she performed. She'd gotten lost in her onstage presence, but now she was back and the real world had come crashing down on her.

Jack took her hand and led her away from the bustling activity on the stage. A woman who'd been introduced as her assistant walked beside her, chattering about a schedule. Jack reached the dressing room and opened the door. Gina went through and he stepped in front of it to block the woman—and the rest of the people who'd been trailing along behind them—from entering.

"Miss Domenico needs to be alone. Go away."

The chatter rose to a fever pitch, but he stared them down hard and they subsided, slipping away into the shadows until it was quiet again. Jack went into the dressing room and closed the door firmly behind him.

He knew Sam and the ladies would be making their way here, but they would wait outside the room until he let them in.

Gina sat in a chair, her body hunched over a table, her head in her hands. There was a bottle of sparkling water beside her elbow. And there were roses everywhere. He blinked. They hadn't been here when the concert started, but then what did he know about being a pop star? He walked over to the nearest one and flipped the card up. "You rock, Gina. Love, Barry."

Her manager. If Barry were a little younger and a little less flamboyant, Jack might wonder about the relationship between them. But there was nothing to wonder, considering Barry acted more like a best girlfriend than anything else. Barry had also, Jack noticed, let his eye wander appreciatively over the team earlier.

If you liked that kind of thing, there were certainly a lot of muscles and tattoos among the HOT guys. And Barry definitely seemed to enjoy the view. He'd also seemed more than a little intimidated by their presence. He'd taken Gina aside for a quick conversation and then looked more tight-lipped than ever when it was over.

No, definitely not happy with the military muscle, even if he did like to look.

"Are these all from Barry?"

Gina looked up, her eyes red-rimmed. "Probably not, no. Sponsors, record executives, admirers."

Jack eyed the flowers suspiciously. It was in his nature to consider all the ways in which someone could get to Gina, and there were a thousand places to hide a bug here.

He put his finger to his lips to keep her from saying anything about Eli or the kidnappers. Her brows drew down but she nodded. Smart girl.

"Great show tonight. Though I thought the dance numbers were something you wanted to move away from."

She shrugged. "If I want the fans to accept the new music, then I have to give them the stuff they love too. And they are still my songs, so I perform them. It makes the fans happy."

He'd listened to that screaming audience for two hours, so he knew it was true.

Gina stood. "I want to go back to the hotel."

There was a knock and then Barry entered. "Great job, darling," he gushed, going over to kiss her cheeks. "I've got the guy from *Rolling Stone*."

Gina's face fell. "I… I can't right now. I have to get back—"

"Five minutes, sweetheart," Barry wheedled. "You can do five minutes."

Gina looked uncertain. And then her shoulders fell. "All right."

"No," Jack said, fury bubbling up inside him. Her kid was missing and this fucker wanted her to talk to people?

Both Gina and Barry swiveled their heads to look at him. He could see on her face that she didn't want to give any interviews, and he wasn't going to watch her get caught up in endless conversations at a time like this. She might not be a cookie-baking mother, but she loved Eli and she was terrified for him.

"I beg your pardon?" Barry had a terrier-like edge to his voice now.

"You know it's not a good time," Jack said. "Reschedule. Gina needs to get back to the hotel and we need to get on with business. This is far more important and you know it."

Barry puffed up like a rooster. "It's five goddamn minutes. And you're the one who said she had to act normal."

Jack told himself not to punch the guy.

Gina put her hand on the other man's arm. "Five minutes, Barry. That's all."

Barry shot him a triumphant look before giving her a quick peck on the cheek. Then he disappeared through the door.

Jack's temper spiked. "Why'd you fucking agree? He works for you, not the other way around."

She gave him a look that would have made a weaker man cower. "Barry helped me get where I am today. I owe him. Besides, this is *my* career and *my* livelihood. I've worked too hard to get where I am, and if I have to talk to a reporter for five minutes, then I'll do it. It's part of *normal*. That was your idea, by the way, not mine."

"Goddammit, that was earlier! Now you could tell that fucker no and move on."

Her eyes sparked. "I don't expect you to understand.

70

But I also don't expect you to order me around—to order my people around—as if you're the one in charge, either. You got that, cowboy?"

Jack blinked. "Cowboy? I'm from fucking Florida, sweetheart. You see any shit-kickers on my feet?"

"No, but I imagine there's a gun tucked away somewhere on your body. And I know what you can do with that, hotshot."

He took a step toward her. "With what, sweetheart? With the gun? Or the body?"

He wouldn't have thought it possible, but she colored. She took a step back on her teetering platforms and fixed him with a hard look. "If you think for one second I was talking about anything but the gun, you're sadly mistaken. Now either get out and wait for me, or sit down and be quiet when this reporter shows up."

She turned her back to him and went over to fix her makeup. His temper boiled hot.

"Let's get one thing straight, *Miss* Domenico," he said between his teeth. Her spine stiffened, but she didn't turn around. He ranged toward her and she watched him in the mirror, her eyes both wary and curious at once.

He was right behind her when he stopped. He could feel the heat rolling from her, could smell the sweat and perfume of her body. And damn if he couldn't see the outline of hard nipples in that fucking rubber dress.

"Go ahead," she said, her eyes sparking, her chin tilting up. "Give it to me."

Jesus, he wanted to give her something all right. Something hard and long and aching with need. He reached out and put his hands on her bare arms. His fingers wrapped around her entire upper arm.

71

He could smell fear and desire on her and his balls tightened. She continued to stare at him in the mirror. But she didn't try to pull away.

He dropped his hands suddenly, as if her skin burned. "Even if you were thinking about something other than my gun, I'm not interested," he told her. "Not ever again. You're gorgeous and you know it. But you're a fucking liar—and I can't stand a liar."

He thought he saw a spark of pain in her eyes, but then her lashes dropped and her eyes were shielded from him. He almost felt like a dick, and yet he told himself he had every right to be pissed.

Damn, if she didn't make him lose his way. He hadn't started out to say such a thing, but it was out there now.

And it was the truth, damn her. She'd lied and flipped his life upside down.

He turned away and raked a hand through his hair. He didn't like the way she made him feel. He was cool, methodical, and patient. Except he felt anything but cool and patient at the moment.

There was a knock at her door and Jack went over and jerked it open.

A man with short red hair stood on the other side. "Uhhh…" he began.

Gina walked over and the man's eyes widened. Then he swallowed.

Yeah, she had that effect.

He stuck out his hand. "Hello, Miss Domenico. I'm Pete Gibson from *Rolling Stone*."

"Well, hey there, Pete. Please call me Gina."

She was the consummate professional once more as she stood back and swept a hand toward the couch on the other side of the room. Jack almost envied her the ability to be cool when he couldn't seem to find his anymore.

She sank down gracefully and the reporter joined her. But she looked up for a moment, her gaze catching Jack's—and every ounce of pain and fear he saw reflected on her face made him feel like he'd failed her somehow.

EIGHT

GINA HAD BEEN TALKING TO Pete Gibson for ten
minutes when Jack interrupted and told her it was time to
go. Part of her wanted to tell him to go to hell just on prin-
ciple, but she was thankful more than anything. She was
tired and wired, and she just wanted to go back to the hotel
and wait for word from the kidnappers. She'd been able to
lose herself in the music, but now that it was over, reality
lay on her shoulders hard, the dread threatening to crush
her like an old car in a scrapyard.

She gave Pete an apologetic smile. "I'm afraid this
has to be the end of our interview."

He stood at the same time she did, his skin flushing as
she took his hand and gave him another smile.

"It was *so* nice to meet you, Pete. If you need anything else, just get in touch with Barry."

"Yes, thank you, I will."

She let Jack usher her out of the building, his fingers
light against the small of her back. She climbed into the
waiting limo and Jack joined her. It was just the two of
them inside the big space, but the others would soon join

them. The chauffeur shut the door and a few moments later the car began to move away from the curb.

"Where is everyone?"

Jack glanced at her, his expression unreadable. His jaw was stiff. "They went ahead just a few minutes ago. We put sunglasses and a hood on Olivia and raced her to the limo like she was you."

Gina blinked as she realized there hadn't been any photographers lined up and snapping photos when she'd exited the building. Olivia was blonder than she was, but with a hood and glasses, would it matter? The media would see what they wanted to see. "That was a good idea."

"Yeah."

She sighed and turned to look at the lights sliding by the car. She was tired, but the adrenaline moving through her veins also made her jumpy. It was always this way after a concert, but it felt doubly so now.

"How did you pull it off?"

Her head swiveled around to find Jack looking at her with those fathomless blue eyes of his. She could drown in those eyes. "I, uh…" She looked away for a moment to gather her thoughts. "Pull what off?"

"Everywhere you go, the attention is insane. And yet you managed to pull off a pregnancy that no one ever got wind of. How? Or is that a lie and you've said all this to get me and my team to help you?"

Anger flared inside her. And hurt. "You really are a bastard sometimes, you know that?"

He shrugged. "It's a legitimate question, Gina. You're a superstar. You can't take a shower without a news bulletin, so I don't know how you managed to be pregnant and no one found out. You didn't disappear off the face of the planet, after all."

She sighed and rubbed her hands over her knees. If he were anyone else, she'd tell him it was none of his business. But of course it was his business. "I never intended to lie about it, but when I found out I was pregnant, I knew I couldn't face the media firestorm that would follow. I also didn't think it was a good idea based on my last public *romance* and what happened to him. Everyone would assume Athenasios was the father. I didn't want to deal with the Metaxas family—worse, would you have wanted me to have a public DNA test that proved Eli wasn't Athenasios's?"

"You didn't know that at the time."

She shook her head. "No, I didn't. But I didn't want anything to do with the Metaxases. Athenasios didn't run his business alone. His brother Stavros took over the shipping company. For all I know, he also dealt in the same side business."

"So you disappeared."

"I spent time in Italy. Well, an island off the coast of Italy. And I was never big. At nine months, I didn't have a large belly. It was noticeable, of course. But not huge. So I wore a lot of big clothes and I stayed away from people, other than the few I trusted. The doctor was paid well not to leak the news. I 'adopted' Eli later so there would never be any question of who his father was."

"What's on the birth certificate?"

He sounded angry. She didn't blame him, but how could she possibly tell him everything she'd been going through then? She'd been scared and alone and confused. And she'd done what she thought was best for Eli's safety.

She bowed her head and swallowed. Her throat hurt after an evening of singing. "Unknown."

She could see him clench his fist in her peripheral vision. "You had a fifty-fifty chance of guessing the right man."

"It was easier that way."

"When we get him back, you're going to correct that."

His tone said he'd accept no other alternative, and yet she bristled at being told what to do. But didn't he have that right? She'd revealed the truth to him, asked him for his help, so how could she possibly deny him the right to call Eli his? And yet it terrified her, too.

"All right," she said softly.

"I don't even know what he looks like."

Tears blurred her vision. "Can I have my phone?" He'd been holding it for her in case there was a call during the concert.

He handed it over wordlessly. She put in her passcode and called up her photos. She found the most recent one of Eli, taken just this morning before she'd flown to DC. He'd been laughing and playing with his toy train. She'd snapped him when he'd looked up at her, his little blue eyes shining, his blond hair a mop of curls. His cheeks were rosy and fat. Her heart squeezed with all the love she felt for him.

She passed the phone wordlessly to Jack. He took it and sat there staring for the longest time. She managed to force herself to look at him. His profile made her heart skip. He was chiseled and handsome, and she felt again all the chaotic emotions she'd experienced back in that cave three years ago. Such hot, intense attraction. Safety. Belonging.

But of course she'd been wrong about the belonging. As usual.

He swallowed, his Adam's apple moving visibly. "He looks a little like me."

"A lot like you," she said past the knot in her throat.

"Yeah." He punched the button to make the picture go away and handed the phone back to her. "Goddammit, Gina," he finally said, his voice hoarse. "Were you ever going to tell me?"

She dropped her gaze to her lap. She knew what the answer should be. But she couldn't say it. She could only tell the truth. "I don't know."

She leaned her head back on the seat and let a tear escape. Her makeup would run and she'd look like a raccoon, but she no longer cared about her image.

"I should have told you. I know I should have. But I was scared. You were so angry and heartbroken three years ago. You told me what we'd done didn't mean anything. I understood that. And I didn't need anything from you. I didn't want you to think I expected anything."

"I wasn't in a good place then. But that still didn't give you the right to keep him from me."

"No, I know." She spread her hands. "I can't say anything other than I'm sorry. I know it's not enough, and I don't expect you to forgive me. All I want is to get Eli back again. After that, we'll work it out. I want him to know you, if that's what you want too."

It terrified her to think of making Jack a part of their lives, but what choice did she have? Without him, there would be no Eli. Without him, she might never see Eli again.

Oh God, she couldn't think such a thing. She just couldn't. It would kill her if he didn't come back safely.

The dam inside her broke then and she folded over onto herself, crying because she was emotionally wrung out from the concert, from Jack's presence in her life, and from her baby being gone.

For the second time today, Jack pulled her into the hard warmth of his body and let her cry. She huddled into his side, her body shaking with fear and adrenaline and sorrow. Jack ran a hand up and down her bare arm. Sparks shot through her body, warming her. She wanted to lean into him for the whole night, lie against him and let him take on the world for her. What would it feel like to belong to someone strong, someone who could take control and make the world go away for a while?

It was always her against everyone else. She was used to it, and yet she still wished for someone to take care of her every once in a while. She'd never been taken care of. From an early age, she'd been alone while her mother went out to bars and clubs. And then she'd been alone when her mother brought men home and spent time with them instead of her child.

Only once could she recall being the center of her mother's attention. She'd been staying at a friend's house for days because her mother was partying and working, but she'd gotten sick at school and the nurse called her mother. Mom had come for her. She'd taken Gina home, tucked her up in bed, and spent two whole days feeding her soup, taking her temperature, and fussing the way a mother should.

It hadn't lasted. But Gina remembered that time so vividly. She'd been cared for and loved, and the memory of it had kept her warm inside when she felt down. When she'd started to make money, she'd asked Mom to come live with her. But her mother hadn't wanted to leave Bill or Bob or Dan—or whoever it had been then. That winter, she'd slipped on a patch of ice, hit her head on the pavement, and died when the bleeding on her brain hadn't stopped.

Gina felt Jack lean forward and then a box of Kleenex appeared in front of her nose. She took several. "Thanks."

She dabbed at her eyes, the tissues coming away black, and then she dabbed her nose with fresh ones. She turned to Jack. "Can you fix this mess? In case there are reporters still at the hotel."

He grabbed some tissues and held her chin firmly while he tenderly wiped away the makeup beneath her eyes. She didn't want to look at him, but there was nowhere else to look while he tended to her.

He had a day's worth of stubble on his jaw. His blue eyes were hot and piercing as he stared at her. Her heart bumped up as her gaze dropped to his mouth. He had beautiful lips, firm, and as she knew from experience, oh so kissable. He'd performed magic with that mouth. She'd worshipped that mouth.

In a fricking cave on an island. It was like a myth that had happened to someone else instead of her.

Except she had Eli, and now Jack was here, dabbing away makeup and holding her chin with his fingers.

"Best I can do," he growled, leaning back away from her.

"Thanks."

"What the hell is that dress made out of anyway? Rubber?"

Gina blinked. What? "It's polyester and spandex. It looks like leather, but breathable."

"Looks like rubber to me. And not much of it."

She glanced down at the dress. She was so accustomed to thinking of her costumes as just that, costumes, that she hadn't paid much attention to this one once she'd left the stage. Gina Domenico was a sexual bombshell who projected sensuality and utter confidence in herself. This outfit was designed with that in mind. Her breasts mounded high and threatened to spill over while the hem had ridden up to nearly crotch level. It explained a lot when she thought back to Pete Gibson's blushes. And maybe it explained a lot now. Her gaze dropped to Jack's groin.

And he was hard, the long, thick outline of his cock lying against his thigh. It made her stomach clench and her pussy throb with answering heat.

She shook herself mentally. Just because he got hard over a pair of boobs in his face didn't mean anything. He'd told her nothing was happening between them ever again—and she'd told him he was an arrogant prick for thinking she cared if it did.

"And here I didn't think you were interested," she purred, deciding to jab him while he was down.

"I'm not. But I noticed. Hell, every man who likes tits and ass noticed."

Her temper burned. He would never know how much thought and planning went into every little thing she did. And she didn't give a fuck what he thought about it. "Sex sells, baby. Or haven't you heard?"

"Then you're doing a fine job of selling it."

"You're an asshole, you know that? You don't get to judge me or make assumptions about my business just because I'm wearing a dress that makes you hard. Jerk off tonight if you must, but blame yourself, not me."

He raked a hand through his hair and swore. "Look, I'm sorry. You're right that I know nothing about your business. I'm just fucking pissed off and not handling it very well. It's going to take time."

The limo came to a stop and she looked out the window to see they'd arrived back at the hotel. The chauffeur got out of the car and came around to get her door. When it opened, she took his hand and let him help her out. There were no photographers, and for that she was grateful. She meant to walk away, but instead she turned and leaned down to fix Jack with a look.

Because she was still angry, in spite of his apology. She'd believed in him on the island, trusted him, and thought he'd seen the real her beneath the polish and glitz. But he seemed to believe the image now, and that hurt.

"Be sure to stroke it extra hard, you hear? And think of these while you do it, sugar." She rounded her hands over the sides of her breasts. And then she straightened and hurried into the lobby where Sam McKnight waited with Georgie, Olivia, and Evie.

"Where's Hawk?" Sam asked.

"Coming," she replied without a trace of irony.

NINE

IT TOOK JACK A COUPLE of minutes to follow Gina. He had to wait for his hard-on to subside because, yeah, she'd made him hot. He'd been wiping the streaky makeup from beneath her eyes and trying like hell not to look at the way her breasts filled out the deep vee of her dress, but it was impossible not to. He'd never seen such perfect breasts as those creamy swells, and he'd seen plenty. He'd been remembering the way they'd felt in his hands and trying to regulate his response.

It hadn't worked, and that had made him angry. So of course he'd been a dick to her. *Asshole.*

He didn't blame her for that last burst of spite. He'd deserved her anger over what he'd said. His mother had raised him better than to talk to a woman that way, but he hadn't been able to stop once the words started.

He reached her room. Ryan Gordon stood outside the door.

"Hey," Flash said as Jack walked up. "Go on in. They're waiting."

Jack stepped inside the suite and closed the door behind him. Georgie, Olivia, and Evie were talking and laughing. Sam and Matt looked up when Jack entered. Gina wasn't anywhere to be seen.

"Got anything?" Jack asked, though he knew if they had someone would have called him immediately.

"No," Matt said. "Billy's got everything set up next door. We're just waiting now. If they call, we'll find them."

"Nothing to do but wait then," Jack said, shoving his hands in his pockets and standing there feeling a little bit lost and a whole lot irritated—with Gina, with himself, with everything.

"You all right, Hawk?"

"It's a lot to take in at once, but yeah. I'll be fine."

Matt came over and clasped his shoulder. "We'll find these bastards and get Eli back."

"I know." And the fact his team would do this for him when they were between missions and could use the time to relax filled him with uncharacteristic emotion. He wasn't very talkative at the best of times, but he wanted them to know how grateful he was.

He just didn't know how to say it. Matt squeezed his shoulder as if he knew and then turned away.

The door to Gina's bedroom opened and she came out. She didn't look anything like the Gina who'd looked at him with such contempt a few minutes ago. This Gina was scrubbed clean of makeup and her hair was wet. She wore jeans and a T-shirt and her feet were bare. It took him back to the island and the way she'd looked there with her face fresh and her long hair hanging in wet ropes down her back. She'd been purely, simply beautiful, and he'd been enthralled even though he hadn't wanted to be.

"What's the plan now?" she asked, and he recognized the hard-assed businesswoman taking control. It was how she dealt with the world. Her gaze flickered over him and her green eyes grew as hard as marbles. But then she was looking at Matt again and waiting for an answer.

"Nothing we can do except wait for them to call, *chère*. We've got a command center set up next door, and we'll be monitoring the equipment twenty-four seven. When they call, just keep them on the phone as long as possible. We'll do the rest."

She pressed the heels of her hands to her eyes and he got the sense she was trying not to cry again. "All right," she said a moment later. And then she looked at him again and his gut twisted. "What if they never call? What if this is some sick plot to hurt me and they never intend to give my baby back?"

Jack had to clear his throat. "You're rich and famous, Gina. They want money."

Everyone agreed. The women came over and gave Gina hugs. "It's been a long day for you," Evie said. "I think maybe we should leave you to rest."

Gina nibbled her lower lip and he knew she was working to control herself. "Thanks so much for coming with me tonight. And I'm sorry about earlier."

Olivia and Georgie made shushing noises at the same time. "Already forgotten," Olivia said.

"We've got your back, darlin'," Georgie added, sounding an awful lot like Sam.

Gina nodded. Evie looked at Matt. "I guess you know we're staying with you guys tonight."

Matt didn't even argue. "Yeah, figured that. It's a suite and there are a couple of connecting rooms." He took

Evie's hand and they went out the door with the others. Jack stayed where he was, hands still in his pockets. Someone had to stay with Gina and it was understood that someone would be him.

The door closed and the room was suddenly silent. Gina sank into a chair and laid her head back against the seat. "Do I need to ask why you're still here?"

"I'm not leaving, Gina."

Her eyes flashed. "You aren't sleeping with me either."

He snorted. "I think we both know that already."

She let her gaze slide over him. "So did you take care of the problem?"

"There is no problem. I'm a man. I'm used to unrequited boners. Doesn't mean a damn thing."

She arched an eyebrow. "Seriously? You, used to unrequited boners? I'd have thought you had a string of willing women standing outside your door."

He shoved a hand through his hair. "Can we just cut the crap? It's not safe for you to be alone, and I'm the most logical person to be here. He's my kid too."

She deflated like a popped balloon. All the fight went right out of her, and he realized how exhausting it must be to keep up the pretense of toughness long beyond the point where you had to be ready to scream.

"Before you say anything else, I don't wear what I wear on stage in order to turn men on. I wear it because it's what I think is best for my brand. And it's none of your goddamned business."

"You told me you were tired of the dance numbers and the direction people were pushing you in. That was three years ago. If it hasn't changed, then you have no one to blame but yourself."

She nibbled on a fingernail. "I can't change it overnight. And I basically dropped out for two years, so if I have a prayer in hell of keeping my career, I have to keep some of the dance numbers and the high energy. Barry's right that I can't just change everything. What if they don't like me anymore?"

He could only stare at her in disbelief. She was fucking amazing. She had a real voice, not a manufactured one. She didn't rely on audio processors to make herself sound good. He'd like to wrap his hands around Barry's throat for holding her back.

"I can't believe your fans would abandon you, Gina. It's more than dancing and a stage show that keeps them buying your records."

She closed her eyes. "I don't tell you how to shoot a gun, or any of that other super-spy stuff you do, so don't tell me how to do my business, all right?"

She had a point, though he still thought she was wrong. "All right."

He'd thought she would rest, but she shot up off the chair and marched across the room. She wasn't wearing her heels anymore, which made her much shorter than the five-nine she'd appeared to be earlier. He'd forgotten how much smaller than him she was.

But, man, she had a body that wouldn't quit. He dragged his eyes off her breasts and made himself watch her face.

"Why don't they call?" she burst out, throwing her hands out wide. "It's been six hours since they took him. Six fucking hours!"

Jack wished he had an answer for her but he didn't

know what the kidnappers' endgame was. All they could do was wait to find out.

And that didn't sit any better with him than it did with her. He was accustomed to being patient, to spending hours or days crawling into position to take the shot. He was used to waiting for a target to appear in his crosshairs.

But not this time. This time he wanted to charge in and take the bastards out with a barrel against their temples. He wanted to see their eyes when they realized they were done for.

He was seething with hot energy and ready to act. Just as she was.

Yet there was nothing they could do but wait.

"They'll call when they're ready. This is part of the game."

She glared at him. "You said your team didn't handle kidnappings. How do you know?"

"I said we didn't handle *domestic* kidnappings." In fact, they dealt with hostage situations all the time. But not in the States where other agencies had jurisdiction—unless the kidnapping was due to terrorism, and then they could be called in.

Her eyes were shiny but he knew she wouldn't cry this time. She was too angry to cry. "How do you deal with this? The waiting?"

"Honestly, I've never had to deal with it like this. I don't know the people we're sent to rescue. They aren't usually children either."

Though it had happened, certainly. Just a few months ago, they'd had a situation where an American family was taken hostage by guerillas while traveling in South America. They'd gone in hard and Jack had taken out six militants in the space of seconds. The rest of the team had mopped up the other bad guys, they'd rescued the family, then bugged out to the extraction point. In and out and done.

"You think I should have called the FBI."

Yeah, he'd thought that when he first arrived. And he knew it changed after she dropped a bomb on him. But it wasn't just that the kid was also his. It was her utter conviction that she needed him to help her. And then the guys had dropped everything to come analyze the situation, and his gut feeling that this was something other than a kidnapping only grew stronger.

"I did think so. I don't anymore."

"Do you think this has anything to do with the threats?"

His gut had twisted reading the initial reports of the threats against her. Men—and maybe some women—who thought she was their soul mate and wanted to claim her. People who hated her and wanted her dead. People who thought she owed them something because they were positive she'd written songs about their lives.

Most were traceable, and most were crackpots. But there were always a couple that couldn't be identified, and those were worrisome in their own way. However, none of them indicated a mind capable of a plan this intricate, though they had yet to see the original letters. The security company had them and would be sending home over in the morning.

"I don't know for certain, but I don't think so." Her security contractor had been thorough in their investigation of the threats, but there was always a chance they'd missed something.

Gina's cell phone blared then and she jumped. Jack's heart rate shot up. Her eyes were wide as she snatched the phone from the table where she'd put it.

"I don't recognize the number."

"Answer it, Gina. Be calm. Keep them on the phone and find out what they want. Ask for proof of life—shit, don't phrase it that way or they'll know you've got someone on your side. Just ask for proof they didn't harm him."

She nodded. He could see the pulse thrumming in her neck as she slid the answer bar. "Hello."

Her eyes widened as she stared at him, and she nodded hard. Her eyes were glassy as tears welled. "I'll do anything you want. But you have to give me proof you didn't hurt him. I want to know my baby is okay."

Jack wanted to hear what they were saying but they'd agreed earlier that she shouldn't put it on speaker. That was a sure sign she had help, and people could always tell when speaker mode was enabled. They couldn't take the chance. But Billy had tapped her phone and the guys were listening in the other room. He had faith they'd get something.

"Baby," Gina cried out. "Sweetheart, don't be scared. Mommy's coming. Mommy's coming."

She put a shaky hand to her lips and tried to hold in the sob that he knew was threatening. The kidnappers must have taken Eli away from the phone.

"Yes," she said. "I understand. Vegas. The Venetian. I'll be there."

"Couldn't get a lock on them," Billy Blake said. "Fuck!"

He slammed a hand on the table. Olivia stood behind him and put her arms around his neck.

Jack's gut rolled with fear and anger. "Do we even know if they're really in Vegas?"

Gina had said the postmarks on the vilest of the letters she'd gotten had often been from Vegas. It was too strong a coincidence to completely ignore, but that still didn't mean whoever had done this was really in Sin City.

He'd brought Gina next door as soon as they'd gotten off the phone. She'd been shaking and on the verge of hyperventilating when he'd taken her hand and pulled her with him. No way in hell was he leaving her while he went to check in with the guys.

Jack glanced at Gina. Her eyes were glassy and her hands were over her mouth as if she were trying to hold all her feelings inside. He knew what that felt like. He'd been just where she was when his CO and the Red Cross came to inform him that Hayley was dead—trying to hold it all in and knowing he was going to blow at any moment.

He put his arm around her and pulled her against him. She didn't try to move away, which told him she was feeling it pretty hard.

"I can't say for certain," Billy said.

Matt swore. "We can't take military transport to get there."

Jack knew that. It wasn't a military operation and they weren't authorized. And while they weren't precisely authorized to do this either, it didn't involve commandeering a government asset as large as an airplane.

"Can't you call Mendez?" Evie asked. Her eyes were filled with tears too. Jack knew this must bring up bad memories for her considering that her sister had been kidnapped last summer.

"It's not official use," Jack said.

"Fuck that," Lucky MacDonald said. "There's got to be a way."

Gina stirred against his side. He got the feeling she'd zoned out there for a bit, but she was trying to work her way back to the conversation. "I have a plane," she said, her voice scratchy and soft.

Jack's stomach fell. Not in a bad way, but in a holy-shit-they-weren't-fucked way. He tipped her chin up and forced her to look at him. A tear slid from her eye and rolled down her cheek. He had a strong desire to kiss it away. He swallowed the urge.

"You have a plane, babe? A plane big enough for all of us?"

"It's a 737."

"If it's a charter, you'll have to—"

"It's mine."

Holy shit. He was reeling here. Just fucking reeling. This woman owned a goddamned Boeing 737. The rest of the guys whooped.

"That's it. We're breaking it down and getting on that fucking plane," Matt said.

"Shit yeah," Big Mac added.

Relief threatened to make Jack's legs buckle. She had

a plane and they weren't dead in the water. There was still a chance to save their son.

TEN

THE VENETIAN SAT ON THE Vegas strip, a large copy of all the best of Venice in the middle of a desert, but without the timeworn feel or unique charm of the Italian city itself. Gina was impatient to get there. Jack's team had played back the conversation she'd had with the gruff-voiced man who'd told her that she'd better get out to Vegas or she'd never see her child again. They'd gleaned nothing new from it, unfortunately.

Her heart twisted as she remembered Eli's voice. He'd been crying, and that had broken her heart and pissed her off all at the same time. Bastards. She would kill them if she ever got her hands on them.

Jack sat beside her in the limo that raced them from the airport to the city. He was quiet and focused, and she wished she could reach out and grab his hand for comfort. He'd been with her every step of the way. And his miraculous band of military badasses was there too, going ahead of them in a van loaded with equipment. The women—except for Lucky—had stayed behind in DC. Gina kind of wished they'd come along too. She didn't make friends easily, and while she wouldn't call them her friends just yet, she liked how strong and no-nonsense they all were.

Those women were close and she envied the bond. Lucky was the only one who seemed to be on the outside of that circle, but that seemed to be more her doing than the other women's. They accepted her as she was. Gina didn't pretend to know why that was difficult for Lucky, but she understood it. When you were accustomed to being a loner, you didn't easily become a part of a group.

The tall facade of the Venetian loomed ahead. Nerves spiked in her belly. What would they find there? Those men surely weren't holding Eli in a major hotel, were they? Would her baby be there, safe and happy and waiting?

Except they hadn't asked her for anything yet, and she knew they had to. No one went to that kind of trouble without wanting money.

The nerves in her belly fluttered like a million hummingbird wings. Gina swallowed against the nausea threatening her. And then she reached out and took Jack's hand because she had to, because she needed his strength and calmness more than she needed to be a rock standing firm on her own.

Jack turned to look at her, but he didn't pull his hand away. He simply wrapped his fingers around hers and squeezed. It was every bit as comforting as she'd hoped. His skin was warm, and he was strong and solid beside her. He was the rock, and she could be the wave ebbing and flowing for a change.

In all the hours on the plane, he hadn't spoken much. He'd sat with his team for the longest time, never far from her, but engrossed in everything they were planning. He hadn't left her side, but he'd somehow obtained a long case that she recognized. He'd had one similar on the island, and she knew it contained his guns.

"What do you think's going to happen when we get there?" she asked, because she needed to say something.

Jack was looking at their twined fingers. "I don't honestly know," he told her. "Whoever is doing this derives pleasure out of making you do what they want. It's a power play as much as a money grab. Which means it could be personal."

Gina's belly took a dive. It wasn't the first time she'd heard that tonight, but it was the first time anyone had said it to her. She'd overheard the guys talking about it, but when they thought she might hear them, they'd lowered their voices.

"I don't know who would be so angry with me they'd use Eli against me. It's a crime, for God's sake. Who would risk that?"

"Have you jilted anyone recently?"

Her face heated. "I've not been with anyone seriously, but I did date a congressman for a bit. I broke it off when I felt his life was too complicated for me. But he wouldn't risk his career just to hurt me. He wasn't that invested in me. Besides, it was months ago."

Jack was looking at her with new interest. "A congressman? Which one?"

"DeWitt."

"He's on the subcommittee for intelligence, emerging threats, and capabilities."

Gina gaped. "How do you know that?"

"It's the branch of the House Armed Services Committee that oversees anything to do with my job. Believe me, we all know who they are."

She shook her head. "But what's that got to do with me and Eli?"

"Nothing."

"Then why did you ask?"

He shrugged. "Because I wanted to know. You never told anyone about what happened on St. Margarethe, did you?" he added.

Her heart thumped. "Which part?"

"Any of it."

"No. I told you I wouldn't. I didn't want anyone to know I was there when..." She swallowed. "That day."

"That's good. The less your name is associated with Metaxas, the better."

"It's so strange to be here," she said, looking out the window at the neon strip. "Barry wants me to sign a contract that will have me performing here regularly, but I'm just not sure that's the direction I want to go. Still, it's a lot of money."

Beside her, Jack had stiffened. "Why didn't you mention this before?"

She whipped her head around to find him staring at her. Her heart thumped. "What? The contract?"

"Yes. The fact *your manager* wants you to sign a contract that brings you to Vegas, the fact you haven't done it, the fact some of the letters have Vegas postmarks—when do they arrive? When Barry is conveniently out of town?"

Gina gasped. "Barry has nothing to do with this! Why would he? That's ridiculous—I've known him for years; I love him and he loves me. We fight sometimes, but he'd never do such a thing!"

Jack looked furious. "Gina, we needed to know this.

We can't leave any angle unexplored—"

"No!" She jabbed a finger in his chest. "Barry is off-limits. He would never, *never* hurt Eli. Barry loves him, and he's upset about this too. You saw him when you arrived—he was crying with me."

"He didn't seem too broken up after the concert."

She wanted to scream. Yes, Barry had turned into his usual bulldog self, but he cared. And she wouldn't have this man trying to make Barry into some kind of monster just because there was a tenuous connection between him and Las Vegas.

"It's not Barry. There's no way it's Barry. You will not, under any circumstances, upset him with accusations. Investigate him and you'll find out I'm right."

Jack still looked angry, but he nodded. "We damn sure will investigate. But I won't upset precious Barry until we know something."

"You won't upset him at all."

Jack didn't reply. The car slowed and turned into the hotel drive. Gina's pulse thrummed. This was it.

The man on the phone had told her to go to the Venetian, check in, and wait. He hadn't told her to come by herself, so Jack was her bodyguard for the trip since it wasn't unusual for her to have one. And while she might be ticked off at him right now, she was glad he was here.

A uniformed man opened the car door, and Jack stepped out first before holding a hand out for her. She'd changed into a modest black tuxedo pantsuit and low heels. Her hair was twisted into a bun on her head, and she popped on a pair of big sunglasses even though it was the middle of the night. She should be exhausted after the concert earlier, but she was running on adrenaline and fear.

There was plenty of time to collapse later.

Jack still wore jeans and a T-shirt, but he'd put a sport coat over the shirt so he could wear his shoulder holster. It comforted her to know he was armed. And she knew his team was already here. She'd had her assistant book her suite along with the one beside it, so the guys would be setting up equipment and preparing for any contingencies.

She and Jack strode into the grand foyer with the painted dome ceiling and the gold ring sculpture at the center. The hotel was over-the-top ornate, gleaming and perfect in a way that the real Venice was not. She preferred the real Venice.

The staff bent over backward to accommodate her, checking her in and sending her luggage up to her room. A personal concierge was assigned to her, though she protested she might not stay long, and a butler would be at her disposal should she need anything.

Finally, Jack ushered her into the elevator and punched the buttons for their floor. It was late, but people were still awake. She'd managed not to get recognized so far, except by the staff, and she breathed out a sigh of relief as the doors closed and she was alone in the elevator with Jack.

He didn't speak and she didn't either. She was still annoyed with him for suggesting Barry could be involved. When they reached their floor, he took her to the suite and made her stand outside the door while he checked the rooms for signs of intruders. When he was satisfied, he let her inside. Then he took out his phone and made a call.

"We're in … Yeah, copy."

He ended the call and a few moments later someone knocked on the door. He went and looked out the peephole before answering. One of his teammates—a guy they called Iceman—came inside with something that looked like a handheld radio. He swept the room and then moved into the next one. When he returned, he shook his head.

"It's clean."

"What's clean?" she asked.

"Bugs," Jack said.

"You're worried about bugs? Really? At a time like this?"

"Not insects, babe. Listening devices."

Gina colored. *Right*. She'd forgotten who she was dealing with for a second. Or the exhaustion and stress were catching up with her. "I see."

"Thanks, Ice," Jack said.

"Sure thing."

"Hey, why are you called Iceman?" Gina asked. "Isn't that kind of a cliché?"

Iceman looked at her and grinned. "Yeah, it is. Everyone's seen *Top Gun*. But maybe I'm just that cool under pressure."

Jack snorted. "Or maybe he got drunk one time when he first joined the team and kept asking if anyone had some ice, man. It kinda stuck."

Iceman laughed. "Yeah, that'd be the real reason. But you can call me Garrett, ma'am, if you prefer."

"Garrett, then. I'll be different. And thanks for helping me. I really appreciate it."

He gave her a wink and a salute and left. Gina crossed her arms over her middle and turned to look out at the bright lights of the Strip. There was so much happiness here. So much life and sin. And she was outside it, existing from minute to minute as she waited for news of her baby.

She hated this place suddenly. Hated all those happy people.

She whirled away from the window and stalked into the bedroom. Her luggage was laid out on racks, unzipped and waiting for her to select something. But what? Did she go to sleep for a few hours? Stay awake and will the phone to ring?

She heard Jack talking and she knew he was probably telling his team to investigate Barry's connection to Vegas. She understood why he was suspicious, she really did, but it hurt anyway. Barry was one of her best friends in the world, and she refused to believe he could be so diabolical.

A few minutes later Jack came into the bedroom. She thought she should tell him to knock first or something, but she didn't have the energy. The barriers that would normally be there between her and a man just weren't there with Jack.

"You didn't eat enough on the plane. I ordered room service."

"I'm not hungry."

"Gina." He walked into the room and stopped in front of her. His blue eyes roamed her face while her heart kicked up. When he met her eyes again, her breath hitched. "You have to rest and you have to eat. We don't know what's going to happen, and you need to be strong. That's one of the rules on a mission. Take care of yourself or you're no good to your team."

"I'm not part of your team. I'm just me."

"You aren't alone on this. We're here, and that makes you part of the team. I'm ordering you to eat, same as I'd order my spotter or anyone else under my authority, and then I'm ordering you to rest."

"I'm not under your authority." Maybe she should be angry at the way he was talking to her, but she was oddly touched. God, just blame it on stress and a situation outside her control. She needed to push this man away, but she couldn't seem to do it.

"Think of this like the island. I'm the one with the experience. I know what I'm doing. I got you out of there, didn't I?"

She nodded.

"Trust me to get you out of here too, okay?"

"All right."

He lifted an eyebrow. "You gonna eat when the food gets here?"

"Depends on what you ordered. I hate squash, for instance."

"Then I'll call and cancel the squash sandwich."

She couldn't help but laugh even though it had an edge that could turn into panic at any moment. "You didn't order anything of the sort."

"No." He backed away and reached for the door handle. "Put on your pajamas. Get comfortable."

"I don't wear pajamas. I don't wear anything."

He stopped in mid-swing and she wanted to laugh again. She did wear pajamas, but she'd wanted to rattle him. Just because.

"Well, honey, you can come out here in nothing if you want, but it'll probably be embarrassing for you and the delivery person both. Still, you can tip him good and I'm sure it'll be fine."

He shot her a grin before shutting the door behind him. Gina stood there her heart pounding and her pulse skipping and wondered just what it was about him that made her want to get beneath his skin.

ELEVEN

JACK WAS STARTLED AWAKE IN the gray light before dawn. He had always been an early riser, and even though he hadn't had much sleep the night before, old habits had him awake as usual. He blinked a few moments until he remembered where he was. And then he pushed himself upright on one elbow and gazed out at the glowing Vegas Strip arrayed below the expensive suite perched at the top of the hotel. The couch hadn't been half-bad, he decided, as he pushed himself the rest of the way up.

The remnants of the fruit-and-cheese platter he'd ordered last night were on a table nearby. He'd known Gina wouldn't eat much, but he'd wanted her to have something. She'd obliged him by eating cheese and strawberries and nibbling on a slice of pita bread. She had not been naked though. Not that he'd expected she would be, but when she'd said that to him about not wearing anything to bed, his body had responded immediately.

But then she'd come out of the room in a pair of silk pajamas that were actually pretty modest. He'd been disappointed, but whatever. She'd nibbled the fruit and talked about Eli until her eyes started sagging. He'd told her to go to bed, but she'd insisted she was all right.

And then he'd ended up carrying her into the room and putting her into the bed after she fell asleep on the chair. She was lighter than he'd expected, but she wasn't too thin. Her body was solid, if slight. She'd wrapped her arms around his neck and burrowed her head against his chest. He'd had to stop and close his eyes for a second at all the memories she brought up. He hadn't carried a woman to bed in years. Not since Hayley…

When he'd pulled the sheets back and placed Gina on the bed, she hadn't wanted to let him go. But she finally had, and he'd pulled up the covers and retreated to the couch. He'd checked in with the team first, and then he'd sat there staring at the lights and thinking he'd never get to sleep.

He'd taken off his shirt and jeans and stretched out with a blanket, but he didn't remember falling asleep. Obviously he had. Now he gazed across the dim suite toward Gina's room. He'd left the door open on purpose so he could hear her phone ring.

It hadn't, and that made his gut twist a little tighter. It was hard to think of the kid as his—and yet he was deeply invested in this mission to regain Eli. It wasn't that he'd fallen in instant love with the boy—how could he when he'd never met the child?—but it was *something*.

Something strange and wondrous—and scary as hell.

He stood and picked up his phone before walking over to the window and looking down at the ornate repro-duction of Italy below.

"Hey."

Jack turned. Gina stood in the open door, her hair

mussed, her silky pajamas wrinkled and clinging to her form. She was stunningly beautiful even when rumpled from sleep. She looked so real in these moments, nothing like the superstar he'd seen on that stage last night, and he found himself wanting to take her in his arms and hold her.

She walked out of the bedroom and wrapped her arms around herself. The movement pushed her breasts higher and he focused on keeping his eyes on her face. Because, yeah, there was the inconvenient attraction thing too.

"You sleep all right?" He was pretty sure he knew the answer to that question already.

"Not really, but it'll do."

"Maybe you should try for a couple more hours."

"I can't, Jack. I just can't."

"Okay. Then get dressed and I'll order breakfast. We'll see what the guys know."

"I'd rather see what they know now."

He should have expected that. His eyes drifted over her. "You may want to put on a robe then. I'll call them over."

She nodded and went back into the bedroom, and he dragged on his jeans. Gina emerged with a thick hotel robe belted around her waist. Her blond hair was wild and curly and she looked as tempting as a buffet would to a starving man.

Jack called the team. A few moments later, there was a knock on the door. All but two of them filtered inside. The other two—Flash and Fiddler—would be monitoring the equipment in the next room. Jack ordered food for the group at Gina's request, and they sat down to discuss the plan and any modifications. If they had anything on Barry, he knew they'd let him know first. But nothing was said as they discussed the situation.

There just wasn't much they could do without knowing what the kidnappers wanted. They couldn't plan a raid, because they didn't know where Eli was being held. It was nothing but a hurry-up-and-wait game.

And it was beginning to wear on Gina pretty hard. She was staring at her plate as the guys—and Lucky—talked, pushing her eggs back and forth into little mountains. She was tough, but she was also vulnerable. He'd seen that over the last few hours, and it brought out his protective instincts even while he was furious at her for lying to him and for protecting Barry.

Lucky looked hard at Gina's bowed head for a long moment. And then she stood. "Think we should be getting back to it, guys."

Kev looked up at his new wife with an expression Jack hadn't ever thought he'd see on the other man's face. The two of them had spent plenty of time seeing who could charm the panties off a woman first. It had been a contest of sorts, and they'd been pretty evenly matched.

But Kev wasn't charming the panties off anyone but Lucky these days. The guys all got to their feet and followed Lucky's lead. She'd really become one of the team after that mission to Qu'rim. She didn't always go out in the field with them, but when they needed an interpreter, she was there. And she did a damn fine job of translating documents and analyzing intel back at HOT HQ as well.

"We'll be listening," Matt said as he paused at the door. "And we'll be ready."

Jack nodded his thanks as his team leader walked out and closed the door behind him. He turned to find Gina leaning back against the couch, her eyes closed. He went over and took the plate from her lap, knowing she wasn't going to finish her food. She opened her eyes as he did so.

They were troubled, their green depths full of hot emotion she was working hard to contain. He sat down across from her and put his elbows on his knees.

"You okay?"

"I wasn't sure if I wanted kids," she said softly. "I have a sister, but she was put up for adoption when she was a baby. I was two, and they didn't want me. Or maybe my mother didn't want to give me up. I have no idea, really."

She sounded like a hurt little girl and it twisted into his soul. Damn, he didn't want to feel any tenderness toward her. But he did. "Have you ever asked her?"

"My mom died five years ago. And no, I never did." Gina sighed. "I think I was afraid to know the answer. But I always thought if my mother could give up a baby so easily, what if I was like her? What if I had a kid and then resented the intrusion into my life?"

He already knew the answer to that. "You don't, though."

She shook her head. "No, I definitely don't. I hate leaving Eli. I don't often do it, but I was only going to be gone a few hours. I was planning to get on the plane and be home again after the concert. If I'd brought him with me—" She pressed her knuckles to her mouth.

"They would have taken him another time. They were watching you, Gina. This wasn't a crime of opportunity."

She sniffed. "I know. And that's what I don't understand. Who would want to hurt me so much?"

He didn't mention Barry because he knew she didn't want to hear it. And they didn't know a damn thing anyway, so why antagonize her? "I'm afraid that's something I don't know."

"I always have fans who are a little too exuberant. Men who write me letters from prison, or men who send me inappropriate photos of themselves. And then there are the rare ones who track me down at my home. But they aren't usually all that stable to begin with." She looked pensive. "Then there were those ugly threats."

He'd read the report and it made his gut churn. "I know. But whoever took Eli had the resources to hire professionals. The two things might not be connected at all."

Which didn't mean Barry was in the clear, but one thing at a time.

She watched him for a long moment. "You're really handling all of this so well."

"It's my job."

She shook her head. "No, I meant that you must hate me but you aren't letting it show. I appreciate that."

He was watching her with those gorgeous blue eyes of his and her heart throbbed in response. But his gaze didn't waver. If it had, she would have known he was about to lie to her.

"I don't hate you."

If it was a lie, well, he was damn good at it. Because she believed him. She drew in breath to speak, but he cut her off with a raised hand.

"I don't hate you, Gina. But I don't think I'll ever forgive you."

She swallowed and looked down at her lap. "I get that."

And she did. She'd kept the truth from him for too long, and even though she'd told herself he didn't want to know, she had nothing to base that on but three days in a cave three years ago. He'd still been mourning the death of his wife and unborn child. And she'd known that wouldn't last forever. She'd owed him the truth in a much better way than she'd given it to him.

He got to his feet and moved away from her. He'd dragged on his jeans and T-shirt, but she remembered the way he'd looked when she'd first walked out this morning. He'd had his back to her and she'd gotten a full view of a tight ass and a broad back.

When he'd turned around, the view had been even better. He was tall and lean and hard, with the kind of body that could belong to a mixed martial arts fighter. She'd had to drag her gaze off his chest. She hadn't really had time for men in the last few months, and she hadn't missed them at all.

Until now.

Now she just wanted to bury herself in this one's arms and let him hold her until everything was right with the world again. But it had little to do with his being male and everything to do with him being who he was. Jack Hunter. Soldier, hero, badass.

Her phone blared in the silence and she gasped. Then she grabbed for it where she'd set it on the table. Jack was instantly at her side.

"Hello?"

"It's so nice of you to visit Las Vegas. I hear it's excruciatingly hot this time of year." It was a different man than the one she'd talked to before. His voice seemed familiar. He had an accent, a slight rolling of his words from time to time. She thought maybe she'd heard it before, and yet she couldn't place it. She talked to so many people.

Gina's heart pounded. "Where's my baby? What do you want?"

The man laughed. It wasn't a pleasant sound. *"Your* baby, Gina? I thought he was adopted."

Gina swallowed. Jack was watching her with hard eyes and she knew that his team was listening in on their devices. "He *is* adopted, which makes him mine."

"Oh, I'm thinking he's more than adopted," the man said.

"I don't know what you mean."

"I think you do." She heard the tapping of a keyboard. "Jackson Eli Robertson, born at five oh three in the evening, seven pounds, eight ounces. Mother, Regina Marie Robertson. Father, unknown."

Her heart was in her throat. Her eyes burned. Someone had leaked her baby's birth certificate. Barry knew the truth... but no, he wouldn't. She closed her eyes. "Of course I'm his mother. When I adopted him, the record was changed. That happens in some places, you know."

"Yes, but there was no need in this case. Because you gave birth to him in a small hospital on the island of Monterosso. The attending physician was Giovanna Crespini. You left the hospital a day later with your baby. But Gina, you've kept a terrible secret. A secret I know."

Her blood was pumping so hard she thought she might pass out. But she gripped the phone tight and forced the words past the knot in her throat. "What secret is that?"

Jack looked angrier than she'd ever seen him as he watched her. It made her feel there was a glimmer of hope, no matter how tiny. This man was fierce and tough and he would get Eli back. One way or the other, he would do it. She believed it. She *had* to believe it.

The man on the phone laughed softly, and she suddenly knew precisely who he was. She'd heard that laugh before on a windswept Greek night. Her blood froze.

"Your baby is a Metaxas. And he is therefore mine."

TWELVE

"HE'S NOT A METAXAS!" GINA yelled, and Jack's gut turned to ice. *Fuck.* Whoever it was thought that Eli was Athenasios Metaxas's baby. And that wasn't a good thing for anyone involved. He couldn't imagine what they wanted from Gina, but whatever it was, he was seriously fucking pissed now.

Gina's eyes grew big. She started to plead, but her plea cut off abruptly and she pulled the phone away from her ear and stared at Jack. Her face had drained of all color. It took him half a second to realize she was about to drop, but he reached out and caught her in time.

He swept her up in his arms and carried her to the couch where he deposited her as gently as he could. She turned her head into his chest and wrapped her arms around his neck. She wasn't crying, but she was shaking like she'd been outside in a snowstorm without clothes.

He wanted to know what the kidnappers had said, but he told himself to be patient. Even if she couldn't tell him, his team would. And soon. First, he had to hold her and hope the shaking would subside. He might be angry with her deep down, but he didn't like seeing her this way.

"Gina, babe, whatever it is, we'll fix it."

She held him tighter. "He wants Eli. That's all. Not money. Not anything. Just my baby. And me."

Holy shit. He didn't want to think about why this asshole wanted her. He squeezed her tighter. She sniffed and pushed back until she could look up at him. Her eyes were glassy. "He thinks Eli belongs to Athenasios. That I gave birth to Athenasios's baby."

Jack pushed her hair out of her face and tucked it behind her ear. "Who thinks that, sweetheart?"

Her fingers curled into his shirt. "Stavros Metaxas."

Fuck.

"I t…told you it wasn't Barry."

"You did. I'm sorry." Jack's phone rang and he brought it to his ear with a clipped, "Yeah."

It was Kev. "We got the whole thing, Hawk. But it's not going to do us a damned bit of good. The call came from an island in the Caribbean."

Jack knew which island. They all did. St. Margarethe, where they'd taken out Athenasios Metaxas and the terrorist leaders he'd been about to sell arms to three years ago. "Shit."

"Yeah," Kev replied.

There was always a successor. In this case, Stavros, the younger brother. His contacts weren't as extensive and he'd had trouble getting business in the years since HOT had interfered in their last big arms deal. He'd made small deals here and there, but nothing as big as what his brother had been on the verge of achieving. What the fuck did he want with Eli and Gina?

"But where is the boy? Is he with Stavros?"

"Most likely. Billy sampled the audio until he could separate out the streams. There was a child in the background. For what it's worth, he was laughing. And Stavros told Gina he had the boy."

Jack wanted to hit something. Or better yet, shoot something.

Stavros had been toying with her by sending her on a wild-goose chase to Vegas, nothing more. He'd wanted to get her hopes up, make her frantic and biddable—and then he'd cut the ground out from under her and left her swinging. Hell, maybe he'd been behind the letters, but they'd clearly moved beyond that now. Stavros Metaxas had his son. *His* son.

"What else did he say?"

"He believes Eli is his brother's child, but you'll have gathered that by now. He said he's taking him and raising him as a Metaxas. If Gina takes this public, he'll make sure the boy disappears forever. But if she comes to him within twenty-four hours, he'll make a deal with her that ensures she can have access to her child."

A fresh chill washed over Jack. And a spike of anger unlike any he'd ever felt before. "What kind of deal?"

"He didn't say."

"We can't let him get away with this."

"Agreed. But this one's going to take some serious planning. And more than a private plane and some equipment."

"How in the hell are we—"

"Richie's calling the colonel. This is a hostage situation now, bro. And you know what that means."

Fuck, yeah, he knew what it meant. It meant HOT could go after Eli. Because Metaxas was a petty arms dealer who sold weapons to terrorist organizations, and Eli was an American citizen. So was Gina. Metaxas expected her to come to the Caribbean and make a deal. But what kind of deal? And what if he refused to let her leave? So long as he had control over her child, he had control over her.

HOT wasn't going to allow it. *Jack* wasn't going to fucking allow it.

He felt scalding hot tears press against the backs of his eyes, but he wasn't sure if it was because of Gina and Eli or because of his team. Maybe it was all of them.

Goddamn, he loved these guys. "It means we're saddling up the posse," he said.

"Damn straight it does."

"Yippee ki-yay, motherfuckers."

Kev laughed at the line from *Die Hard*. "Let's rock and roll, buddy. We're bugging out."

In the end, it took several hours to get everything together and form a plan. They returned to DC on Gina's jet, and then they needed to go to their headquarters to gather intel and make deployment plans. Gina didn't know what any of that meant, but she knew she had to trust Jack and his team to get this done the right way.

She believed Eli was safe for now, but every minute that ticked by on the clock made her more frantic. Stavros wanted her to come back to the island where she'd con-

ceived Eli. She had no illusions that that was all he wanted. When she'd started dating Athenasios, Stavros had
made her uncomfortable the few times she'd been around
him. Where Athenasios was all charm and politeness at
first, Stavros was nothing but a pig. He'd made her skin
crawl just by looking at her.

She should have taken that feeling as a hint about the
whole family, in retrospect.

If Stavros got her alone, she didn't know what he
would do. Gina shuddered and ran her hands up and down
her arms. It was spring, but she was cold. Evie Baker
looked up from where she was standing at her stove, stir-
ring something. Whatever it was smelled divine.

Gina hadn't wanted to be here, but Jack had told her
she couldn't go with the team to their headquarters. He
hadn't wanted her to return to the hotel, so Matt called
Evie to come and pick her up. That had been over an hour
ago now.

Evie smiled. "You change your mind about that coffee? I can whip it up in no time."

"That would be nice," Gina said. Because she was
cold and the coffee would be hot. She let her gaze wander
the kitchen and great room of Matt and Evie's house. The
kitchen was huge, with commercial appliances, and the
great room had soaring wood ceilings from which an iron
chandelier was suspended. It looked like a European cot-
tage, all warm and homey.

Gina's heart squeezed at the thought of having a
home. She owned six houses, and she enjoyed all of them,
but not one of them had the same feeling this one did.

Evie started the coffee brewing and set a plate of
cranberry bars on the island. She fixed a serious look on

Gina. "I know you must be frantic. Being here with me doesn't help, but it'll work out. The guys know what they're doing."

"I know they do." Gina took a cranberry bar and bit off a corner. "I feel like I should be doing something, though."

"I know the last thing you want is advice, but try to save your energy during these down times. You'll need everything you've got once you go after your boy."

Gina nodded and Evie turned back to the stove to check her sauce. A few moments later, the coffee was done and she poured them both a cup. Gina fixed hers with cream and lifted the hot cup to take a sip.

"How do you do this, Evie?"

"It's not too hard. You just need really good coffee—"

"I didn't mean the coffee." Gina swallowed. "I meant... *this*. This life. Where you wait for Matt while knowing he's doing something dangerous."

Evie smiled. "Oh, you never really get used to it. But Matt doesn't go out on many missions anymore, so that helps. He directs a lot of operations, and sometimes he still goes in the field. This time will be one of them, I'm sure." She shrugged. "You just go about your business and have faith that your man knows what he's doing. Matt wouldn't cater an event for forty Junior League ladies, and I wouldn't strap on a gun and go after the bad guys."

"Lucky does it."

"Lucky is different." Evie nibbled her lip for a second. "I know it's none of my business, but Hawk—Jack—is a good guy. He's quiet. Enigmatic, maybe. But he was hurt pretty badly when his wife died, or so Matt tells me. I think it's made him more cautious than usual. But when he's with you, well... he seems a little different, that's all."

Gina had a lump in her throat. *Was* Jack different with her? And was that a good thing or a bad thing? "Eli is his son. Did Matt tell you that?"

Evie nodded. "It was a shock to everyone, I think."

"Including Jack." She lowered her gaze, unwilling to see the condemnation in the other woman's eyes.

But Evie reached out and put her hand over Gina's. "Hey, I'm not judging you. You had your reasons, and they're none of my business."

Gina pulled in a breath. "Thanks. But I should have told him before now. I just didn't know how. He says he'll never forgive me."

She didn't know what made her confess that, but Evie squeezed her hand and Gina was glad she'd shared. She was so accustomed to doing everything alone, to making her own way and being in charge of her destiny. It was lonely, but she did it. She sometimes wondered where her little sister was, but she had no idea who had adopted her. Her mother hadn't kept any paperwork—or maybe she hadn't known either. Gina had no idea if the adoption had been open or closed.

"Men say things in the heat of anger that they later regret. Give him time, Gina."

"He saved me three years ago. I wouldn't have made it out alive if not for him. And I didn't repay him very well, did I?"

"It's not an easy situation, I'll grant you that. But Eli is a real person, and he's half you and half Jack. For his sake, y'all will have to figure it out."

Her chest ached. "You sound so positive that we'll get him back."

Evie smiled. "That's because I am. I've seen the team in action before, and you have too. We know what they can do. Have faith in that."

Gina gripped her coffee cup in both hands and let the warmth flood her. "Have you been with Matt long?"

Evie's smile turned dreamy. "My whole life." Then she shook her head slightly and laughed. "Okay, not quite. But I've loved him since I was about eight, I think. We grew up together. He was my best friend when we were kids. Then he left me and went to join the Army." She shrugged. "I didn't see him for ten years, and then we met again last summer."

"Wow. Clearly it worked out though."

"Yes. We'll get married at Reynier's Retreat some-day."

"Reynier's Retreat?"

"It's Matt's family's home. An elegant antebellum mansion with giant columns and a front veranda unlike any you've ever seen. The gardens are divine."

Gina felt a pinch of envy. Not over the house so much as the way Evie was so happy—and also how she had a place where she belonged.

"Where's home?"

"Rochambeau, Louisiana. It's a small town, kinda nutty, but I love it. I have to admit I didn't always, but I do now. My mama and sister and all my family are there. I think Matt and I will live there one day."

"That sounds wonderful."

"It is. You'll have to come visit sometime."

Gina swallowed. "I'd like that."

Evie laughed. "If you walked into Mama's salon, half the ladies in Rochambeau would be scandalized to their roots and the other half would think they'd just witnessed the second coming."

Gina couldn't help the laugh that burst from her then. "I remember small-town living. We never stayed long in one place, but that sounds about right."

Evie looked curious. "Where's your family from?"

Gina shrugged as embarrassment settled in the pit of her stomach. "I don't really have any. There was just Mom and me, and she's gone now. She was a teen mother and her family threw her out. She never spoke about them."

"I shouldn't have asked."

"No, it's fine." And it was, except for the little hole in Gina's heart. "That's life."

Evie straightened and went over to the liquor cabinet where she grabbed a bottle of whiskey. "How about we doctor this coffee up a little bit, hmm? I make a mean brandied coffee."

Gina pushed her cup toward Evie. "Sounds like a plan to me."

"We shouldn't take her." Jack sat at the conference table in the ready room and stared at his teammates. They were giving each other looks they clearly thought he was missing. He wasn't missing a damned thing. "She's a civilian and she's not trained."

"But Metaxas wants her there. And if she's not there in twenty-four hours, we don't know what he'll do," Billy said. "We can't risk the kid's life."

"We can get in and out before the deadline." He didn't want to risk Eli's life—but he didn't want to risk Gina's either. He needed space on this op, and that was something he wasn't going to get if Gina was there. His usual calm had gone MIA.

And they all knew it.

Kev leaned forward, elbows on the table. "No guarantee we can. You remember that place. Metaxas's compound is on an isolated peninsula. There's no easy way in or out."

"It's not that damned isolated. There's a city on the other side of the island." But there was a mountain between the peninsula and the city, and only one twisty road that connected the two.

Jack knew what they were saying made sense, and yet he couldn't help having a visceral reaction to the idea of Gina going to Metaxas. Of her being in that house again and being in danger. There had to be another way.

But there wasn't. He knew it. They knew it. And they were looking at him with sympathy, waiting for him to admit what they all knew. No one said anything.

Jack threw down the pen he'd been tapping on the table and let out an explosive breath. "All right, fine. We have no choice. She goes."

The door opened and Colonel Mendez walked in. Everyone shot to their feet and snapped to attention.

"As you were," he said.

Everyone sat. Mendez walked over and looked at the maps arrayed on the table. Then he glanced up at the slide on the screen which showed the aerial view of Metaxas's compound and another view of the island. It was a large island with a flourishing tourism trade. But that was on a different part and not easily reachable from the side where Metaxas had built his house.

"This is a tricky one," Mendez said as walked up to the screen. Then he turned back to them. "On many levels."

He sank into his usual seat and let his hard gaze slide over them. It lingered on Jack, and that wasn't something he liked very much. In all the years with HOT, he'd never actually been the object of Mendez's scrutiny. He did his job, he kept his mouth shut, and he stayed out of trouble.

Clearly, that era was over.

"Not asking how the kid is yours, Hawk," Mendez finally said. "Though I figure I already know."

"Yes, sir," Jack said, keeping his gaze on the colonel's face. There was no denying what everyone knew. And no denying when it had happened either. They all remembered those three days when he'd been isolated with Gina and waiting for the team to extract him.

Mendez's gaze slipped on by and Jack's breath slowly left his body. The colonel had been known to make lesser men cry. Jack didn't think it was possible with him, and yet he really didn't want to find out.

"This mission isn't completely regulation, but we're going anyway. Turns out Stavros Metaxas has been a busy man lately. He's entered into negotiations with the opposition forces in Qu'rim."

Jack could see Lucky stiffen out of the corner of his eye. She'd done a lot to stop the violence in Qu'rim, but unfortunately it had taken on a life of its own. The Freedom Force was effectively dismantled, but there were always other groups waiting to take its place.

The Qu'rimi Opposition had been infiltrated long ago by militants. They were severely weakened after Al Ahmad's defeat, but they weren't dead yet. An influx of weapons would only prolong the violence.

Jack's blood began to hum. If Metaxas was negotiating with the Qu'rimis, he was a target. And Jack was the one who'd get to pull the trigger.

But Mendez's gaze swung back to him. "Brandy's taking point on this one."

Jack's anger surged. His spotter was a good sniper, one of the best—but he was better. *The* best. And this bastard was his. "Sir, I respectfully disagree."

"You don't get to disagree, Hawk. You're emotionally compromised and we don't have an order to kill. I need to know that my sniper will obey orders."

He thought of the last time he'd taken out a Metaxas. He'd done the job—and then he'd done more than he was supposed to. But Gina was alive because of that choice, and he didn't regret it.

"All right."

Mendez raised an eyebrow. "All right?"

"All right, sir," Jack amended.

The colonel's eyes flashed. "I shouldn't let you go on this mission at all."

Jack's gut clenched hard. But he didn't open his mouth. Mendez was testing him. Looking for a fight. Looking for weakness.

He wouldn't show it.

Finally, Mendez nodded. "I'm not that cruel. But I expect you to follow orders and do the job properly."

He stood then and everyone followed suit, snapping to attention until the colonel walked out.

The guys all looked at each other, their expressions grim. "You heard the man," Matt said. "Let's bug out."

THIRTEEN

GINA SAT IN ONE OF the plush leather club chairs on her plane and scrolled through her phone, looking at pictures of Eli. Jack was nearby, chin on his fist as he brooded. They hadn't spoken in about an hour now. It was hell being near him like this and not knowing what to say.

It was almost like being back in the cave together, except there hadn't been any bad blood between them then and conversation had flowed freely. She'd been scared, but he'd kept her mind off it and she'd talked about so many things. Not everything, but almost.

Now she had no idea what to say to this man. The father of her child. The soldier who made her belly clench and her sex ache with one hot look. What was wrong with her? She had no time for this kind of thing. No time for speculation and memories of the heat they'd shared.

But he was Eli's father, and it was inevitable she would remember how that had happened. Especially since they were returning to the island where they'd made Eli.

Her heart squeezed at the thought of going back into the lion's den. She didn't want to go, and yet she had no choice. Stavros had told her she would never see Eli again if she didn't come. So she was on her way and terrified about what awaited her.

But she was determined too. She wasn't letting Stavros have her baby. She would do whatever it took to get him back.

The rest of the team was on another plane, traveling a similar route. Jack would stay in contact with them, but she and Jack were essentially on their own. She'd thought they would travel together as they had to Las Vegas, but Jack had explained it was better to go separately. It was always possible Stavros would have her watched when she landed at the airport, and if she emerged from the same plane as Jack's team did, Stavros might know it. That was a risk they couldn't take.

Gina closed her eyes and imagined having Eli back safe and unharmed.

Jack blew out a breath and her eyes snapped open. He'd seemed agitated from the moment she'd met him on the tarmac at the airport, and it hadn't changed much since.

"Penny for your thoughts," she said and then wanted to bite her tongue because it was so lame.

Jack slanted a dark look at her. "It's nothing."

Gina sighed. "Then stop looking like someone peed in your cornflakes. You're making the flight attendants nervous."

She didn't know that he was, but it was something to say. Besides, neither of the attendants had been back here in half an hour. They knew not to disturb Gina unless she buzzed them. She liked her quiet time for reflection when traveling. Not that it happened often, considering she usually traveled with a retinue. Except for the flight staff, they'd all been left home this time.

Thank God.

Barry was off to Hawaii with a new lover, none the wiser that he'd been the object of Jack's suspicion for a few hours. Gina had no engagements for a couple of weeks, so it had been easy to leave the posse behind— even her usual security firm's men because now she had Jack and his team.

"I'm not making them nervous."

"Then where are they?"

He moved his hand. A moment later one of the attendants appeared, smiling broadly, and Gina knew he'd pressed the button to summon her. This girl had red hair and pink lipstick and she sashayed her way toward Jack.

"What may I get you, sir?"

Her voice was bright and cheery and Gina wanted to snap at her. Except that wasn't fair and she would do nothing of the sort.

Jack's gaze drifted over the girl, lingering on her chest for a moment, and Gina's face heated. "I'd like a soda, Stephanie. Thanks."

Stephanie. He'd been looking at her name, not her chest. Or maybe he'd been looking at both.

"Yes, sir." Stephanie turned toward Gina. "And you, ma'am? Can I get you anything?"

The *ma'am* made her feel old, though it was simple politeness. "Sparkling water with lime."

"Yes, ma'am."

Stephanie disappeared again, her rump swaying invitingly in her dark blue skirt.

"She's cute," Jack said.

Gina lifted an eyebrow and tried to look disinterested. "Is she? I hadn't noticed."

Jack chuckled, and Gina flipped a page in the magazine sitting on the tray in front of her.

Stephanie returned a few moments later with drinks and snacks. Once they were settled, she gave them her bright smile and disappeared again.

Jack grabbed a handful of pretzels. "Didn't look nervous to me," he said before popping them into his mouth and chewing.

"She's a good actress."

Jack laughed. "No, you're just a poor liar."

Gina crossed her arms and glared at him. "Fine, she's not nervous. None of them are. Clearly, your problem is with me—and I'd appreciate it if you'd get over it so we can get Eli and get home again. After that, you can be pissed at me all you like. But right now you're making me jumpy and I don't like it."

Whoa, where had all that come from?

But then Jack opened his mouth, and any embarrassment she might have felt flew out the window.

"You're right, my problem *is* with you. But it's not what you think, Gina. I know my job and I'm good at it. What I don't like about this op is you being here. I'm worried about what Metaxas wants, and I'm worried about keeping you safe."

Her heart thumped and her breath shortened. He was worried about her? "Oh."

His eyes flashed. "Yeah, *oh*. I don't fucking like this, and I don't trust Metaxas. I argued for leaving you behind, but I was the only one who wanted that. So you're here, and I'm with you instead of where I ought to be."

She closed her eyes for a second. She'd known he was pissed about being with her instead of with his team. Of course he was. The dude was fricking Rambo or something. "I didn't ask for a babysitter."

"No, but you got one."

Anger bubbled inside her. "Do you think I like this situation any better than you do? Stavros has my baby and I'm terrified about what he's going to do once I get there. I won't need a fucking babysitter then, asshole. I'll need the man who shot all those bastards the last time and saved my life!"

She shot to her feet and glared down at him. Yeah, she understood why he was pissed at her. She'd kept the truth from him when she shouldn't have, but now they were here, on their way to Stavros and whatever crazed plan he had, and she didn't need to deal with Jack's anger on top of her fear and anxiety about Eli and what awaited her on St. Margarethe.

Jack rose. He towered over her and she hated that. "I'm not going to let anything happen to you," he growled. "But I'd prefer you weren't there so I could concentrate on getting Eli back and stop worrying about you."

Her heart throbbed, but she told herself not to read anything into it. "Don't worry about me. I'll take care of myself."

"The way you did the last time?"

"I ran into you, didn't I? I'd say I did a pretty good job."

He took a step closer to her, his nostrils flaring. "And what about in the compound, Gina? What about when you're at his mercy?"

"I'll do the best I can. You'll be there."

Or so she hoped. They'd decided that she would call Stavros's bluff when they arrived. He wanted something from her. They didn't know what that was, but Jack and his team seemed to believe she had a bargaining chip. It wouldn't get her much, but they believed it would earn her some concessions. For one, they thought she should insist on meeting him in the city. They didn't believe he would agree to that, but it was the first step in insisting she be allowed one bodyguard.

That bodyguard was Jack. If Stavros refused, then she didn't know what she would do. But that was a bridge they'd cross when they got to it.

"*Maybe* I'll be there. But what if I'm not?"

Her stomach churned.

"I'll do what I have to do to survive." Her throat ached, but she knew deep down that was the case. She'd do what it took to buy herself time and to keep Eli safe until Jack and his team arrived. No matter what it was, she'd do it.

And Jack seemed to think so too. His jaw tightened. "Will you fuck him, Gina? Give him a taste of that sweet pussy if he asks for it?"

She wanted to gasp in outrage. But she didn't. Worse, her pussy throbbed with heat. Damn him anyway. Judgmental asshole. She bared her teeth. "I'd fuck the devil himself if it got me what I wanted. Don't you know that, baby?"

"Yeah, I know it."

And that was the last straw, no matter that she'd taunted him. They'd spent three days together waiting for rescue and they'd only had sex on the last day. She'd thought he'd seen beneath the glitzy tough-girl veneer, but he hadn't. He'd said the words so matter-of-factly, like she was the kind of woman who'd achieved everything she had by screwing her way to the top. It was the kind of thing the tabloids liked to say about her, and it made her utterly furious.

She didn't know what she was doing when she closed the distance between them and swung her fist at his head.

He caught it before it connected and spun her around until her back was to him, her body pressed against his, her ass wedged tight to his groin. His arms wrapped around her and he held her hard against him.

"I hate you," she spat. "I wish I'd never met you."

His breath was hot on her neck. "Likewise, babe." But his cock was growing against her and her stomach twisted tight.

Oh, it wasn't fair. Gina closed her eyes and tried to will away the arousal sweeping through her body like a flash fire. Why did he affect her this way? Why, when he was such a jerk? He'd been so wonderful and tender the last time, but this time he was an arrogant prick and she hated him.

Except that her body didn't. Her body recognized his and responded. Her nipples tightened until the lacy fabric of her bra was almost torture.

"Let me go."

He did as she asked, letting her go so quickly that she stumbled forward and would have fallen had she not caught herself on the chair. She whirled on him, angry and hurt and frustrated.

"You bastard. Don't you ever touch me again!"

"Or what?" he said. "You'll get too excited?"

Gina stiffened her spine and glared at him. "Fuck

you, Jack Hunter. Fuck you for the asshole you are."

Her pride stung and her heart ached. It didn't matter that she donned a tough exterior with him. She was wounded by his indifference and his casual assumption that she could give her body to a man like Stavros without any remorse or feeling.

Not that she was going to choose Stavros. And it truly angered her that Jack thought she could, or that he believed her body was somehow more sacred than his as a bargaining chip. She had no doubt he'd screw some modern day Mata Hari for information if he needed it.

"I told you I'm not interested, babe. But thanks for the offer."

And that made her utterly ballistic. *Jerk. Asshole. Fuckhead.*

She wanted to prove to him, more than anything, that he wasn't the tower of strength he thought he was. He was a hypocrite.

"Not interested, huh? What's going on in your jeans, hotshot?"

His gaze hardened. "Told you before, if you're gonna display the tits and ass, it has an effect."

"I'm wearing jeans and a T-shirt, jerk."

"And I can see every curve and bump."

She put her hands beneath her breasts and hefted them. "Oh, you mean these? Yeah, they're such a nuisance."

"Gina." His voice was torn between a growl and a plea, and she felt a reckless surge of adrenaline in her veins.

"Oh, I'm so hot," she whispered, pulling her shirt from her waistband and lifting it. "The infamous Gina

Domenico who gangbangs ten men before going on stage every night."

"Gina."

She knew she should stop, but the tone of his voice spurred her on. Like he was aching something fierce. Like she was torturing him.

"Yeah, you know me, baby. Just a girl who can't control her urges."

"For God's sake, I didn't say that."

"Didn't you?"

He only glared at her.

She suddenly wanted to win this contest between them. She wanted him panting and gasping, and she wanted to walk away and leave him hard and unfulfilled.

Gina whipped the T-shirt over her head and tossed it on the chair. "Oh, my urges are out of control."

Jack moved so fast she couldn't get away from him before he had his hands on her shoulders. But instead of yanking her into his arms, he turned her and pushed her toward the back of the plane. Toward the bedroom that was there.

"Are you taking me to bed, big boy?"

He pushed her forward. "Yeah, something like that."

She walked down the aisle, laughing softly. When they reached the door, he yanked it open and thrust a hand against the frame to steady himself.

She leaned into the door and gave him a smile. "Don't you want to come in?"

His Adam's apple moved. "No."

She let her gaze drop to his crotch. The outline of his cock was long and firm, and a surge of wetness flooded her.

"Doesn't look like that to me."

"Gina."

She lifted her gaze and found him looking at her with a combination of heat and fury that made her stomach clench. "What?"

"You don't want me. You're pissed off at me. And you're trying to make me pay for it."

"Aw, does it hurt?"

"Nothing I can't handle."

She had no idea where it came from, but she reached out and ran her hand over his cock. It leapt at her touch. "Or I could handle it."

He couldn't quite stifle his groan. "What game are you playing with me?"

His words chilled her, reminded her of her mission. "You're hard for me, Jack. You want me. You want to sink deep inside me and fuck me hard. *Me*, Jack. Not Stephanie. Not some other woman. Not Hayley. *Me*. And you hate that about yourself. You can deny it all you like, but you want me. Be man enough to admit it."

He was silent for a long moment. And then he swore long and hard. "I'd like nothing better than to strip you naked and fuck you until you scream. I want to lick you and suck you and make you come. But so does every man who sees you on that stage, Gina. I'm one in a million to you—and I know when I'm being played." His eyes raked over her, his look disdainful, and she felt small, as if she'd lost control of the situation after all.

Her throat was tight. She'd trotted out the persona, large-and-in-charge Gina, and it was coming back to bite her in the butt.

He shook his head. "And even if you weren't playing

me, you lied to me. I can't forget that."

She tried to be nonchalant, and yet it hurt. "So that means sex is out of the question, I take it? No licking after all?"

He reached out and ran a finger over her jaw. "I'd lick anything you wanted me to lick. But it'd be meaningless. Is that really what you want?"

She swallowed, her heart thumping. *No*. "Maybe I do."

He bent toward her then, his lips so close to hers that her breath razored in and out of her lungs while she prayed he would kiss her. Where had her determination to humiliate him gone? Oh, she had no idea. All she wanted was his mouth on hers. On her body. Everywhere.

And then his mouth touched hers and she whimpered. His lips licked across hers, fanning the flames of a desire she'd tried to convince herself she was in control of.

She wasn't. She *so* wasn't.

He pulled away, his mouth a hair's breadth from hers. "You're just a paper tiger, babe. And I'm not scared."

He backed away, staring at her for a long moment. And then he turned and walked up the aisle.

FOURTEEN

JACK WAS PISSED. AT HIMSELF. At Gina. And he hurt. His balls ached with the need to spend inside Gina's gorgeous body. He flopped into the seat and adjusted himself to take some of the pressure off. It didn't do much good. His body was tight, the testosterone raging through him and demanding release. This was no way to embark on a mission.

But what the fuck was he supposed to do? Spread her out on the bed and lose himself in her willing body?

Yes.

No. Jack clenched his fingers into a fist and closed his eyes. She'd brought up Hayley. She'd told him he wanted her instead of sweet Hayley—and she was right, which angered him even more. He'd loved Hayley with his whole being, and he'd thought he died when he lost her. His life had closed in on itself like a rare flower deprived of sunlight.

And he hadn't opened back up again. He'd existed in darkness and loneliness, and he'd been just fine.

He was still fine. Except he wanted the woman he'd

just hustled back to the bedroom more than he could remember wanting anyone in a long time. He wasn't deprived when it came to sex. He had plenty of numbers in his contacts list and he could call up a dozen women who would be happy for a one-night hookup.

Which he'd probably do if he weren't on a plane over the ocean, winging toward an island in the southern Caribbean. Jack put his forehead in his hand and concentrated on breathing deeply. *Fuck.*

"Can I get you anything else, sir?"

He looked up at the woman standing over him. She was a redhead, busty, and had a pretty smile. She wasn't wearing an engagement or wedding ring. He could flirt with her. He could take her to the lavatory and join the mile-high club.

She was looking at him expectantly, and he realized she'd unbuttoned her blouse another two buttons. Her cleavage was nice. Inviting.

He shook his head. "Thanks, uh, Stephanie. But no. Nothing else."

Her smile dimmed. "Just let me know if you change your mind."

"I'll do that."

She picked up his glass and napkin and disappeared up the aisle. Jack let out his breath. Jesus. What the hell was wrong with him? He could have cleared his head with Stephanie, released some tension.

But, goddamn, it hit him like a ton of bricks that he actually felt some sort of loyalty to Gina in this moment. Like he owed her something. She'd fucking lied to him about his child, and he thought he owed her something? She was screwing with his head, sobbing on him one minute, teasing him the next, begging him to touch her and acting all vulnerable and confused when he didn't.

He couldn't do this. He couldn't go into this mission with his head so muddled. Mendez had accused him of being emotionally compromised, and it hit him hard that he was, that his life was changing because a woman he'd made love to three years ago had had his child.

Jack got up and stalked through the cabin. He had to tell her they needed to stop fighting each other. That this was too important and he needed her to be straight with him. Utterly straight.

He reached the door and stopped, uncertain for a second. And then he rapped on it. When she didn't answer, he jerked it open. She wasn't in the room. His heart throbbed. She couldn't have gone anywhere, but it was a reaction to her absence just the same. He took a step forward.

And then he saw her in the adjoining bathroom, her body bare, her arms over her head as she twisted her hair up and pinned it. She'd turned on the shower. It was an amazing shower for an airplane, a space big enough to hold six people. There was even a full-sized bathtub. It hit him again just how rich she was. How out of his orbit she was.

He was a boy from a working-class family in Florida, and she was a superstar. She looked into the mirror then and saw him. Her hands stilled on top of her head and her mouth fell open. Her nipples were hard little points and her waist dipped in before flaring over her hips. He wondered if she was wet, if her body had responded to his when she was caressing him or if it really was all a game.

Her hands slowly fell to her sides. And then she

turned, her arms crossing over her breasts. Which was ridiculous because her pussy was still bared to his gaze. That little triangle of dark blond hair. The dip of her belly and plumpness of her lips.

"What do you want?"

He couldn't speak. "I…" He shook his head, but it didn't clear. She was still there. Still beautiful. Still tempting. His balls ached harder than before. His cock was thick and full. All he could do was tell her the truth.

"You make me ache, Gina. You make me not care about consequences."

Gina's throat was dry. Jack was looking at her with that same combination of pain and anger he always seemed to look at her with and it made her heart hurt.

Tears filled her eyes and she shook her head. "I don't want you to hate me. That's not what I want."

"I don't hate you. I told you."

"You're here against your will. You'd rather be with your team—or with anyone but me."

He blew out a harsh breath. "I'd rather be with them because I want you safe, Gina. You aren't a special operator. You shouldn't be here."

"But Stavros wants me."

He swore. "I know. And I don't want him to have you."

Her breath hitched as she took his meaning. "We

don't know that's what he wants—"

"Whether he does or not, it makes me sick to think of you with him."

She dropped her chin and looked at her feet. It occurred to her that she was naked, and that she was doing a poor job of hiding her body from Jack. She reached for a towel and pulled it over herself.

"I don't want to sleep with him. I won't." She swallowed. "Unless it's the only way to save Eli."

He crossed the distance and tilted her chin up until she had to look him in the eye. His gorgeous blue eyes were troubled. "I don't want him to have you. I don't want anyone to have you."

Her heart squeezed tight and butterflies swirled in her belly. "Why not?"

"Because I'm a jealous bastard. Because I want you, and I'm not sharing." He cupped her jaw. "Do you understand me? I don't share."

"I'm not yours, Jack."

He reached for the towel and carefully stripped it away. She didn't stop him. And then he circled a nipple with one finger. The steam in the bathroom had made her sweat, so his finger glided slickly around the sensitive flesh.

"I think you are, babe. I think you want to be."

"You're too full of yourself."

"I'd like to fill you."

Her pussy throbbed. Oh, how she wanted that too. But it was dangerous with Jack. So dangerous. She'd given herself to him before. Given him her heart. And he hadn't even known it. Those three days in the cave had been the most honest exchange she'd ever had with a man—but he wasn't in the same place she'd been, and when he'd told her it couldn't go anywhere between them, she'd retreated into the pop-star persona that insulated the real her from the world. It hadn't ended well, but she'd never stopped thinking about those three days.

About this man.

"What changed your mind?"

"Stephanie."

Gina didn't like the flare of jealousy in her soul. "Why, did you make a move and she turned you down?"

He pinched her nipple and she sucked in a breath. "No. I turned her down."

He lifted his other hand and cupped her breast. The shower continued to steam.

"I'll fire her," Gina gasped as he tweaked her nipples.

Jack lowered his head and licked one stiff nipple and she shivered. "That's harsh, babe. I think you should thank her."

She clutched his shoulders as he continued to lick and suck. Her eyes threatened to roll back in her head it felt so good. "Why would I do that?"

"Because she made me realize how much I wanted you. Only you."

"Jack," she gasped as he glided a hand down her body and slid his fingers between her lips.

"God, you're wet."

He pushed a finger inside her and then another. His thumb skated over her clitoris and she wanted to scream. Instead, she bit her lip. His fingers moved rhythmically, sliding in and out of her body and driving her arousal higher. She was strung tight, but she knew she could go tighter still. And she knew the release would be incredible.

"Jack, please."

"Please what, sweetheart?"

She gazed up at him, her breath catching hard in her chest, and knew what she needed more than anything. More than orgasms, more than his body pounding into hers, more than her next breath.

"Kiss me. I need you to kiss me."

His mouth crushed down on hers, his tongue thrusting between her lips and stroking against her own. Gina's arms went around his neck, but when she met the cloth of his shirt, she began to tug it upward. He broke the kiss long enough to rip it off his shoulders and over his head. Her hands splayed over his muscles, clutched him like a lifeline, while he kissed her as if he were starved for her.

She was certainly starved for him. She couldn't hide it any longer, couldn't deny it. He was everything she'd wanted, everything she remembered. His mouth was sweet and hard and demanding. He kissed her like he owned her soul, like he would accept nothing less.

The man kissed like a god.

He stopped stroking his fingers into her and then he lifted her and set her on the counter. The marble was cold against her ass, but she didn't mind. The rest of her was so hot it didn't matter.

She hoped he'd open his jeans and plunge inside her, but he didn't. She clung to him while he kissed her hard, his fingers shaping her, playing with her nipples, her pussy. And then he broke the kiss and she whimpered.

"I have to taste you."

Her heart hammered in her chest, her throat, as he dropped to his knees and pressed hot kisses against the inside of her thighs. And then he spread her open with his fingers and ran the point of his tongue from her clit to the wet seam of her pussy and back again. Gina swallowed the scream that gathered in her throat. Her fingers clutched the edge of the counter and her back was against the mirror. The steam from the shower glistened across her body.

And across his. His skin rippled with ink and muscle and he pushed her legs wider until she had to perch her feet on the counter to brace herself.

And then he licked her again, his hot tongue gliding against her in just the way she liked. He slid a finger inside her while he licked and sucked her clitoris. Gina's breath came in hot gulps as she tried to hold back the tide. She wanted to enjoy it, wanted to linger in the sensuality and amazing feelings he was making happen inside her.

She should have told him no. She should have refused him. Because sex with Jack turned her inside out and made her want things she couldn't have. Like him. He'd told her he would never forgive her, but he was clearly capable of having sex with her.

"You taste good," he said. "So fucking good."

And then he found the tight rim of her anus and pressed a finger just there, just barely—and it sent her over the edge. Gina's body exploded in a wave of heat and sensation. Her orgasm ripped through her, making her cry out, but Jack didn't stop licking her until she gripped his hair and pulled him away. She was too sensitive, too raw, her body too splintered to take another second of torture.

Gina put a hand over her eyes to shield herself from his gaze. What the hell had just happened? She'd come unglued, her emotions breaking free of the box she tried so hard to keep them in.

She was afraid of what he'd see in her eyes, so she

kept hers face covered and worked on breathing evenly while her skin rippled with the aftershocks of her pleasure.

"Gina, you okay, babe?"

A lump formed in her throat and she shook her head because she was afraid she'd sob if she tried to speak. What was he doing to her? How was it this was the man who affected her so deeply even after so many years?

He pulled her into his arms and she laid her head against his chest and wrapped her arms around him. He smelled good, clean and fresh like soap, and she clung to him. Eventually, he pushed her back until he could see her eyes.

"You okay?"

Her heart pinched tight. "Yes."

"I'm sorry for being a dick earlier. That's what I came here to say. Not for this." He shook his head. "But you were naked, and I lost my mind. Seem to do that a lot with you."

She reached for the button to his jeans. "I like it when you lose your mind. It feels good."

He laughed, but his eyes remained deadly serious. "I'm not sure we should do this, Gina. Sex clouds thinking, and sex with you shuts my brain down entirely."

She slipped the button open and started working on sliding the zipper down. His cock pressed against the fabric as she eased the zipper open until finally he was overflowing the opening.

"It's a little too late to put the genie back in the bottle, don't you think?"

FIFTEEN

YEAH, IT WAS DEFINITELY THAT. Jack wanted to lose himself inside her body for hours on end. They didn't have hours, but they had a little while. If he could have her now, maybe he could clear his head enough to get on with this mission. What had he told her? That it drove him crazy to think of Metaxas touching her?

Fuck, yeah, it did. The genie was definitely out of the bottle, and in more ways than one. He'd told her she was his. That he was jealous and he wasn't sharing her. Where the hell had that come from?

He didn't know, but as she leaned forward and pressed her mouth to his abdomen, he knew he'd spoken the truth. He was jealous. Completely and utterly, and it twisted him up inside to realize it.

He knew this thing between them wouldn't last. He didn't see them building a life together. How ridiculous was that idea anyway?

Even if he could forgive her, he had HOT and she had her privileged existence. But he would be a part of Eli's life; that much he knew. He just didn't know how it would happen yet.

"Jack," she said against his skin, her mouth moving up his body to his pecs. She wrapped her hand around his cock, but the soft cotton of his underwear was a torturous barrier between her and his flesh. Then she fastened her lips over his nipple and a shock of sensation shot to his toes.

Jesus Christ.

He gripped her by the hips and picked her up. Then he toed off his shoes and walked into the shower with her. He didn't care that his jeans were getting soaked or that she must surely think him insane. But she was holding him tight, her head tilting back as she laughed.

He set her down and she shoved at his jeans until his cock sprang free. Her eyes widened, her mouth going slack. "Oh, you are beautiful. I want to taste you now."

He took her wrists in one hand and pushed them above her head. "No way, gorgeous. You do that and I'm done."

She twisted in his grip. "No fair. You tasted me."

"And now I want to fuck you." Except, dammit, he didn't have a condom. He stood there as disappointment rolled through him, cursing himself silently. Gina was biting her lip. They both knew what had happened the last time, even with a condom.

"I'm on the pill. I wasn't before. And I'm not promiscuous, no matter what you think."

Her words made him feel like an asshole. "I don't think that."

But he'd implied it, and they both knew it. Because he was confused and pissed and insane with jealousy and, yeah, guilt. After all this time, the way she made him feel still had the power to make him feel like he was betraying Hayley.

He cleared his throat. "I'm clean, too. We get tested for the job. I never, uh, do this without protection."

"I know."

Her gaze dropped and he could feel the tension between them changing into a different kind. One less about sex and more about emotions. He didn't know how to respond to that, so he tipped her chin up and fused his mouth to hers. When he let her wrists go, she wrapped her arms around his neck and arched her body into his. Her hard little nipples pressed against his chest, and he cupped her full breasts in both his hands. God, she was lush.

The water was starting to cool, but he didn't mind it. He needed something to slow down this fire in his blood. Still, he felt her shiver and he reached out and flipped the taps closed.

"I want to take you in a bed," he growled against her neck, nipping her softly, her gasps making his cock ache. "You deserve a bed."

The last time, he'd taken her on the sandy floor of a cave. They'd been wedged tightly together, rocking into each other frantically. It had been hot and desperate and sexy—but not precisely comfortable or leisurely.

Not that they had the luxury of leisure now, either. But they had comfort.

"I want you wherever I can have you," she replied, nipping him back.

He took a moment to shove his jeans into a sodden lump on the floor, and then he scooped her up and carried her the few steps to the bed. They were soaking wet as he laid her down and came down on top of her, but he was too far gone to care.

"You're gorgeous, Gina. A wet dream come true," he told her, pressing her breasts together and sucking her nipples in turn while she writhed. "I want to do everything to you. At once."

"Yes. Oh, yes."

Their mouths met again and he reached down to hook an arm around one of her knees and draw her wide open. She wrapped her other leg around his ribs, gripping him tight.

And then she reached down and grabbed the head of his cock, guiding him into her wetness. He groaned as he sank into her, and then he stilled. He just wanted to feel this for a few seconds. The way her body held him, the slickness of her flesh, the mingling of their breaths as they kissed. She was hot in all the right places, welcoming and soft.

He could feel her heart beating hard where her chest pressed against his. It gratified him to know she was affected by this thing between them too.

"Goddamn," he said, breaking the kiss and cupping her jaw in his free hand. "You feel amazing, Gina."

"So do you." She smiled, and it was tentative enough that his heart twisted hard in his chest. How could a woman like her be uncertain about herself at a time like this? She was a goddess, a fucking sex kitten, and he was pretty much the luckiest man alive at this moment—even if a part of him still ached because she'd kept the existence of his kid from him.

"Am I hurting you?"

"No."

He flexed his hips, sliding deeper into her hot wetness, and groaned. "How do you want it, babe? Hot and fast? Slow and sexy? I'll do my damnedest to give you exactly what you need."

She reached up and ran her fingers over his mouth. "How do *you* want it, Jack?"

His laugh was broken. *Any way he could get it.* "I asked you first."

She slid a hand between them and cupped his balls. "I want you to come as hard as I did."

Her heart felt as if it would pound out of her chest as she gazed up at him. She wanted him to lose control the way she had, to break apart helplessly while she watched and knew she was the one who'd caused it to happen. She wanted to see raw pleasure in his eyes, and she wanted to see the vulnerability she felt reflected back at her.

But he was more in control than she was, even though she literally had him by the balls. Jack would never show her those things, and her heart ached even while it craved more from him. She was in so much trouble here. So much.

She couldn't seem to find the barrier she'd erected between them before. It was gone, shattered into a million tiny pieces, and she was afraid he could see everything she felt.

I love you.

It whispered in the air between them, even though she

was the only one who could hear it. Because she was the only one who felt it. It was confusing to love a man you felt like you'd known your whole life, but who in reality you didn't know at all. But she felt safer with Jack than she'd ever felt with anyone else. That meant something.

Her belly clenched into a knot. Not a bad knot, but an oh-my-God-I-love-this-man knot.

"Gina," he said—growled, really. "I could spend a week in bed with you and not do nearly everything I want to you. But no matter what I do, I guarantee I'm going to come hard. And probably sooner than I'd like."

"Then we'll just have to do it again."

He grinned, and then he moved his hips and stroked into her. Gina couldn't help the gasp that rolled through her. "Hold on, babe," he told her. "This is going to be good."

He went slow at first, building the pleasure, spinning it out between them. He let go of her leg, let her move until she had her legs high around his back, her ankles locked together.

He moved faster then, rocking into her harder and harder. Their bellies slapped together, sweat rose on their skin, and still the pleasure didn't stop. Gina didn't think she could go any higher, but he took her there again and again. She got close to the peak, closer, until her body was impossibly tight and she was begging him—loudly, desperately—for release.

"Is it enough?" he asked. "Do you want to come?"

"Yes, oh, yes."

Jack lifted her ass with one broad hand, bringing her hard against his body, his cock finding her sweet spot deep inside and stroking it. She tumbled over the edge with a long cry, falling into a pleasure so deep and consuming that she didn't ever want to emerge. Jack moved faster then, pumping mercilessly into her until she felt him coming deep inside her. His body stiffened as he came and he held her hard against him, rocking into her over and over.

He didn't shout—she hadn't expected him to shout—but he groaned deeply and brokenly, and she knew he'd lost as much control as he was capable of losing.

Gina put her arms around him as he collapsed against her. He made sure to roll his big body so that his weight was on his hip and shoulder, but he still lay on top of her, covering her. She ran her fingers up and down the muscles of his back. He was slick with sweat, but so was she. The air was cooling, but not quickly.

He moved a hand against her belly, her hip, and then down to her pussy where he toyed with her clit while she began to writhe her hips, faintly at first and then with more urgency.

Jack laughed. "Greedy girl."

"Shut up and make me come."

"I can do that." He did, his fingers moving expertly and quickly until she shattered yet again, her chest heaving as she tried to calm her racing heart one more time.

"You should come with a warning."

He lifted himself on an elbow. "I do."

"Really? Where?"

He pointed to a tattoo on his pec. "Right there. Says Caution, dangerous."

She peered at him. And then she slapped him. "It does not."

He laughed. "No, it doesn't." He lifted his arm and rolled off her then, and a sharp feeling pierced her heart at the name running along his ribcage when he put his arm over his face. *Hayley.*

She hadn't noticed that before. Had he had it on the island three years ago? She didn't know, but he certainly had it now. Gina's throat tightened. "I can't say I expected this to happen," she said lightly, trying to keep it surface deep between them even though she wanted to go farther.

But he didn't.

He lowered his arm and gazed at her. "Can't say as I did either. I'm not sorry, though."

"Neither am I."

They looked at each other for a long moment. The silence was awkward, but she didn't know what to say. Just when she was ready to fold herself into him, to lie against his warm body and fall asleep for a few minutes, the captain came over the intercom.

"Miss Domenico, we've been cleared for landing at St. Margarethe Airport. We'll start our approach and be on the ground in approximately thirty-five minutes. Flight attendants, please prepare the cabin for landing."

Jack was looking up at the ceiling, his expression far away. When he turned his gaze on her again, his eyes were noticeably cooler. Her belly fell into her toes. She felt as if the last hour hadn't happened at all—or maybe it had happened with another man, because this one didn't look in the least bit happy or satisfied anymore.

"Jack?"

He swung his legs from the bed and stood, gloriously naked, his muscled body still glistening with sweat. "Showtime, babe. Better get dressed."

SIXTEEN

JACK TOOK A QUICK SHOWER and dressed in a fresh pair of jeans and a T-shirt before going back to the main cabin and strapping himself in. Gina was a few minutes behind him, but she was seated too by the time the captain began the final descent into St. Margarethe. They didn't speak as the plane set down on the runway.

The lights of the city and the airport glittered as they whizzed by. It wouldn't be daylight for a few hours yet. They were still within Metaxas's twenty-four-hour deadline, so the plan was to check into the hotel and rest for a few hours before calling him—and hope the team could extract Eli and make the whole thing moot.

Jack could see her fidgeting out of the corner of his eye. She was nervous—but was it because of him or because they'd arrived?

Hell, he didn't know up from down anymore. He was out of his depth with her. It was hard to believe he'd been lost in her sweet body just a few minutes ago. That he'd been stroking hard into her and feeling like the top of his head would blow off. He'd felt the power of that orgasm all the way to his toes. His balls still tingled with after-shocks, and his cock threatened to grow hard again just thinking about it.

Fuck. Why couldn't this thing between them be normal? Why couldn't she be a waitress or a nurse or someone he'd met at the gym? They could go out for drinks, dinner, fuck each other stupid on a regular basis, and walk away when they were done.

But this? This was hard-core. She got to him deep down, in his gut, in a way no one since Hayley had. Not that he felt the same way for her as he did for Hayley, but there was more to it because of the circumstances. He was smart enough to know that's what it was. He'd crossed a line with her three years ago, and there'd been consequences.

His gut clenched as he thought of the way he'd spilled himself inside her just a few minutes ago. She'd said she was on the pill, but if a condom hadn't worked the last time…

Shit.

Jack scraped a hand through his hair and fixed his gaze on the movement outside the plane's window. What the hell was he doing with Gina? Why did he always seem to give the universe the finger when he got inside her?

He wasn't that reckless. Ever. He was cool, methodical, and thorough. Yeah, he had sex with other women. But he used protection and he pulled out when he came.

There'd only ever been one woman for him, and that woman was gone. He didn't want to go through it again with someone else. He had a child with Gina, and he would deal with that, but this thing between them wasn't anything more than hot sex and short-circuited brains. He needed to remember that the next time his cock tried to do the thinking for him.

The plane came to a rolling stop and the seat-belt light went off. Stephanie came into the main cabin. "The door is open if you'd like to exit, Miss Domenico. Someone from immigration will meet you inside. Your bags will be delivered to the Margarethe Crown Hotel."

"Thank you." Gina stood and shouldered her handbag. Her hair was damp and messy, and she'd pulled on jeans that looked as if they'd been painted on. She wore a lemon-yellow silk top with a white cropped jacket and heels that made her seem tall again.

It hit him just how rarified her existence was. They'd just landed in St. Margarethe on her private plane. The captain spoke directly to her when he made announcements. The flight attendants arranged for her baggage to be taken to the hotel and came to inform her personally that she could leave the plane.

The room at the hotel was no doubt the best available, and if there wasn't a bottle of Dom Pérignon in an ice bucket waiting for her, he'd be stunned. Jack grabbed his backpack and followed Gina down the aisle and out the door. The captain was waiting for her, of course, but at least that was somewhat similar to flying commercial. The flight staff thanked you for flying their airline as you stepped off. In this case, the airline was hers and the staff was comprised of her employees.

Surreal.

They went through immigration—a brief affair since St. Margarethe didn't require a visa and didn't much care about things you brought to the island so long as they were legal—and then they were in a hired limousine and heading toward the hotel.

When they reached the hotel, they checked in and took the elevator up to the suite. It wasn't as luxurious as the suite at the Venetian, but it was still nice. Jack let his gaze wander the room—and of course there was a bottle of champagne. He went over and picked it up.

Not Dom Pérignon. Cristal.

He set it back down.

"What now?"

He turned to find Gina standing on the white plush carpet in her heels, staring at him. She'd removed her jacket and her arms were folded over her middle. It made her breasts even fuller, if that was possible.

His dick started to tingle.

"You should sleep for a while. I'll check in with the team."

She dropped her gaze for a second. "I figured that much. But I was talking about... what happened. On the plane."

As if he didn't know. A chill seeped into his veins, but it didn't calm him the way it usually did. "What do you want to happen?"

She sighed and turned away from him. Then she sank down on the couch and crossed her legs. It was a casual move, yet he didn't get the impression she felt very casual or at ease with him just now. Her green eyes fixed on him. They were wide, filled with a hurt that went deeper than she let on.

"You're Eli's father. I want you to be a part of our lives, and yet this complicates things."

"How? It's sex, Gina. Not a proposal."

Her eyes flashed. "And that's not complicated? I've

157

dated one man since Eli was born, and he was never a part of Eli's life. But you will be."

Jack blew out a breath. "Do you really think now's the time to discuss this? We have to get Eli back first. We can talk about the future after we've done that."

Her jaw tightened. "All right. But I want to know one thing first."

"What's that?"

Her gaze dropped to her lap. "I want to know if you're over Hayley."

His belly was a ball of lead. Pain ricocheted out from his heart, across his nerve endings, and settled in his temples, pounding out a rhythm. "Over Hayley?" He sounded hoarse, and her head snapped up, almost as if he'd slapped her. "I met Hayley in elementary school. I rubbed dirt in her face and she told the teacher. I had to write sentences on the board. I didn't like her very much then, but that changed. I asked her to junior prom. She wasn't my first kiss—or my last—but she was my first in every way that mattered."

His throat was tight. How to explain what Hayley had been to him? What he'd wanted out of life with her? And how miserably he'd failed. She'd never asked him to leave the Army, though he'd spent plenty of time away from her. But she hadn't known what he did because it was top secret. What he never knew was why he'd kept doing it when he had her to go home to. That was the guilt that sometimes tore at him at the most unexpected times.

Gina clasped her hands in her lap. "Then I suppose the answer is no. Thanks for being honest with me."

Somehow he felt like he'd disappointed her. And he didn't like that feeling either. "She's been gone for nearly four years. I miss her, I still think about her, I wonder if our baby would have been a boy or a girl, and I wonder if he or she would have had Hayley's smile. She had a great smile." He stopped and shook his head. "Why are you asking me this?"

She dropped her gaze, but he didn't miss the way her eyes glistened. "Her name is on your ribcage, near your heart." She shrugged. "I wondered."

"So why didn't you ask me then?"

"I didn't see it until right before we landed. I didn't think it was appropriate, given the circumstances."

No, it wouldn't have been. But he still felt like he had to explain. "It's ink, Gina. I wear her name because she's important to me, because she helped make me who I am. Don't try to turn this into something it's not. It's not about you, or me, or Eli. We'll deal with our shit, but Hayley's not a part of it."

She got to her feet. "Great to know. I'm going to bed."

Jack watched her walk out of the room, her hips swaying in that come-to-mama way she had, her head held high, her back straight. She was something else, that woman. And he had no idea how to handle her or how to begin to address everything that lay between them.

Gina woke the next morning with a start. She sat up in bed, certain she was supposed to be frightened and not quite sure why. And then everything that had happened to this point downloaded into her brain, and she threw back the covers and grabbed a hotel robe before hurrying over and ripping open the door to her bedroom.

Jack looked up from the table, his blue eyes raking over her. An array of weapons sat on the table in front of him, dark and gleaming. Boxes of bullets were stacked up on one side and her heart thumped.

"Are we robbing a bank?" She didn't know why she thought she'd find herself alone, but she had. And it had scared her. Except he was here, bent over his weapons and looking lethal. Since when did the sight of a shirtless man polishing guns make her feel happy?

She pulled her robe tighter and walked toward him.

He glanced at the table and back at her. "Just getting prepared."

"I doubt Stavros will let you arrive packing heat."

"His men will find some of them. But they won't find them all."

She didn't bother to ask. "Have you heard from the others?"

"Stavros has fortified the compound. Security there is five times as tight as it was three years ago."

Her heart thumped. "And what's that mean for us?"

"It means it's taking more time to get into position than we anticipated."

Gina's mouth was dry. "We're running out of time."

He nodded. "Yes."

She bit her lip and tried not to let her fear show. "What if he insists I come alone?"

Jack got to his feet then. There was something comforting about the way he towered over her. But he didn't reach for her. He stood there and gazed down at her, his body radiating leashed energy. "Don't borrow trouble, Gina. Let's just take it one thing at a time."

"I should shower and get dressed."

His gaze slipped over her body, back up again. Her nipples tightened and her core melted at that look. But he wasn't about to let his icy reserve crack again. "Yeah, you should. We need to be ready to move."

She could feel his eyes on her back the whole way, and when she reached the bathroom, she shut the door and stripped out of the robe while the shower heated. She watched the door in the mirror, wondering if he would come through it like he had on the plane, but it stayed firmly shut. Gina showered alone, her hands slipping over her soapy flesh, gliding over her nipples and between her legs, reminding her of Jack's touch. She closed her eyes and bit her lip—and skated her thumb over her clitoris again and again until her body shuddered and she had to bite back a moan as she came.

She dressed in a shirtdress and heels before twisting her damp hair on her head and pinning it up. Then she returned to the living area of the suite and found Jack standing with his back to her, his hands in his pockets while he gazed out at the city below. He was wearing a jacket with his jeans and she knew he had a shoulder holster. God only knew were else he was packing a weapon.

He turned when he heard her heels on the tile and her heart skipped. He was so incredibly handsome and so remote. Had he really held her close and made love to her only a few hours ago? Had he let down his guard long enough to gasp his pleasure in her ear?

It didn't seem possible, and yet she knew it had happened. Heat blistered her cheeks as she thought about pleasuring herself in the shower just now. But Jack didn't know she'd been thinking about him and making herself come.

As if that made it better.

His brows drew down. "You look flushed. Everything okay?"

"I just took a shower. I'm hot. But everything's fine."

"You should have used cooler water."

It wouldn't have helped, but she didn't tell him that. "I'll remember that for the next time," she snapped.

He shook his head as if she were a silly child. "You ready for this, babe?"

She lifted her chin. "As ready as I'll ever be."

"Then make the call."

SEVENTEEN

THERE WERE PERIMETER ALARMS RIGGED around the property, starting about a mile out and getting denser as they got closer to Metaxas's compound. Billy Blake had them pinpointed on his computer, but disarming them took time. Time they didn't have.

Nick Brandon remembered the spot where he and Hawk had hidden before, but he couldn't reach it. In the aftermath of his brother's death, it seemed as if Stavros Metaxas had systematically hunted out every possible perch and rendered it moot with infrared equipment and alarms. There was no way to get close enough to take a shot. Not without a week's notice anyway.

"They're on the way," Matt said.

"Did Metaxas let her bring Hawk?" It was Lucky who'd spoken. She didn't usually go on this sort of op with them, but she'd insisted on this one because she figured Gina might need a woman along. For what, Nick didn't know.

"He agreed to it. But that's not really a surprise. He's bringing them into a fortified compound. One man is easy to disarm."

Iceman snorted. "Guess he doesn't know Hawk."

"Truth." But Matt didn't look happy. He gazed at the computer screen on the table in the yacht's main cabin and frowned. "He's never gone in after his own son before."

No one said anything, probably because they couldn't imagine what that was like. Nick's gaze flickered over the team. To his knowledge, none of them had any kids.

"Guess we're going with Plan B," Lucky said, and the guys all looked at her. She whipped her T-shirt over her head to reveal a pink bikini top. Her breasts were spectacular, Nick decided. And then he decided he'd better not look or Big Mac would kill him.

In fact, Big Mac was glaring at them all as Lucky shimmied out of her jeans and stood there in one smoking-hot bikini. Her skin was scarred along her arms and back, but it didn't detract from her beauty in the least. She was tanned, toned, and hot enough to make water steam.

"I'll be lounging on deck like the rich bitch I am," she said with a grin. "Fetch me a drink, would you, sweet cakes?"

That last was directed at Kev who miraculously didn't get pissed. "I'll do better than that. I'll rub oil on your back."

Ryan Gordon wasn't called Flash simply because of the obvious superhero reference. He was also pretty reckless at opening his mouth—flashing his teeth—when it would be better to keep it closed.

"Man, how in the hell are you going to manage that without losing focus? This ain't your honeymoon, bro."

Kev's eyes narrowed. "You want to keep those teeth of yours, jackass?"

Ryan held up both hands. "Hey, if you can do it without getting distracted, you're a better man than I am."

"Already fucking knew that," Kev growled.

Lucky put her hand on her husband's arm. "Seriously, you're getting pissed over this? First, he has a point—you do get distracted easily when, uh..." She cleared her throat. "Second, Flash, darlin'," she said, turning her smile on him and mimicking her husband's accent. "You remember what I did to Al Ahmad?"

Jeez. Nick's balls tightened involuntarily, as did every man's in the cabin. They all knew what she'd done to the terrorist.

Flash automatically cupped his hand over his groin. "Lucky, with all due respect, you're the last woman on earth I ever want near my package."

"Damn straight," Kev said.

"Ladies, Jesus," Matt interrupted. "Can we focus here? Sorry, Lucky," he added, but she was used to their banter by now and simply nodded. "All right. Lucky's going to lie on deck and make us look like party boys on a joyride. The rest of you know what to do..."

The helicopter set down on the same pad where Jack had shot the engine out of another one three years ago. Palm trees and pines swayed in the breeze the rotors whipped up, and the Caribbean sparkled just a few yards away. The same long dock was still there, but there was no yacht tied up to it this time.

Jack glanced at Gina. She'd put on red lipstick and giant sunglasses and looked every inch a star. But the corners of her mouth were tight, little grooves cutting into her skin on either side of her lush lips.

He wanted to squeeze her hand and then he wanted to take her in his arms and kiss her, but neither was appropriate any longer. He was her bodyguard, a hired gun meant to give her peace of mind when she came face-to-face with Stavros. Except they both knew there was no peace of mind here.

If Stavros wanted, he could have Jack killed and throw his body to the sharks. Jack hoped that wouldn't happen, at least not before he got a look at his son. He'd tried to keep Eli's existence in the abstract for as long as possible, but now that he was faced with the prospect of actually seeing the kid he'd fathered three years ago, his nerves were stretched tight.

Not that he would let that affect him. No, he was a special operator for a reason—he was cool under pressure and he had a deadly accurate aim in all kinds of conditions.

A man in a white jacket and black pants came forward and opened the helicopter door. Another man stood with a tray that contained a single champagne flute and a red rose.

Jack didn't pat the gun on his ankle or the one tucked under his arm, but he wanted to just the same. And then there was the one he'd put on Gina. She hadn't seemed comfortable with the idea, but she'd watched him with those big green eyes of hers while he'd tucked it into the thigh holster he'd strapped onto her pretty leg.

"This thing won't go off, will it?" she'd asked when he'd stepped back and let her dress fall.

"No. But don't pull it no matter what. It's for me, not you."

She'd propped her hands on her hips. "The damn thing's between *my* legs."

He'd grinned. "I know. Guns and pussy. Two of my favorite things on earth."

Only he knew why she'd sat there with her legs slightly apart during the helicopter ride, and it had made him hard to think about it. The gun should be on the outside of her thigh, but he couldn't take that chance with Metaxas, so he'd put it on the inside. He kept picturing the grip rubbing against her panties whenever she moved, and it turned him on. Though really the gun was too low for that or she wouldn't be able to walk. Still, what an image.

Gina exited the helicopter with the butler's help and Jack joined her. He stood respectfully behind her, his gaze sliding over the grounds of the compound. There were men on the roof, men in a guard shack on the perimeter, and cameras everywhere. Metaxas had erected a concrete wall on either side of the compound, but he'd left the water approach open. Of course, because it was pretty.

And because he didn't expect anyone to come in that way since it was obvious and easily defended.

"Champagne, miss?"

Gina took the glass with a smile and Jack felt a knot of panic harden in his belly. But she didn't drink it. When the man tried to hand her the rose, she waved him off and Jack was forced to take it instead. He wanted to throw it down, but no sense antagonizing Metaxas just yet. Besides, it made him look like a trained lapdog and that could be an advantage.

The man led the way toward the house. Before they passed inside, two men with machine guns stepped out. They insisted on patting Jack down—and relieved him of his weapons as expected—but they didn't touch Gina. Jack let out a breath as they passed into the darkened coolness of the house.

They were shown to a long room that overlooked the lawn and beach. Gina set her untouched champagne down while Jack gazed out across the blue Caribbean. He didn't see any boats bobbing on the water, but he knew HOT was there somewhere.

"Ah, Gina, how lovely to see you again."

Gina spun around as Stavros walked into the room. He wasn't quite as tall as Athenasios had been, or as broad, but he was unmistakably a Metaxas with his dark slashing brows and curly hair. And he was just as dirty as his brother had been, trading illegal weapons for cash and not caring how many people got hurt because of it.

"How dare you?" Gina spat, and Jack felt the first prickle of alarm slide down his spine. She stalked toward their host, her body vibrating with fury, and Jack wanted to snatch her back against him and pull a gun on Stavros before he could hurt her.

But Jack didn't move, and Stavros didn't look anything other than amused.

"You took my baby off a street, Stavros! You traumatized him! I want to see him right now."

Stavros's face darkened. "You are in no position to demand anything!" He leaned toward Gina, his teeth bared. "You thought you could keep Athenasios's baby a secret from me? From the family?"

Gina, God, don't say it. Don't.

He knew she was seething, that she wanted to tell this man again that Eli wasn't a Metaxas, but they'd talked about this. If Stavros learned that Eli wasn't his brother's, he would have no incentive to keep any of them alive. For now, he wanted the kid—but if there was no family connection between them, what was the point?

Yeah, she'd shouted it at him over the phone in Vegas, but he clearly hadn't believed her. And why would he? If she insisted now, the game might change.

She dropped her gaze and went for demure. Jack breathed a sigh of relief.

"I did it to protect Eli," she said.

"*I* will protect him now," Stavros said angrily. "And I will protect you."

Gina's head snapped up. "I don't need your protection. I have my own."

Stavros's gaze flicked to him. "This is your protection?" He snorted. "I let you bring him because it made you feel better, but my men have disarmed him. What kind of protection is that?"

"I don't need your protection, Stavros."

"And I think you do."

She lifted her chin. "From what? Random stalkers? Overly enthusiastic fans?"

Stavros reached out and ran a finger along her cheek and Jack stiffened. He kept his expression neutral, his eyes on a fixed point on the wall. But he saw everything, and he wanted to strangle this man for daring to touch her.

"I know you were here that day, Gina. The day Athenasios died."

She paled. "I don't know what you mean. I wasn't

here. I left after we docked that day—"

His hand was over her mouth now and Jack's gut twisted. "Hush, Gina *mou*. Do not tell me that lie. I know. Maria was here, too. And she told me everything."

"Who?"

"The maid, my dear."

"She's mistaken."

"She was not mistaken. She was very clear. I made her repeat it before she died."

"Sh…she died? How did it happen?"

"It was necessary. For your safety. There are men who would not be happy if they knew you were here when their brethren died."

"What men?" Her voice was barely audible.

He didn't answer. "Let me protect you, Gina. Let me keep you safe…"

Stavros had his hands on her shoulders and he was leaning toward her again. Jack closed his eyes and told himself not to react. Not to go over and throw the man against the wall. He'd be dead if he did that, and Gina would be on her own. She was smart and strong, and she could take care of herself up to the point where he had to intervene. And he would let her do it so long as he could.

She put her hands on his chest and pressed her cheek to his shirt. "Oh, Stavros. Thank you."

She was cutting off the kiss, Jack told himself. Her eyes met his, just briefly, and he saw the abject fear in them. She'd done the only thing she could think of to prevent him from kissing her, but she hated the fact she was standing in this man's arms.

Stavros wrapped his arms around her, held her close. And then he dipped his head and pressed his nose to her hair. Jack's blood ran cold.

"Athenasios was a part of some terrible things. He knew terrible men. They will want revenge if they know. I've done everything I can to keep your secret, but if they find out…"

Gina managed to extract herself from his arms. "Revenge for what? I don't know anything!"

She paced away from him while Stavros clenched his fists at his sides and watched her with hot, greedy eyes. Jack could see on the other man's face that he wanted to possess her. That he had no intention of letting her go.

Crap, where was HOT?

Stavros Metaxas was the incompetent younger brother who'd lived in the elder's shadow. But he'd inherited the business, and now he wanted the woman his brother had been with, the woman he'd thought had given birth to his brother's baby. Stavros wanted to possess her as if she were a status symbol. As if having her would somehow make him better than Athenasios.

That's what this entire thing was about. He'd kidnapped her child to force her to come here. To force her to become his. So that he could one-up a ghost.

A fresh chill spread through Jack's gut. He wouldn't let it happen. He'd told her he was jealous, and he was. She belonged to him. When he'd been buried inside her, when she'd been screaming his name and shuddering around his cock, he knew she was his. And he couldn't imagine her being someone else's. Not even for the sake of this deception.

"You were here," Stavros said. "You escaped while others died. How did you do this, Gina?"

She wrapped her arms around her middle. "I took a

car and drove. And then I got stuck and I walked until I found the beach. I had to hide in a cave, but on the second day there was a fisherman—and he took me to Iron Bay. I called Barry and he arranged everything." She sniffed. "But why did you take my baby, Stavros? Why didn't you come and talk to me about this in person?"

Stavros's expression hardened while she spoke. "Eli is where he belongs, and now you are too." He walked over and took both her hands in his. "We're getting married, Gina. If you want your baby back, you're going to marry me."

Gina's skin went white and her mouth fell open. Jack's teeth were going to crack.

"M...married?"

"Yes," Stavros said, his voice cool and deadly calm. And then he snapped his fingers and a door opened. A priest walked in, followed by two acolytes. "Married. Right here. Right now. That is the deal."

EIGHTEEN

"I... I NEED TO SEE Eli first," Gina said, her throat so tight it was hard to get the words out. She couldn't quite credit that Stavros was standing here with a priest and telling her she was going to marry him. Now, this very minute.

And yet she didn't doubt that he meant it—and she couldn't see how she was going to get out of it.

Stavros's dark eyes were hard. He'd always made her skin crawl and now was no exception. He grabbed her hand and tugged her toward the priest. She stumbled on her spiked heels and fell against him. She didn't dare to look at Jack as Stavros righted her. He took the opportunity to run his hand over her breast while he was at it and she wanted to puke on his expensive loafers.

But that would do her no good.

"After we're married," Stavros said, giving her a smile that threatened to make her throw up anyway.

Gina dug in as he pulled her forward. *No, oh please no*. How could she do this with Jack here? How could she possibly do this?

"I really think Eli should be a part of this ceremony," she blurted. "He's a Metaxas, and you're going to be his father. He should witness this moment when his family comes together."

Her heart hammered in her throat, but she prayed he didn't notice the fluttering of her pulse. He terrified her— but that's because she now realized he was utterly cracked in the head. She'd thought he was creepy before, but now she knew he was mad. Or maybe he wasn't mad in the conventional sense, but he was definitely out of touch with reality in the areas where he wanted to create his own reality.

And if she could play up to that, he might let her see her baby. She didn't know if Jack could stop this, but maybe if she stalled a little bit, his team might arrive for backup.

He'd told her he usually went in with a radio link, but they hadn't been willing to risk it for this operation so he was working blind. But HOT knew where they were because he had a GPS tracker on his phone—and an extra one on his body, just in case. Stavros hadn't confiscated their phones, probably because he didn't see how that was an issue for him out here on his remote peninsula. Who the hell were they going to call anyway? The cops?

Not likely, and Stavros knew it.

"Perhaps you are right." Stavros stared at her thoughtfully for a long moment. "Tell Patricia to bring the boy," he said to one of the guards standing at the door.

The man disappeared and Gina's heart thudded. A bead of sweat trickled between her breasts. She could feel the gun against her thigh. It was a solid hunk of metal against her body, weighing her down and reminding her that she wasn't as vulnerable as Stavros thought. So help her God, no matter what Jack had said to her about the gun, if Stavros tried to rape her, she would shoot him herself.

It only took a few minutes, but a woman walked into the room carrying Eli, and Gina burst into tears as she rushed toward her son.

"Mama!" he cried, stretching his little arms out, and Gina grabbed him and held him close while she sobbed.

She needed to get it together, needed to be strong and get through these next few minutes with Stavros—and with Jack—but she couldn't stop crying. And that made Eli start to cry, which forced her to snap out of it damn quick.

She pushed his hair off his forehead and kissed his little cheeks.

"Oh, baby, Mommy's sorry. Don't cry, sweetheart. Mommy's happy. See?" She forced a smile, though she was shaking desperately, and Eli hiccupped a couple of times. Then he collapsed onto her chest and hugged her tight.

Love flooded her. She would do anything to keep him safe. Absolutely anything, including marry Stavros if that's what it took

Gina managed to glance at Jack, and the look on his face pierced her heart. She hated this for him. Hated that he had to see his son for the first time like this. He couldn't hold Eli, or talk to him, or do anything but stand there stiffly and pretend to be completely unconcerned with everything going on around him.

He was about as important as the furniture to Stavros, and she supposed she should be thankful because it meant

Stavros had dismissed him as useless.

"Give him back to Patricia," Stavros ordered coldly. "And let's get on with it."

Gina hugged Eli tight. She wanted to refuse. She never wanted to let Eli go again, but if she didn't hand him over, she risked his safety because Stavros would have him taken by force. She kissed Eli's cheeks and gave him to the woman standing there with her arms out. Eli started to cry again, reaching for Gina, his little face turning red as he screamed.

Stavros was beginning to look furious as Eli's screams didn't cease.

"Please let me hold him," Gina said. "He'll be calm if I'm holding him."

Color slashed Stavros's cheeks. "Do it then."

Gina took Eli back and he buried his head against her neck. She was furious and frightened, and yet she had to pretend everything was okay. She turned toward the priest and stood there quietly, rocking Eli in her arms and just letting herself be in the moment with him.

He was safe. *Safe.* And he was hers.

"Begin," Stavros ordered, and the priest opened his Bible.

"We are gathered here today to join this man and this woman in holy matrimony…"

"Holy Christ, Lucky," Kev said as his wife untied her bikini top and dropped it on the teak decking.

"Shut up, handsome." She stood and waved toward the men on the shore. "Woohoo!" she screamed like a college coed on spring break.

Nick had to hand it to her. Lucky not only crushed balls—terrorist balls—but she had elephant-sized balls of her own.

She reminded him of a woman he'd gone to sniper school with. Victoria Royal had a stripper's name and a stripper's hot body. All the guys had wanted her, but she'd wanted nothing to do with any of them. She'd been his only real competition there. A fiery redhead with rain-gray eyes and a mouth he'd wanted to kiss senseless before watching it wrap around his cock.

But if Victoria had disliked all the men in sniper school, she'd hated him especially. He wondered what had happened to her. Last he'd heard, she'd left the Army and disappeared into obscurity. Probably went back home, married some guy, and started popping out kids.

Nick stroked the stock of his Mk12 SPR sniper rifle where it lay against the side of the flybridge and tried to be patient. It was a risk coming in here like this, but it was their only choice. Nick let his gaze run over the yacht's gleaming reflection in the water. Damn shame, but this baby was going to get a few bullet holes in her before the day was done.

Men along the shore—men who were clearly supposed to be guarding Metaxas's compound—watched Lucky with the kind of slack-jawed focus that only bare tits could cause. The yacht glided up alongside the dock and Flash threw out a line. One of the stupid bastards caught it and tied it off.

"Hey, y'all," Lucky said, strutting across the deck while Kev tried not to look as if he would kill someone. "Is this Leon Barton's place? I swore we wouldn't be late, but my stupid boy toy here can't read a map. Can you believe it? Has the party started yet?"

"Uh, ma'am, you've got the wrong place. You really need to turn around and go."

Lucky managed to look crestfallen as she put her hands on her hips and thrust her breasts out. Nick decided to enjoy the show since everyone else was. Plus Kev couldn't see him. Like most of the guys, he didn't often think of Lucky as a woman since she was one of the team—but times like this... Well, shit, it was impossible not to realize how fucking hot she was. Kev was one fortunate bastard.

"What? Are you sure?" Lucky turned and glared at Kev as if it was all his fault. He was standing there in board shorts and reflective Ray-Bans, a beer in his hand, looking like a hapless good ol' boy out for a sail with a high-maintenance woman. "You know, you've got a big dick, but you're fucking stupid as hell," she said disgustedly.

Then she turned and walked back over to her lounge chair where she picked up an oversized T-shirt and slipped it over her head. Nick was almost sorry the show was ending—not only Lucky half-naked, but also Lucky giving Kev hell because that sure was amusing—but another show was about to begin. And that one was going to be fun for them all.

As soon as Matt gave the signal, Nick lifted the rifle and started picking off targets.

She was stuck at the part where she was supposed to say "I do."

Gina stood there with Eli tight in her arms and swallowed hard while the priest waited for her to speak the words that would bind her to Stavros.

Dear God, *Stavros*. She closed her eyes and fought down a wave of bile. Jack was behind her, quiet and deadly and solid. She wanted him to take the gun from between her legs and put a stop to this. She needed him to act.

But he didn't. No one did. They simply waited.

"Gina," Stavros said, his voice a warning.

"Y...yes," she said. "I d...do."

Her heart cried out in agony when she said the words. She'd never been married before, and she didn't want to marry Stavros. She wanted it to be Jack standing beside her. Jack who she promised to love, honor, and cherish.

But it was Stavros, and her belly churned. She could get through this if she had to, but please God, please don't make her have to have a wedding night with him. She'd thought she could do it if she had to, but after the things she'd experienced with Jack, she would rather die than give herself to this man.

The priest turned to Stavros and started to ask him the questions that would bind them together. But there was a shout outside and then another. The sound of gunfire shattered the air and Stavros whirled. But then he grabbed her and Eli and dragged them toward the door where one of his personal bodyguards stood with drawn weapon and dead eyes.

She turned to look over her shoulder at Jack. He was looking right at her, his eyes sharp and hot and filled with fury. Her heart skipped a beat at the look on his face. His eyes slid to the guard, then back to her—and then he was in motion, rushing toward her, tumbling onto the floor in front of her. A second later, his hand was on her thigh—and the gun came free from the holster.

He aimed between her legs and the gun exploded twice in succession. Gina couldn't even scream it was so sudden. Eli did, however, and she hugged him tight and tried to reassure him.

"Get down, Gina," Jack ordered, and she dropped to the floor as he fired again and again.

Her gaze met the priest's across the room. His eyes were wide as he made the sign of the cross. His acolytes were huddled together on the floor, praying.

Outside, the gunfire was rapid and strong, and Gina prayed that Jack's team were the ones winning. If they weren't, then she didn't think that she and Jack and Eli would be trekking across the island or holing up in a cave. If Jack's team wasn't winning, they were all dead.

Something exploded nearby, and Gina gasped. A huge fireball roared upward into the blue sky, and men screamed and shouted.

Jack got to his feet and went over to the door. There were four men lying on the floor and Gina's gaze darted between them as she prayed Stavros was one of them.

He wasn't, and her heart sank like a stone.

"Come on," Jack said from the door, and Gina got up and followed him. He handed her a gun he'd taken from one of the dead men, and she realized he had the rest of them on his body.

"I don't know how to use this," she confessed as Eli wrapped his arms around her neck and held on tight. He'd stopped crying and she thought maybe he was fascinated by all the noise and commotion rather than scared now.

Jack gave her a look. "Seriously, babe?"

"I'm a pacifist."

He snorted a laugh. "Jesus. Don't point it at anything you don't mean to kill, all right? When you're ready, flip that button on the side near the trigger—and squeeze."

She nodded.

"Now hold on to my jacket and follow me, okay? We're getting out of here. Just don't shoot me."

"That's the last thing I want to do." She'd rather kiss him. And if they got out of here alive, she would do a whole hell of a lot of kissing him. And other things. They started down the hallway. "Where's Stavros?"

He didn't look at her. "He got out. But we'll get him."

They didn't encounter anyone as they moved through the house. The staff was hiding. Jack had taken out four of Stavros's hired men. If there'd been any others still in the house, they'd probably gone outside to defend the compound.

When they reached an exterior door, Jack stood there for a long moment and listened. Gina's heart pounded hard as she waited. She didn't know what he was about to do, but then the door burst inward and Gina screamed. Jack had two guns in his hands when someone in a black suit and helmet came through the other side. She thought Jack would start shooting, but instead he lowered the weapons.

So did the man in the suit. It took Gina a second to

recognize Iceman, but when she did, her knees went wobbly. She dropped the gun Jack had given her and sagged into the wall, holding her baby close and trying to keep it together.

"Metaxas?" Jack asked.

Iceman shook his head. "Not sure. But we got to get moving, dude. Big Mac, Lucky, and Brandy are holding them off out there at the yacht, but if Metaxas has reinforcements coming, we're in big trouble."

As if to punctuate that point, the soft thumping of a helicopter in the distance began to grow louder. "Is that us?" Jack asked.

"No."

"Then let's get the hell out of here."

NINETEEN

JACK KEPT GINA AND ELI between him and the wall as they made their way across the compound. There were trees on fire, and black oily smoke rose into the air. It stank, but it also provided cover as they ran. Iceman led the way, and they soon met up with Knight Rider and Billy the Kid, who flanked them and kept them protected as they ran down the dock toward the yacht. Gunfire erupted from the trees and Jack felt a stinging hot sensation pierce his thigh. He knew he'd been hit, but he had enough adrenaline and fury to propel him down the dock and onto the yacht. Iceman and Knight Rider slashed at the ropes with their knives while Big Mac gave the engine juice. As soon as they were untethered, the yacht shot backward as Big Mac worked the thrusters.

Brandy and Flash set up covering fire as they kicked up to higher speed and blasted toward the open channel. Over the mountain, two helicopters appeared as they came closer to the compound. The place had been shot to hell, and the diesel tanks that stored fuel for the generators were on fire, lighting the sky and crawling tree by tree toward the house. It would reach the house in a few more minutes, and then the roof would burn.

Jack stayed outside to help with the covering fire, grabbing a rifle and aiming toward the trees. When the next shot flared bright, he targeted the light and fired. He did it again and again—and then the compound simply exploded, a giant fireball whooshing into the sky. The shockwave rolled over the yacht, but they were far enough away it didn't affect them.

Jack stared at the fire raging out of control and knew Metaxas couldn't have survived that. And yet he'd wanted to shoot the bastard personally, goddammit. He'd taken their son, and he'd tried to force Gina to be his wife. When Jack thought about that slimy bastard touching her…

Someone put a hand on his arm and he jerked. Matt was staring at him with lowered brows. "You're hit."

Jack glanced down at his leg, at the hole in his jeans and the blood welling through the tear and seeping into the fabric. "Yeah, so?"

"So? Get inside and get that taken care of. I think we got it out here."

And they did, because the yacht was traveling fast and the water cleaved before the hull like butter under a hot knife. The shore was receding quickly and the bullets had stopped coming. The men who'd been on the perimeter of the compound would probably still be alive, but they damn sure wouldn't care about an escaping yacht with the whole place burning around them.

Jack tried to see the helicopters, but they weren't visible through the smoke. He didn't hear them either, but that didn't mean they weren't there. "They can still come after us by air."

Matt shook his head. "Get inside, Hawk. If they come after us, I'll let you take them down. Between you and Brandy, I think you could shoot the fucking Air Force out of the sky. I'm not worried."

But he didn't want to go inside the yacht's cool interior. Because it meant he'd be facing Gina—and the kid he'd fathered. He thought he'd wrapped his head around that, but seeing the boy—hearing him cry for his mother—had gotten inside Jack's heart and twisted it up tight. He didn't know what to do, what to say. He had no frame of reference for this. When he'd had a job to do—save Gina and Eli—he hadn't had time to think about it.

But now?

There was a child inside who belonged to him. What the hell was he supposed to do about that? In the abstract, it had been easy to tell Gina she wasn't keeping him out of Eli's life. But in reality, what the hell could he give this kid that she couldn't? Maybe she'd tell him he could be a father, but he didn't see where having one of those had mattered much in his life. And since he hadn't had the best example, how would he know what to do?

He set the rifle down and rubbed his hands over his face. Then he turned and hobbled down the side of the deck toward the interior door. As the adrenaline from their flight faded, the wound would hurt more and more. He knew that, and he didn't look forward to it.

The yacht was big and luxurious—albeit a little worse for wear now that it'd been in a pitched battle—because the team had wanted to look like the kind of people who could sail the Caribbean without a care. He knew it had bedrooms in the interior, and he hoped like hell that Gina had retreated to one of them. Then he could get this wound doctored and deal with her later.

But that wasn't the way it was going to be. She was sitting in the main living area when he walked in. The cabin was furnished with gleaming cherrywood finishes and cream leather couches. A dining table sat at one end, its polished surface reflecting the chandelier that hung overhead. It was the kind of yacht she could afford. The kind of life she could give Eli. What did he have that compared to any of this?

Her head snapped up at his entrance, her eyes boring into him. She had Eli on her lap, and he was crying and saying things Jack didn't understand while Gina tried to soothe him.

"I know, sweetie. I know. Mommy's here now." She rocked him back and forth, but he still cried. Jack's gut twisted. She was trying to make him stop crying, but her voice sounded as if she might cry any minute herself. Jack's heart pounded so fast he thought it might burst from his chest. He felt too many things standing here, watching Gina and his son, and he didn't know how to make sense of the tight ball of emotion in his gut.

Gina gasped, and he knew she'd seen the blood soaking his jeans. It was almost a relief, because it gave him something new to focus on.

"Jack, you're hurt!"

"It's not bad," he told her, though he really knew nothing of the sort. Thigh wounds could be dangerous if they hit a major artery, but since he was still breathing and not losing consciousness, he figured he was okay.

Iceman grabbed his bag and started pulling out the medical gear. "Take 'em off or I'm cutting them off," he said as he pointed at one of the couches.

Jack hesitated. "Maybe you should take Eli back to one of the rooms," he said to Gina. "This might be a bit much for you."

She was still rocking Eli and her hand came up to shield his face, though he was actually looking the other direction. "We're staying."

"Hey, Eli, look at this," Lucky said, holding up a stuffed animal. Where in the hell had she gotten that?

Eli's crying turned into a hiccup. He reached for the animal and Gina let him go so he could crawl onto the cushion beside Lucky, who kept saying things to him, and he smiled as if he hadn't just been crying a moment before.

"Who's a good boy?" Lucky said, and Eli banged the toy on the couch as Lucky looked up at Gina. "Go sit with Jack if you want. I'll play with Eli."

Gina frowned as she looked at her son and then back at him. "Just for a minute," she finally said, and then she stood came over to his side.

"You don't have to do this," he told her, his voice low and rough. "Take the kid and go."

"You didn't leave me. I'm not leaving you."

Goddamn, she was stubborn. He unbuttoned his jeans and dropped them to the floor. Might as well get this over with then.

"Oh, Jack," she said, her voice soft and sweet. Her eyes filled with tears and he glanced down, wondering if maybe he was dying or something and he just didn't know it yet.

But, no, he was only bleeding.

"Nothing I haven't been through before."

He sat back on the couch and Iceman started cleaning

the wound. He gave Jack a shot for pain, but Jack still had to clench his fists around the edge of the couch as the other man probed the wound for bullet fragments.

Gina sat beside him and he turned to look at her. "You can hold my hand," she said softly.

"That's not a good idea." Because he didn't want to squeeze her hand off when the pain was too much.

She put her hand on top of his fist. "Okay, then I'll just do this."

"Gina, go take care of Eli. You don't want to be a part of this."

"Actually, I do." She looked over at Iceman. Something unspoken passed between them, and he went back to probing the wound.

"Jesus, Ice," Jack hissed after a few seconds. "Can you do that any faster?"

"Almost done."

Just when Jack was ready to yell something seriously foul, Ice straightened. "You're clear. The bullet went clean through."

His gloved fingers were covered in blood as he reached for a syringe, and Gina looked a little pale.

"Who's helping who here?" Jack teased, and her gaze crashed into his.

She took a breath. "I'm helping you, you big sissy."

"Right."

Now that Ice was done probing, Jack unwrapped his fist and let her slip her fingers into his. His heart thumped in response to her soft skin against his hand. He shouldn't let himself get used to this, and yet he liked it when she touched him.

"You're a badass, Jack Hunter," she said. "I'm thinking of writing a song about you."

He laughed, though Ice was still doing shit that hurt. But it wasn't as bad as the probing, so at least there was that.

"Oh yeah? What's it gonna say?"

Her eyes sparkled, but he wasn't sure if it was humor or tears. "I'm not sure yet. But it'll be flattering."

"That's good."

Ice gave him another shot and pronounced him done. "Better get into one of the cabins and lie down. That shot's going to knock you out in about ten minutes."

"I'll be fine here," he said. "What if I'm needed?"

If those helicopters came after them, he would need to be ready with a rifle. Everyone on the team was an expert marksman, but Jack was the best.

"I think we can handle it for a while, Hawk." Ice looked at Gina. "Can you get him to go, please?"

She glanced over at Eli, who was now moving the animal along the floor like it was a car. Lucky grinned. "I've got this. We're having fun. Take the big sissy to a room so he'll sleep it off and the rest of us can do our jobs. We'll be right here when you get back."

Gina got to her feet and tugged on Jack's hand until he stood too. "Come on, Jack. You heard them. Let's go."

Jack sighed. "Fine. I'm going. But when you fuckers need something shot, you'll be sorry you sent me away."

Gina put her arm around his waist. He didn't need to lean on her, but he liked the sensation of her next to him enough that he didn't stop her. He hobbled toward the staterooms with her, and she opened one and helped him inside. When the door snapped shut, he yanked her into his arms. She gave a little gasp, but her arms went around his neck.

"It killed me to stand there during that sham of a wedding," he said, his mouth against her skin, moving along the smooth column of her throat. He didn't want to be saying this, and yet he couldn't help it. It was as if any guard he'd had on his tongue had disappeared when Iceman gave him that shot.

He was still mad at her, dammit. And yet he couldn't seem to dredge up that anger when she was in his arms.

"All I could think about was you and Eli," she said. "Getting out of there with you both. Kissing you again…" She stood on tiptoe and slanted her mouth over his. Her tongue slipped inside and rolled against his.

He pulled her back toward the bed, his cock hard and aching. She arched against him, her hips rolling into his and making him groan at the sweet pressure. His leg hurt like a son of a bitch, but he thought if he could just get inside her, it would all be better.

"When you said 'I do' to him…" He pushed her back until he could see her eyes. "I wanted to smash something."

Her fingers slid along his jaw. "Jack…" Her gaze dropped and her lashes fanned over her cheeks. Her gorgeous blond hair had come loose during their run to the yacht and it hung down her back, wild and curly.

He tipped her chin up and made her look at him. "What is it, babe? Are you pissed at me because I didn't do anything to stop him?"

She shook her head. "If you'd tried any sooner, he would have killed you. And that would have killed me."

His heart was starting to pound, and so was his head. He tried to smile, but he felt like his gut was filled with broken glass. So many emotions were swirling through him and he just couldn't separate them all. Damn Iceman and his painkillers.

Jack glided a thumb over her lips. "No, it wouldn't. You're a survivor, Gina. You'd keep on living and you'd forget all about me."

"That's not true. I couldn't forget you. Not ever." She put her hand over his mouth when he started to speak. "There isn't anyone else like you, Jack Hunter. There's only you." Her hand fell away and her voice dropped to almost a whisper. "And whether you like it or not, I've fallen in love with you."

If she'd shot him in the belly, he couldn't be any more stunned. His jaw fell open and he couldn't think of one damn thing to say. Not one...

She squeezed her eyes shut. When she opened them, her lashes were spiky with tears. One fell free and slid down her cheek, and his heart ached.

"There, I've said it. I love you. Whether you like it or not, now you know. So stop with the no-illusions speech. I have plenty of illusions for us both, so please don't shatter them just yet, okay?"

All he could do was kiss her.

TWENTY

GINA TOLD HERSELF NOT TO be hurt that he didn't say anything. He was kissing her, and that meant something. Or maybe it didn't. Maybe he was just hot for her body and he wanted to shut her up. No matter what he said about seeing her with Stavros, that didn't mean he'd forgiven her. Or that he envisioned a future with her.

He reached for the hem of her dress, and she broke the kiss and put a hand on his chest. "Wait. You're hurt."

As if that was the only reason not to do this. But she had no idea how he was still standing, much less trying to get into her panties. If she'd been shot, she'd be in agony.

His blue eyes gleamed. "Yeah, I'm hurt—and I'm going to burst if I don't get inside you."

"You're also drugged up, and Garrett said you'd be asleep in ten minutes. We've used up five."

"Babe," he said on a sigh, "I'm not going to fall asleep when I've got you wrapped around me. After, hell yeah, but not during."

He ran a hand up her thigh, stopping when he reached the holster. She'd forgotten she was wearing it, which said something, considering she didn't really like guns all that much. She thought back to the way he'd yanked it from the holster and fired, and a shiver slid down her spine. Jack was one lethal dude. His team called him Hawk. She didn't have to be a genius to figure out why. He'd hit everything he'd fired at, even when he'd been firing from between her legs with his vision partly obscured.

"Damn, that's so fucking sexy. I want you to wear that while I'm inside you."

She put her hands on his chest when he tried to kiss her again. She was wet and hot, and under ordinary circumstances she'd want nothing more than to fall on this bed and let him rock her world again.

These circumstances definitely weren't ordinary. Plus she was still reeling from telling him she loved him. Her emotions were wound tight, and she didn't think she could handle sex with him right now, even if they weren't fleeing from the bad guys.

"Later, Jack. I want you too, but I'd like us to be in a bed that's not currently part of an escape plan."

He swayed on his feet before shaking his head and fixing his gaze on her face. "Yeah, maybe that's a good idea."

The bed was behind him so she gave him a little push—and he crumpled onto the mattress. His eyes were glazed as he looked up at her. He looked so adorably confused that she wanted to laugh. Well, he'd been warned, hadn't he?

"Go to sleep, Jack. We'll talk about everything when you wake up."

"'Kay," he mumbled before turning onto his side. A second later, he was snoring softly.

Gina stared down at him. Her belly churned with hot emotion and she pressed a hand to her mouth. Dammit, she was in so much trouble here.

There was a soft knock on the door. Lucky stood on the other side, her expression soft and concerned. "You okay?"

Gina sucked back hot tears. "Not really."

Lucky peered past her to where Jack lay on the bed. "He'll be out for a while. I just wanted to let you know that Eli fell asleep on the floor. I made a pallet of blankets, and he's tucked away in front of one of the couches." Lucky gave her an encouraging smile. "If you want to talk about it, I'm a good listener."

"Are we being followed by Stavros's men?"

"Doesn't seem like it, no." She shrugged. "The compound exploded, Metaxas is MIA, and the orders have stopped flowing."

"Is he dead?"

"It would be a miracle if he wasn't. Identification of all the bodies will take some time though."

Gina went into the hall and closed the door behind her. She wanted to stay with Jack, and yet it was probably better if she didn't. She needed the space to think and prepare for when he woke up again. And she needed to be with her baby.

"Do you do this kind of thing often?"

Now that they were safe on the yacht and Jack was taken care of and sleeping, it was starting to sink in that she'd been shot at as she'd run across the compound. In the moment, she'd had no time to think about what was happening. Her entire focus had been on keeping Eli safe.

But now, when she could replay it all, she could see

Stavros's evil face, feel his hot breath on her skin and read the disgusting intention there. And then there'd been gunfire, bodies falling, and her and Jack creeping through the house until Garrett had burst in.

She couldn't even recall the run across the compound, not really. She'd had Eli in her arms, the air had been thick with smoke, and all she could do was keep up with Jack while he fired his weapon and got her closer to the yacht.

When they'd jumped onboard, her heart had been pounding so hard she'd felt faint. She tried to remember when Jack had been shot, but the truth was she didn't know. She didn't recall it at all. Seeing the blood on his skin, watching Garrett clean it, had brought back to her forcefully that what they did was dangerous. And they hadn't just been doing it for her.

It's what they did on a regular basis. And this woman did it with them.

She was pretty, but not quite as soft as Evie, Georgie, and Olivia had been. Her eyes said she'd seen things. She was watching Gina carefully. "It's the job," she said. "We do what we have to."

"You could be killed. Your husband…"

"I know." She shrugged, though Gina didn't think she felt in the least bit casual about that statement. "But that's what makes it important. We help people. We stand up for people who can't stand up for themselves. And we try to rid the world of assholes like Metaxas who think it's okay to get rich by selling guns to people who will use them to hurt others."

"I didn't know he was in that business at first. Athenasios, I mean. He was handsome, a bit thrilling in a way…" She felt like she was babbling, and she pulled in a breath to steady herself.

Lucky put a hand on her arm and squeezed. "We all make mistakes."

Gina's gaze landed on the fine scars on the other woman's arm. She didn't say anything, but Lucky withdrew her hand and turned her arms over, baring the network of scars to Gina's sight.

"You never know what life is going to hand you. I got these, but they don't define me. They did for a while, though. I was afraid of people. Afraid of being touched or touching. And then I got stronger and I stopped letting it rule my life." She put her arms down again and looked plaintively at Gina. "Don't apologize for your experiences. They brought you Jack, and they brought you Eli. That can't be all bad, right?"

Gina blinked. She hadn't thought of it like that at all. She'd just been embarrassed that she'd let a man like Athenasios fool her so completely. But yes, if she hadn't come to St. Margarethe with him three years ago, she wouldn't have met Jack. And she wouldn't have Eli.

"Right," she said, and the other woman smiled.

"Let's get back up front. Jack will sleep it off for a while yet."

Gina glanced over her shoulder. "He'll be okay, right?"

"Iceman said the wound was clean and the bullet went through the outer fleshy part of his thigh. Basically, it winged him. But it'll hurt like hell, and he'll have to stay in bed for a while, but he'll be okay. If it makes you feel better, he's going to the hospital as soon as we get home. Standard procedure."

"Somehow, I don't think he's going to like that."

Lucky laughed. "Probably not."

Jack's head hurt when he woke. A side effect of the medication Iceman had given him. He sat up carefully, his head and leg pounding, and blinked at his surroundings. He wasn't onboard the yacht anymore. The whine of the engines told him he was on a plane instead. Gina's plane? He threw the covers back and swung his legs toward the floor.

Pain radiated through his body and he stopped moving, cursing instead. Shit. Not the first time he'd been shot, but he always hoped it was the last. It fucking pissed him off. He was the one who did the shooting, not the one who got shot. And he knew what a well-placed bullet could do to a body, so he was damn glad that whoever'd shot him wasn't as good with a gun as he was.

He focused on the walls and recognized the door to the bathroom where he'd found Gina naked. His body responded to that memory, his dick hardening in spite of the pain throbbing through him.

Jack scrubbed a hand through his hair. He remembered her telling him she loved him on the yacht, but he wasn't sure if he'd dreamed it or not. He tried to concentrate on the memory, tried to separate it out and determine if it was real or his imagination. But he couldn't be sure.

He dragged himself to his feet. Someone had put a pair of his jeans on the small couch next to the bed. He grabbed them and tugged them on. He was no longer wearing a shirt, and he suddenly realized there was an IV bag hanging nearby, dripping drugs into his system. He hadn't noticed it at first, but now he could feel the chill in his blood.

He pulled the needle and tubes free and blood ran down his arm. He swore and stumbled toward the bathroom, grabbing a towel and pressing it to the vein.

"Goddammit, Hawk," someone said, and Jack turned and hobbled back into the bedroom. Iceman was standing there with a syringe in one hand and a fresh bag of fluid in the other.

"I don't need that shit," Jack said. "It gives me a headache."

"Then I'll give you something for the headache."

Jack pointed. "If you make me sleep again, motherfucker, I'll shoot you when I wake up. Got it?"

Iceman ranged toward him like a bear on the prowl. "Yeah, fine. Just let me look at that."

Jack snatched the towel away. The blood flow was lessening. Ice grabbed his bag from the corner where Jack hadn't seen it sitting and took out a first-aid kit. He cleaned and bandaged the puncture, took out a different bottle of medicine and a new syringe, then drew out some fluid and jabbed Jack in the arm none too gently.

"Ow, fucker."

"You'll live," Iceman said. "It's tramadol for your head. And Benadryl too, so if you get sleepy again, too bad."

"Where are we?"

"Almost home."

"Why are we on Gina's plane?"

Iceman snorted. "Because she had one. And because she refused to leave you while we waited for our ride."

Jack blinked. "The whole team here?"

"Yep."

"Anything I need to know?" He didn't have to spell it out because they both knew what he was talking about.

"Nothing at all."

Jack shoved a hand through his hair. "Did Gina say that Stavros tried to force her to marry him?"

"Yeah—and that's some fucked-up shit."

Jack's gut still roiled at the memory of her standing there, Eli in her arms, saying "I do" in a too-quiet voice. He shook away the darkness flooding him. "He knew she was there three years ago."

"It's not a surprise, right? There were others there who knew. They would have told him."

"I know… Jesus, I wish I'd put a fucking bullet between his eyes."

"Richie called Mendez. He's got Intel sifting the chatter for any mentions of Gina from any quarter. So far, there's nothing."

"Yeah." Jack started toward the door, but his leg nearly gave out and he slapped a hand against the wall to steady himself. He cursed long and low.

"You need to lie down, dude."

"I'll be fine if I sit. Just help me out to the main cabin."

"Nope, not happening. Lie down, and I'll send whoever you want this way."

Jack swore again. And then he shoved over to the bed and sank onto the mattress. He hated being weak. When he'd been sick as a kid, his mother still took him to daycare. These days you probably couldn't get away with that, but back then the woman running the daycare had stuck him in a room by himself with a television and books and left him alone. He'd had to listen to the other kids play and scream with laughter, and he'd hated it. Even if he didn't talk a whole helluva lot, he liked to be in the same room where the action was.

He wanted to see Gina. To lay eyes on her and Eli and know they were well. But he'd rather do it in a crowd because this ball of emotion that sat in his gut was a damned volatile thing. He had no idea when it would explode or what the fallout would be when it did. It scared him, and that wasn't something he was used to.

He pulled in a breath. "Richie and Big Mac."

Iceman shrugged. "Wouldn't have been my first choice in your shoes, but whatever."

TWENTY-ONE

GINA TRIED TO BE PATIENT while Matt and Kev went back to the plane's bedroom to talk to Jack. Eli was asleep in the seat beside her, and she worried her lip between her teeth while keeping a hand on his back. When Iceman had said Jack was awake, she'd been halfway out of her seat when he'd told them that Jack wanted to see Matt and Kev. Her heart had fallen to her toes, but she told herself it was perfectly normal. They were the leaders of the team, and they would be able to tell him everything that had happened since he'd passed out.

She began to tap her fingers on the armrest and watch the GPS tracker on the screen in front of her. They'd be back in DC before too long. And then what? She knew that Jack had to go to the hospital for evaluation, but what was she supposed to do? Wait for him in a hotel somewhere? Go home and pretend none of this had happened?

She heard voices, and then Matt and Kev were coming back up the aisle. She bolted to her feet. Matt looked as if he might say something, but then he just stood aside and motioned with an arm for her to go. She hesitated as she glanced down at Eli. She wanted to take him to meet Jack, and yet she wasn't sure yet what Jack wanted.

"I'll watch the kid," Nick said from his seat across from her. "You go."

"Thank you."

Gina went back and opened the door. Jack looked up from where he was sitting on the bed, his blue eyes hot as they met hers. Her heart thumped at the sight of all that bare, tattooed flesh, and then she walked in and let the door shut behind her. There was silence in the room, other than the smooth growl of the engines vibrating along the plane's length.

"How are you?"

He shrugged. "I've been better."

She moved toward the bed, her belly churning as she thought about the last time she'd been in this room alone with him. He'd owned her body in this room, and then she'd realized that he owned her heart.

"I was worried," she said, feeling the tightness in her throat that indicated tears.

"Nothing to worry about."

She wrapped her arms around her waist. The last time they'd left St. Margarethe with his team, she'd hadn't seen him again for three years.

"Thank you for everything," she said softly, and his eyes narrowed. He looked... wary.

"Sounds like good-bye, babe."

"No, of course not. I just meant that you saved me. Again."

He patted the bed. "Come here, Gina."

She thought, vaguely, that she shouldn't be obeying commands—but she went and sat on the bed beside him anyway. He twirled his finger. She turned around, and then he dragged her back against him. On the side that said Hayley. She closed her eyes and tried not to think about that. She curled into him and put her hand across the taut flesh of his abdomen.

"Does it hurt?" She couldn't see his skin since he was wearing jeans now, but she remembered the blood and the way his face had turned white while Garrett probed the wound.

"Like a bitch." He ran his fingers up her arm, down again. "How's Eli?"

She pushed away until she could look up into Jack's face. "He's fine. Maybe a little bit clingy."

His expression clouded. "Understandable."

"Yes, definitely." She pulled in a breath. "When do you want to meet him? Really meet him, I mean?"

He closed his eyes and rubbed his hand across his forehead. "Later."

She tried not to let that one word sting, but it did. "I thought you wanted to be a part of his life…"

"I do. But maybe it needs to wait until after the hospital, okay?"

"We could go with you."

His brows drew down. "You can't. It's Walter Reed, and you aren't family."

She didn't know what showed on her face then, but whatever it was, it was enough to make him swear.

"I didn't mean it like that," he told her. "It's just military bullshit that has to be taken care of first since we've been on a mission."

She dropped her gaze. "All right."

He tipped her chin up until she was forced to look at

him. "I'd give you the keys to my apartment, but I somehow think it's a little plain for your taste."

"I've lived on the street, Jack. I doubt your apartment is that bad."

His eyes searched hers. "No, but you aren't the same woman you were then. All it takes is one person to recognize you and there'll be a mob outside the door."

"Then I'll stay at a hotel."

He nodded. "Yeah, that's probably best."

"Will you call me when you're discharged?"

"I'll call."

She leaned against him again, pressing her cheek to his bare skin. He was warm and firm, and he made her feel safe. He twisted a lock of her hair around his finger and her throat tightened. She felt like they should be talking, but she didn't know what to say.

Hayley's name burned into her subconscious. It was against her body, but she could picture it running along his side, the loops and curved lines, the blackness of the ink against his tanned skin. A permanent reminder that he loved another woman—and always would.

It had been three days and Gina hadn't heard a word. She'd taken a suite at the Ritz and she was getting tired of living in a hotel with a rambunctious little boy. Cassie had offered to come to DC, but Gina had told her it was fine. She'd wanted to be alone with Eli for a while, though it would be nice if they could both get out of this room for an afternoon at least.

She sighed as she looked out the window at the city. She wanted to take Eli to the National Mall, walk among the monuments, and just be a tourist for a change.

But that wasn't possible. Even if she could manage it without being recognized, she couldn't get over the fear that someone would step out of the shadows, point a gun at her, and demand that she go with them. Or, worse, that someone would take her baby and leave her standing there on the street alone and frantic. Stavros was dead, but that didn't stop the fear.

Her security firm had sent a man over, but the truth was she only trusted Jack right now. Darren was as big as a house, quiet, and definitely intimidating—but he wasn't Jack. She hadn't wanted anyone in her space right now, but she couldn't send him away. He was in the lobby, waiting for her to call him if she wanted to go out.

Barry had called and tried to set up interviews, but she'd refused them all. It wasn't unusual of her to withdraw from the public eye, but it hadn't been the plan with her new album dropping soon. Barry just sighed and told her to let him know when she was ready. He hadn't said a word about the new contract.

She didn't know if she would ever be ready. The hotel phone buzzed and she jumped a mile out of her skin. Eli was on the floor, watching cartoons and playing with his toys. She swallowed her racing heart as she picked up the phone. The only call she wanted was Jack's, but he wouldn't call the hotel when he had her cell phone.

She'd started to call him a dozen times but told herself to be patient. Chasing him wouldn't do any good. And it would only make her seem desperate. She wasn't used to being the one waiting, so she'd done nothing.

"Miss Domenico, there's a man here to see you," the front desk clerk said.

"I'm not expecting anyone." Not since she'd sent Darren the bodyguard downstairs.

The sound was muffled while the clerk spoke to the man. Then she came back on the line. "His name is Jack Hunter, ma'am."

Her heart kicked up and butterflies swirled to life in her belly. "Can I speak with him?"

A second later, Jack's gravelly voice was in her ear. "Hey, Gina."

"Why didn't you call me?"

"Calling you now."

"Not really."

"Do you want me to come up or what?"

"Yes."

"Then tell this woman it's a yes."

"Miss Domenico?" He hadn't even given her a chance to reply before he handed the phone back to the clerk.

"Yes, please send Mr. Hunter up."

She hung up the phone and stood there for a second, uncertain what to do. Then she hurried over to the mirror and released her hair from the banana clip she'd put it in. She shoved her fingers into the messy strands and shook it out, then wished she was wearing something besides jeans and a T-shirt. She'd gone for comfort instead of style; that much was obvious.

There was a knock at the door a few minutes later, and she swallowed her trepidation before peeking through the hole. It was Jack, looking moody and hot as always. She pulled the door open and tried to be cool.

"Hi," she said.

He tipped his chin. "Hey."

She let her gaze slide over him, gasping when she noticed the cane.

"It's not permanent," he told her.

Her fingers gripped the door. "Are you coming in?"

He hobbled inside and she shut the door behind him. Her first instinct was to kiss him senseless, but he didn't seem prepared for that, so she kept her hands to herself.

"It's been three days," she said. "I thought you'd changed your mind."

He had the grace to look uncomfortable. "I should have called you sooner." He looked around the room, though he didn't comment on it. Maybe she should have picked a less expensive hotel.

"Met your security detail in the hallway."

"I thought he was in the lobby."

"Is that really a good place for him?"

"I don't see why not."

One corner of his mouth turned down. "Thankfully, he does. I almost didn't get past him. Darren's a good guy, and his firm has a good reputation. I'm glad you have him."

"I feel bad he's in the hall. I should let him in."

"I sent him downstairs for dinner." He patted his side. "I've got this shift."

Her heart thumped. Of course he was armed.

Gina moved toward the living room and Jack followed, prompting Eli to look up when they walked over. His little eyes were wide and fixed on Jack. Gina prayed he wouldn't burst into tears at the sight of a stranger. He'd been a little sensitive the last couple of days when room service came by, and she didn't know how he'd react.

When she turned to look at Jack, he was staring back at Eli and her belly churned. "Jack, meet Eli."

He shook his head slowly. "How did Metaxas not see it?"

"What?"

Jack's gaze flickered over to her before turning back to Eli. "Me. I was standing right there in front of him, and you were holding Eli."

She knew he was talking about the resemblance.

"Not everyone can see the truth when it's staring them in the face. I'm thankful for it, quite honestly, because if he'd realized…" She shivered involuntarily.

"Yeah."

She pulled in a breath as Eli went back to playing with his toys. The noise of the cartoon filtered into the room, its bright sounds out of place when they were discussing such darkness.

"I haven't told him you're his father. I wasn't sure how you wanted to do this, so I thought it was best to wait."

"I can't believe he's mine. I see it in his face, and I still can't believe it." He turned to her, his blue eyes full of emotion. "We were together once, we used protection, and he's here. Hayley—"

He stopped speaking abruptly and she bit down on her cheek. He seemed lost in his own thoughts and she hated to see him suffer. "What, Jack?"

There was a well of suffering in those blue eyes. "You don't want to hear it."

"I *do* want to hear it."

He looked at her for a long moment. "Hayley had trouble getting pregnant. She wanted a baby pretty badly, and I wasn't always there when the time was right. We tried for over a year."

"I'm sorry."

"It's not your fault."

"I know. But it hurts you, and I care about that."

He sank onto the arm of a chair and stretched his leg out. "She found out she was pregnant the day she had the accident. I was forward deployed, but we were cooling our heels at the base, so when she called, I was there."

Gina didn't quite know what to do, so she put her hand on his shoulder. She hadn't known that he'd learned of the pregnancy the same day as the accident.

"The accident happened about an hour later, but I didn't know for hours. Takes time for that kind of thing to filter through channels."

She couldn't stop herself from stepping into him, from putting her arms around his neck and hugging him tight. One of his hands came up and splayed across the small of her back.

"You don't need to hear this. It's in the past, and there's no going back."

"I think she must have been very happy that day."

"Yeah, I think so too. I just hope…" His hand tightened on her for a second. "I hope it happened fast, you know? They said the impact killed her. I just hope that's true."

She held him for a long while. The television blared, Eli played, and Jack just sat there staring at his son, his arm around her waist. It was almost companionable and she closed her eyes, laid her cheek against his head, and wished the circumstances were very different.

"Mama," Eli called, and her eyes snapped open.

"What, sweetie?"

"Cheese, Mama. Want cheese."

"Okay, baby. Let me see if we have some." She went over to the refrigerator and found the bag of string cheese she'd had sent up. She tore off a strip and opened it, then took it back and handed it to Eli after she'd started the process of peeling the cheese. He stood up now and leaned against the couch while he looked up at Jack.

After Gina handed him the cheese, he occupied himself with tearing off the strips and eating them. Then, when he got to a strip he couldn't make work, he thrust the cheese at Jack. Not at her, but at Jack.

Gina's heart lodged in her throat as Jack reached for the cheese.

"What's wrong, buddy? Can't peel it?"

Eli nodded as Jack took the cheese and peeled it, then handed it back to Eli. This time, Eli moved closer until he was standing at Jack's feet and bracing himself with a hand on Jack's knee.

Gina wanted to sob. She pressed a hand to her mouth and stood there breathing deeply while Jack talked to Eli. He slipped off the arm of the chair and down into the seat.

"Want to sit with me?" he asked.

Eli nodded and Jack picked him up. After a second, Jack settled him into the crook of his arm. Eli ate his cheese and watched cartoons. Jack dipped his head, sniffing Eli's hair. But then she realized that his body shook and tears rolled silently down his cheeks.

"Jack?"

He didn't look at her. He just held up a hand as if to silence her, and she knew he didn't want her comfort. She didn't blame him, but it still hurt. Gina shuffled into the bedroom to give him time alone with Eli. She stood there numbly until her body began to tremble and the tears she'd been holding in broke free.

Jack wasn't the only one whose heart was breaking.

TWENTY-TWO

GINA WAS SITTING ON THE bed when Jack walked in with a sleeping Eli in his arms. She swiped beneath her eyes and sat up, muting the television as she did so. It had been nearly an hour since she'd left him with Eli.

And Jack didn't look as if he'd fought an emotional battle at all. No, he looked like a battle-hardened warrior dominating her bedroom with a small child cradled tenderly in his arms.

"Where do you want him?"

Gina sniffed and got to her feet. "There's another bedroom." She led the way back across the suite and into the room where she'd put Eli. She'd wanted to keep him with her, but she'd finally decided it was important she treat him as if everything were perfectly normal. He had his own bedroom at home, so she'd gotten a suite with two rooms.

It was hard to put him to bed every night and walk back to her own room, but she'd done it. She'd left a light on in the living room and both doors open so it wasn't quite so bad, and Eli seemed to be adjusting.

Gina tugged the covers back and Jack laid Eli on the bed. Then she pulled the sheets up and tucked him in, sliding his stuffed lion in beside him. He clutched it and yawned before burrowing deeper into the pillows. He never once opened his eyes.

Jack left first and Gina followed. She pulled Eli's door most of the way shut before turning to find Jack raking a hand through his hair and rolling his neck to pop out the kinks.

"Thanks for sitting with him."

"He's beautiful, Gina."

"Well, that's half you." She tried to make the words bright, but his expression didn't lighten.

"Sitting here with him, I realized..." He shook his head. "I missed a lot, didn't I?"

Her throat ached. "Yes, and I'm sorry."

He sank onto the couch, then leaned forward and put his head in his hands. "I wasn't in the right place anyway. I wasn't ready. I was pissed as hell at you for keeping him from me. But now I'm not so sure how I feel... It's a lot to process."

Her heart thumped. "Are you ready now?"

He lifted his head. "I don't know. I want to be."

"All you can do is try." It was a lame answer, but it was all she had. He hadn't said he forgave her, but if he understood, just a little bit, then maybe there was hope.

He snorted as his gaze drifted around the room. "And how would this work, babe? You're a superstar. Rich, famous, with the world at your feet. Just look at this hotel room." He lifted his hand, let it fall again. "I'm a soldier. It'd probably take an entire month's salary for me to afford one night here. And you've been here three."

She swallowed. Of course this would be an obstacle between them. She'd be naive to think it was only about her lie or about Hayley. Her life was fundamentally different from his and they couldn't ignore it. "Does the fact I have money change who I am? Who you are? If I had nothing, would it be easier for you?"

"I don't know. Maybe."

Those simple words made her mad. They negated her whole life. "I worked hard to get what I have, Jack. And it's damned misogynistic of you to want me to have nothing so you'll feel more comfortable about the whole thing. You're Eli's father, for God's sake. Isn't that more important than who has what?"

His eyes flashed. "Yes... but are you gonna drop everything to accommodate my schedule? Fly halfway around the world when I have a week off? Stay in my apartment while your adoring fans cluster outside and clamor to see you? You can't even walk down a street without a mob, Gina. Fuck."

It was all true, and yet she really didn't want to think about it right now. "I don't want to fight with you. Not tonight."

He got to his feet and limped toward her. It hit her that he'd taken a bullet for her. He'd done everything he could to get her and Eli away from Stavros, and now he was here and her heart ached because she wanted him so much.

But she didn't know how to make it work. They were so different. He put his hands on her arms, his gaze intense and hot.

"We weren't supposed to happen. It was an accident of timing and bad luck."

He had no idea how much his words wounded her.

"So I'm bad luck, huh?"

His eyes closed. "That's not what I meant."

She shrugged out of his grip. "It's okay, Jack. I can take it. You don't want to be with me. You're in this by accident because you had the misfortune to use a condom that didn't work. And then I called you up, all crazy like, and told you three years after the fact that you have a child. It's a lot to process. I get that."

His jaw tightened. "You sure do know how to push my buttons. No one else has ever pissed me off quite as much as you do. Yeah, you lied to me and that hurt, but I'm trying to see it from your perspective. I was a dick to you three years ago, and I made you think I didn't care if there were consequences to our actions. That was wrong."

Her eyes filled with tears. "Does that mean you forgive me?"

"I'm working on it."

"That's what you say about everything," she cried. "And you know what? You piss me off too. You aren't perfect, Mr. Hotshot Sniper Man. You're no picnic to deal with."

He was glaring at her. "Maybe I should go, let us both cool off."

She folded her arms over her chest. "Maybe you should."

He started toward the door, but then he stopped and turned back to her. "Is this really what you want? Because I got a whole different vibe from you on the yacht, I gotta say."

Her insides quivered. How could she begin to tell him what she wanted? Him and her and Eli as a family. But that would be baring too much of her soul just now.

"What do you want me to say, Jack? I already know what it's like to hand you my heart on a platter and get nothing in return. I'm not crazy about repeating the experience."

He shook his head. "I thought I dreamed that… And I didn't give you nothing."

"You thought it was a dream?" She'd poured out her feelings and he hadn't known it was real. Just her luck.

"I wasn't sure. I was pretty drugged up, I guess, and I couldn't remember what was real and what wasn't. But I didn't give you nothing. I know that much."

"No, you tried to have sex with me. I guess that's not nothing. It's just not quite what I was looking for."

"I'm trying, Gina. This isn't easy for me."

"You think it's easy for me?"

He shoved a hand through his hair again. He looked golden and rumpled, like he'd just gotten out of bed, and her body insisted on reacting even though she didn't want it to.

"Nothing about this is easy, babe. For either of us."

She didn't say anything and he went to the door. Then he stood there with his back to her, his hand on the knob. He let his forehead rest on the door, and then he swore.

When he turned around and strode back to her, she was frozen in place. "This is fucking ridiculous," he growled, yanking her to him.

And then his mouth slanted over hers, his lips firm and demanding, his hands gripping her hips and pressing her into his body. He was firm, big all over, and she melted into him in spite of her wish not to. Couldn't she resist just a little bit?

But no, her arms went around his neck and her traitorous body arched into him like she'd been deprived for too long. Had it only been a few days since they'd made love? It felt like months.

His hands shaped her, gliding over her hips, her thighs, her waist, and then up to cup her cheeks. His tongue stroked into her mouth, finding hers and sliding against it over and over. She might have moaned. She might have melted.

No, she *was* melting, her body liquefying, heat pooling between her thighs, her pussy aching for his touch. For his possession.

"Gina, fuck. Why is this the only thing we do right? God, what you do to me…"

What she did to him… She could feel it, his cock a hard bulge in his jeans, pressing against her belly. She wanted to feel him moving inside her again, wanted to strip him bare and take him in her mouth before watching his eyes as he slid into her body.

But it scared her too, this wanting. Because while she was certain he wanted her equally as much, she wasn't certain there was any emotion behind it, no matter what he said about forgiveness and trying. For Jack, it was sex. Hot, thrilling, mind-blowing sex. But how much of that could she take before her heart simply shattered? Was the collateral damage worth it?

He flexed his hips and she saw stars. Yes, maybe it was. Maybe some hot sex was just what she needed after the stress of the last few days. Maybe she didn't care what motivated him so long as he was hers for a few hours.

"I'd pick you up and carry you to bed, but I think my doctor would frown on that." His mouth moved over her neck, his breath hot against her skin.

She sucked in a breath and pushed him back until she could see his eyes. They were a little confused, a little glazed. She liked that.

"You have to know I want you," she said. "You kiss me and my brain goes to sleep while everything else wakes up."

"Is that a bad thing?"

She curled her fingers into fists in his shirt. "I don't know. Maybe."

His grip eased, but he didn't let her go. "Then tell me what you want, babe. If I can, I'll give it to you."

She bit her lip. What she wanted was to get naked with him as soon as possible. But another part of her wanted to be more than a body, more than a hot, mindless fuck. He could have that with any woman. She wanted more. She *needed* more.

"I want to sleep with you. *Just* sleep. I want to lie in your arms, and I want to wake up with you beside me. That's all."

"Damn." He let out a low whistle. "You don't want much, babe. Just to cripple me with the worst case of blue balls I'm likely to ever have."

She dropped her gaze to his chest. It wasn't going to be a picnic for her either, but it was important. She knew that. For once, they had to be together and not let sex cloud their thinking. Her emotions were on edge, and if she was that vulnerable, that open to him while he worked her body and made her feel like the center of his universe, then she didn't know if she'd ever recover.

"I didn't say it would be easy, but if you don't want to…"

"Hey." Jack tipped her chin up and gave her a peck on the nose. "I'll risk it."

"You will?"

He nodded. "Lead me to the torture chamber, mistress."

He had to be insane. But the happiness in her eyes was worth the price. It surprised him that he wanted to make her happy, but they had a kid together and she was a part of his life now. And her happiness mattered. She was gaping at him a little bit, her jaw slightly open, her green eyes blinking as if he were an illusion that might disappear.

And then she took his hand and led him into the bedroom. He took in that giant, king-sized bed with a glance and his gut clenched. Damn.

"I think I need to establish some ground rules here," he said, and she turned to look at him, surprised. "If I'm going to survive this, we have to keep our clothes on."

"Okay." There was a little frown line on her forehead, but he didn't really think she wanted to do this naked any more than he did. He hadn't been the only one breathing hard back there.

"And we're staying on top of the covers."

"What if I get cold?"

"You aren't going to get cold. I'll be wrapped around you."

She gave him a shy grin that he didn't expect, but it lit him up inside in ways he couldn't quite believe. Yeah, he was attached to her. There was no doubt about it. He'd tried to walk out, but the truth was that he couldn't do it.

But what kind of attachment was this? And how could it ever go anywhere?

Didn't take a genius to figure out why they were a doomed pairing. He could crawl for days to get into position, live in conditions that would horrify her. He stayed hidden in mud and rain and filth, waiting for the target to appear in his crosshairs.

Gina owned an airplane. People hung on her every move as if she made the sun come up every morning. She'd left a reporter dazed and confused in Jack's presence. And then there was the arena full of fans who waited for hours—days—to get two hours of her company.

How would he ever fit into that life? Why would he open himself up to that kind of attachment only to have it crash and burn? He'd been on that emotionally devastating roller coaster before, and he wasn't sure he wanted to go there again.

And then there was the kid. *Jesus*. He was already a mess where the boy was concerned, and he hadn't even seen it coming.

Jack had been overcome when Eli climbed onto his lap to watch cartoons. It was the kind of emotion he hadn't experienced in a long time. He'd felt, for a minute, like the kid was everything in the world to him. He'd heard that having a kid changed you—hell, Hayley used to talk about it all the time—but he'd never really believed it.

Stop thinking.

He kicked off his flip-flops and leaned the cane

220

against the nightstand before crawling on top of the covers. Gina was still standing there with her arms crossed over her chest, watching him. He wondered if she knew she was looking at him like he was an ice cream cone.

Shit. Best not to think about that either.

He patted the bed. "Come over here, babe."

She shook her head. "You have to let me put on pajamas. These jeans will get uncomfortable."

"I'm wearing jeans."

His worn Levi's were soft and kinda loose though, and her jeans were clearly of the painted-on variety. Not that he minded. Plus it would make it impossible to get his hand inside them during the night. Still, she looked kinda miserable, so he sighed.

"Fine." He pointed an accusing finger and she smiled. "Neck to ankle, Gina. Flannel. None of that silky bullshit with lace."

She laughed. "It's June. I don't have flannel pajamas in June."

"No silk."

Her mouth twisted. "I'll see what I can do."

She disappeared into the bathroom. He tried not to think about the last time he'd been in a bathroom with her. All that silky skin and moist heat. He'd lost all his good intentions that time.

She returned faster than he expected, clad in a long shirt that went to her knees. It wasn't silky. But there were no pants.

"Ankles, babe."

She looked down. "Can't you deal with calves and ankles? The rest is covered."

"Nope. Find some pants or the deal's off."

She frowned. And then she went over and pulled a pair of yoga pants from a drawer. She tugged them on, then sighed and pulled out another T-shirt before disappearing into the bathroom again. When she came back, she was wearing a fitted workout shirt rather than the long one she'd worn before.

This one, however, revealed the flaw in his plan.

"Where's your bra?"

She popped her hands on her hips. "You didn't say I had to wear a bra. Honestly, Jack, are we sleeping or hibernating here?"

He frowned. "Come on, then. But if you wake up with my hand up your shirt, don't be shocked."

She got on top of the covers and came over to curl into his side, facing him. He put an arm around her… and kept his eyes on the far wall instead of looking down into the gaping neck of her shirt.

She put a hand on his abdomen and his muscles tightened. "What?" she said, looking up at him.

"Your hand. I'd really like it a few inches farther south, so that's just fucking torture." His eyes narrowed at the innocent way she batted her eyelashes.

Jack hooked his hands beneath her arms and flipped her before she could do anything more than squeal. Then he tucked her firmly against his body, his front to her back, before putting his mouth to her ear.

"Spooning, that's all you get, babe."

She turned her head to the side to look up at him. "Thanks for staying."

He dropped his mouth to her cheek, left a soft kiss there. "I wanted to stay."

She put her head down again. "I wasn't sure. When I

didn't hear from you, I thought maybe..." She put her hands over one of his where it wrapped around her stomach. The other one was beneath her head. "I thought you'd changed your mind about Eli and me."

He could hear the hurt in her voice and it made something throb inside him. It hadn't been easy staying away, but he'd needed time to think. He was still thinking.

"I haven't changed my mind."

Hell, he had to make a decision first. And that wasn't proving to be simple at all.

TWENTY-THREE

GINA WOKE UP ALONE. FOR a moment, she couldn't remember why that was a bad thing. And then she bolted upright, her heart pounding. It was still dark outside—but there was light coming from the living room of the suite. She climbed from the bed and drifted toward the door.

The television was on, the sound muted, and Jack was sitting there in the pale glow, flipping channels and looking dark and unapproachable. She glanced around, but Eli was nowhere to be seen. He was still sleeping, then.

"Jack?"

He looked up, his gaze flickering over her before going back to the television. "Couldn't sleep."

She went over to the couch and stood beside him. Her fingers ached to slide into his hair, but she kept them to herself. "It's my fault, isn't it? I shouldn't have asked you to sleep with me."

"I liked lying there with you." His voice was a low growl that slid into her blood, her bones. He shrugged. "Sometimes I don't sleep so well. Comes from years of training to be awake at odd hours and take catnaps, probably."

She sank down on a chair nearby. "How did you end up joining the Army?"

He gave her a wry look. "We talked about this three years ago."

"But you didn't tell me everything."

He tossed the remote down and turned to her, one arm along the back of the couch, the other on the side. "I had to get away from home. I didn't want to stay in Florida and be like my parents, working long hours at jobs I think made them miserable. Dad was a restaurant-supply sales-man and he traveled a lot. Mom was a paralegal in a busy attorney's office. My entire childhood was a blur of day-care, babysitters, and being alone after school once I was old enough. I wanted adventure, and the Army seemed like the thing."

She pulled her knees up. "You grew up shooting, though. That was kind of an adventure, right?"

He nodded. "My best friend's dad was a hunter. He took us with him when we were old enough. Taught me how to shoot. I was good enough that he got excited and started taking me to shooting tournaments. I won a few of them." He looked wistful for a moment. "My parents never went to a single one."

"Then they missed out. I'm sure you were amazing."

He snorted softly. "I was good then. I'm better now."

"You have to be." She thought of the men falling down around her three years ago—and the men from just a few days ago. No, he didn't miss. It was a lethal skill... frightening even.

His eyes flashed. "I know what you're thinking."

"You do?"

"You're remembering that night three years ago. You had no idea what was happening, but you witnessed terrible things. I'm sorry for that, but you have to know they weren't nice men."

Gina closed her eyes. It *had* been terrible. The snap of the bullets came after the men had fallen to the ground, their heads split open like melons. She hadn't known, at first, what was happening.

And then she'd feared for her own life when she'd realized they'd all been shot.

"I know they weren't." She pulled in a breath. "Does it ever bother you? Killing people?"

"You asked me then and my answer's still the same. It's a job. I do what I'm ordered to do. And I trust that the people making those decisions have damn good reasons. We don't take lives lightly, Gina."

She knew that, and yet it seemed like the kind of thing that could weigh on a person after a while. "Is it something you want to keep doing for the rest of your life?"

He looked away. "I don't know. But I take it a day at a time. I learned that four years ago when my life changed in an instant."

An awkward silence descended between them, and Gina finally got to her feet when he didn't say anything else. He was looking at the TV again, flipping the channels mindlessly.

"I should go."

He looked up as she walked by—and then he caught her hand, pulling her up short. Her skin sizzled with heat. Her breath caught painfully. She closed her eyes. Dear God, she was jealous of a dead woman. It was so wrong, but it was the truth. She was jealous of the hold Hayley still had on him. And she couldn't look at him, couldn't let him see that emotion in her eyes.

"Don't go."

She swallowed. "I think I should."

He turned her hand over and pressed a kiss into her palm. "I take my life one day at a time because every day could be the last when I'm out in the field. But today I want to be with you."

Tears pressed against the backs of her eyelids. She wanted to ask him about tomorrow, but she was afraid of the answer.

He stood and cupped her jaw in his broad hands, forcing her to look at him. "I don't know that I can give you what you need, but I want to try. I want to be there for you and Eli."

Her stomach fluttered like it was filled with a thousand tiny butterflies. He hadn't said he forgave her, but maybe he was getting closer. Maybe, one day, he would. "We want that too. Very much."

"I wish I could have been there when you had him. That was a lot to go through on your own."

She swallowed. "I didn't know whose baby he was then."

"I know... but I still wish I'd been there. You shouldn't have been alone."

She searched his gaze. "I wish you had, too."

He pressed his lips to hers. It was a soft kiss, a sweet kiss—and yet she couldn't help the little tendril of excitement that unfurled within her. She put her hands on the waistband of his jeans, tugged his shirt out, and let her palms flatten against his hard belly.

"Gina," he groaned. "Don't."

"But I want to be with you. I *have* to be with you."

His eyes were hot as he pushed her back. "You sure about that? It's not what you asked for a few hours ago."

"I know. But you gave me what I wanted when I asked for it. Now I want something else."

She pushed his shirt up until she could press her mouth to the corrugated muscles of his abdomen, then ran her tongue over those ridges, loving the way he shuddered beneath her.

He slipped his hands into her hair, his fingers tightening. "Gina. God."

"I love the way you feel. The way you taste. I want to make you come." She thought he might insist on being noble, but he grabbed her hand and hauled her toward the bedroom.

"Don't want our kid walking into the room for that."

He pushed the door most of the way closed behind them, and her heart squeezed at that little bit of thoughtfulness for their child. Eli usually slept the night away, but if he woke up, he'd come looking for her and she didn't want him to find a closed door. She wasn't worried he'd walk in on them in here since he'd call for her the whole way if he woke up.

The room was still dark, but their eyes adjusted until it wasn't so dark after all. The light from the television flickered into the room. Jack took his gun out and put it on top of the high dresser near the bed. "Guess I'm going to need trigger locks in the future," he said, and her heart melted that he was thinking of a future with them.

Gina grabbed his shirt again and lifted it over his head. He tried to kiss her, but she ducked out of his grip and went down on her knees, tugging at his belt and zipper until she got his jeans open and pushed them down his hips.

"I want to be inside you," he growled.

She thrust her hands into his underwear and gripped him. He was hot and hard, and he gasped as she squeezed lightly. "I want this first."

"I'm not coming that way, Gina."

She laughed softly. "You're the strangest man. I thought most men loved blow jobs."

"It's not that I don't love it…"

Whatever else he might have said was cut off when she freed him and ran her tongue along the underside of his cock. He was salty and musky, and she ran her tongue over him again, tasting the bitterness of his pre-cum on her tongue. And then she slipped him into her mouth and listened to him groan.

His hands went to the back of her head, but he didn't force her to take more of him than she could. She wanted to hear him groan her name and gasp as he lost control. Her body throbbed with need, her pussy tingling as she swirled her tongue around the head of his cock.

She wrapped a hand around the base of him. He was big enough to fill her hand and still leave plenty of room for her to take as much of him as she was able before her gag reflex kicked in. She moaned as she pumped her hand up and down in time with her mouth. She'd never done this to him. They were together once on the island and once on her plane, and this was the first time she'd had the opportunity.

She could feel the pressure gathering inside him, feel the tightening of his balls as she cupped them with her other hand. His hips jerked as he moved with her—and then he stepped away from her, gently removing her hand from his cock as he did so.

"Not this time," he said, lifting her up and stripping her top over her head. His hands cupped her breasts, his fingers softly pinching her nipples. They were already spiky and so sensitive.

She reached for his cock again, held him in both hands and pumped slowly while he played with her breasts.

"You like that," he said when she gasped as sensation streaked down into her toes.

"You already know I do."

He pushed her yoga pants down until she stepped out of them. She thought he would tell her to get on the bed, but instead he turned her and bent her over until her torso lay on the silky sheets. Her ass was in the air, and he bent and pressed a hot kiss into the small of her back. And then he licked a trail to one of her cheeks, nibbling and kissing it before moving on to the other.

The sensation was already exquisite, but then he took it over the edge when his fingers slipped between her legs and found her clit.

"So wet," he whispered against her back. "So hot."

He pinched her clit the same way he'd pinched her nipples, and Gina cried out softly. If it felt good on her nipples, the feeling was magnified a thousandfold here.

Jack straightened then and she felt the head of his cock pressing into her, opening her wet folds wider and wider as he invaded her body. But, oh, what a good invasion.

An amazing, wonderful invasion. When he was fully

inside her, he bent over her and kissed her shoulder. He didn't move immediately, and she loved him even more in that moment. He was taking care of her, making sure she could handle him. He didn't just shove his way in and pump mindlessly until he came. He made sure she was primed, as if she were a virgin instead of a woman who'd been sucking him off only minutes before.

"I love the way you feel wrapped around me," he said. "It's good with you, Gina. So fucking good."

He began to move then. It was slow and intense at first, and then her body relaxed and he took it a little faster, a little harder. His hands gripped her hips, keeping her steady—and then he slipped a finger beneath her, found her clit, and started stroking it in rhythm to his thrusts.

Gina arched her back and held on, gripping fistfuls of the sheets as he pounded into her. The pressure inside her body grew tighter and tighter, like someone had wound a toy almost to the breaking point. When he let her go, she would fly.

But Jack wasn't ready to let that happen just yet. He changed the tempo, moved his fingers away from her clit and down to where they joined together. Gina cooled, but only marginally. The spiral ride she'd been on had nearly been to the top but suddenly began floating back to the bottom again.

Before she reached it, he pulled out of her and turned her over. They fell to the bed together, face-to-face, and he took her mouth passionately. She ran her hands over the damp skin of his back, his arms. He kissed her hard, stoking her passions higher, making her desperate for him.

And then he hooked both arms behind her knees and spread her wide open. When he plunged into her this time, she was ready. There was no gentle stroking this time, no teasing. They were both fully aroused and in need of hard, good sex.

Their bodies slapped together, their groans twining, their sweat mingling. Jack pushed her legs even wider— and that's when her body caught fire. His cock found that bundle of nerves deep inside her at the same time the angle worked the nerves in her clit.

Gina came hard, her entire world dissolving into nothing but voices and breaths and sensations. She knew she screamed. She knew she sobbed his name. Her breath shortened until she had to remind herself to breathe.

Jack lifted her a little bit higher—and then he ground his hips into her, his body jerking as he shot deep inside her. His neck was arched, his head thrown back, his eyes tightly closed as he spilled everything he had. When it was over, he let her legs go and braced himself above her, resting on his elbows.

He lowered his head to kiss her, and she lifted up to meet him as if he were her only source of oxygen. He kissed her slowly, leisurely, his body still hard deep inside her. He flexed his hips and she moaned, still so sensitive.

His mouth trailed to her throat, her ear. "You do things to me, baby. Amazing things. I don't think I've ever come that hard in my life."

Gina couldn't help the small smile that curled her lips. "Then we need to repeat the experience. See if it's true."

"Fuck, yes."

She ran her fingers over his jaw, threaded them into his hair. She loved the feel of him, the scent of his skin, the way he dominated her body in a totally delicious way.

Her chest ached with everything she felt for him. She wanted to tell him she loved him, the same as she'd told him on the yacht, but she didn't want there to be any awkwardness.

And she feared there would be. She would say the words, her heart on the line, and he would kiss her without responding. Then he would encourage the fire between them until they lost themselves in it. She would enjoy the sex, but she would know, deep inside, that he didn't feel the same as she did, and it would affect things between them.

"I'm ready whenever you are," she whispered against his cheek.

He rocked into her then, and she couldn't stop herself from moaning at the way he filled her. She wouldn't have thought it possible considering how drained they'd both been, but he took her to the edge much quicker than she thought he could, driving her across the bed with hard thrusts until she saw stars behind her eyes.

She gripped him tight, her legs wrapped around his back, his hand beneath her ass, lifting her to him as he made her body sing. And then he crashed over the edge with her, groaning long and hard, her name a broken sound as he poured himself into her.

TWENTY-FOUR

JACK TOOK A SHOWER AND slipped back into the same clothes he'd worn yesterday. He hadn't expected to stay, so he hadn't brought anything else with him. His body ached, but mostly in a good way. His leg still throbbed, and he certainly hadn't done it any favors when he'd made love to Gina over and over.

But, God, she made him feel good. And she terrified him too. Because there was something about the way he felt when he was buried inside her that was more familiar than he liked to admit. He'd only ever felt this way with one other woman, and even that was different from how he felt with Gina.

Because Gina and Hayley weren't the same, and he wasn't going to feel quite the same. But did this mean he actually loved Gina?

He didn't know. He *liked* her, definitely. Maybe more than liked her. But love?

He thought about Hayley and all the time they'd spent together. They'd had years, even if they'd only been married a short time. She'd been such a good person... and she would have loved Gina. He knew it in his bones. Yeah, she'd loved the music—but she would have really liked the person. Evie, Georgie, Olivia, and Lucky liked Gina. She could have been an entitled bitch to them, but she hadn't been. She was warm and friendly and approachable. Even a little bit awkward, maybe.

It made her endearing, and he thought Hayley would have approved of his being with her.

When he went out into the living room, Gina was there with Eli, and his heart just kind of stuttered for a moment before it started pounding a little bit harder than before. Eli was eating cereal and watching television, and Gina was on her phone, picking at a plate of eggs and arguing with someone.

There was another tray with a silver lid and he knew she'd ordered him breakfast. He could hardly credit that he was at the fucking Ritz. Or that the woman sitting across the room was more than just someone he'd had sex with last night. He cared about her, he knew he did.

She looked up and realized he was there. "Barry, I have to go." Barry must have argued again because she rolled her eyes. "No, I have to. … We'll talk later. … Yes, of course. … Love you too."

She set the phone down and smiled. "Hey."

"Hey." He limped over and sat on the couch beside her. "So Barry's up to his usual tricks, huh?"

He was glad the man hadn't been involved in the kidnapping because it would have killed Gina. HOT had investigated him thoroughly, and he'd definitely not been the one to send the letters. Probably they weren't connected to the kidnapping at all and were just the random work of an obsessed stalker. She'd had a few of those over the last few years.

She laughed. "He's planning on world domination, as usual."

"Have you told him you don't want to dominate the world?"

"He knows. He just thinks if he keeps talking, I'll do what he wants. We're like brother and sister, really. Fight over everything but love each other just the same."

He didn't pretend to understand that kind of relationship, though it made him think of what she'd told him about her sister who'd been given up for adoption. He'd asked Mendez about that, asked if he knew anyone who could maybe find her. The colonel had looked at him with those unfathomable eyes of his and said he couldn't guarantee anything but he'd see what he could do.

Gina reached for the tray and whipped the cover off. "Bacon and eggs with hash browns. I didn't really know what you like, but I figured it had to be at least one of those things."

"I like them all."

She sat back when he unrolled the napkin and laid it on his lap. "I can cook a pretty mean omelet," she said, "but I rarely get the time."

He forked eggs into his mouth. Yeah, he felt a little pinch of annoyance because she made him think of his mother when she said that, but he knew it wasn't a fair comparison. Gina had the luxury of ordering food in and still spending time with her child. She wasn't ignoring Eli the way his parents had ignored him. He knew better than that after all the time he'd spent with her in going after their son. She was a good mom.

She reached out, ran her fingers over his arm. Her

touch was light, as if she expected him to push her away. Instead, he took her fingers and kissed them before letting her go again.

"I'm thinking about buying a house here," she said, and he turned to look at her. Her green eyes were so serious, her brow creased in worry, as if she expected him to say something negative.

He put the fork down. "That's a good idea."

"I thought it would make it easier for you to be with Eli."

"And you."

She smiled. "And me."

He reached out and caressed her cheek. He liked touching her. "Day at a time, babe."

"Yes."

He picked up his fork again, feeling vaguely dissatisfied with his reply. Yeah, life was a day at a time, but didn't he know that he wanted more of her? And he damn sure wanted to be with the kid. Why was he still hedging his bets?

"What do you want to do today?" he asked instead.

"I'd like to get out of this hotel. I'm going a little stir-crazy."

He understood why she'd stayed locked up, but the threat was gone now that Metaxas was blown to bits. She could use a day out. They both could. "We could go to the Eastern Shore, drive to Waterman's Cove or St. Michael's. They're small, out-of-the-way towns with charm. Wear some sunglasses and a wig, and no one will ever know it's you."

She laughed. "I'd like that. But what about your leg?"

He shrugged. "It'll be fine. I'll take it easy. But no

limousines, babe. Too ostentatious."

"No, I want to ride in your car." She frowned. "What kind of car do you have, anyway?"

He leaned back on the couch and gave her a serious look. "You ever see that movie about the cartoon cars that live in a little town?"

She frowned. "Wait… yes, I know the one you mean." She glanced at Eli. "Best not to say any names, you understand. Someone will want to watch the entire thing right now."

"Right. Remember the tow truck? The beat-up one that barely runs? It's all rusty and falling apart—and more than a little bit redneck?"

She arched an eyebrow. "Uh, yeah…"

"That's my car."

She blinked a few times. And then she grinned. "Okay. Sounds fun."

He let her sit there looking at him all goofy-like while his heart thumped and a hot feeling spread through his stomach and down into his groin. Jeez, she was something. She could probably buy any car she wanted, and she was content to ride in his fictional rusty piece of shit.

"I'm kidding, Gina. I drive a classic Mustang. You won't be embarrassed to be seen in it."

She actually looked disappointed. "Well, hell, I was looking forward to the rusty truck."

"We'll stop by a junkyard. I'll buy you one."

She reached out and took a piece of bacon off his plate. He didn't stop her. He liked watching her sitting there with her knees drawn up, munching on it. It was companionable. He hadn't had that with a woman in a long time. It almost made him content.

"Such a romantic," she said between bites.

"That's me, babe. Romantic to the core." He picked up another piece of bacon and held it up for her to take a bite when she finished the one she'd stolen. After she took a piece, he bit into it. "Sharing my bacon with you. I'd say that's hard-core romance."

Eli got up and toddled over. He walked right up to Jack and put a hand on his leg. "Bacon?"

"You like bacon, buddy?"

Eli nodded in that exaggerated way kids had. Jack tore a piece of the bacon off and gave it to the boy. He stuffed it in his mouth and went back over to plop down in front of the television.

Gina was smiling when Jack looked at her. His belly clenched tight. Yeah, there was something right about this. Being here with her. With his son. The past was fading, and the future was beginning to take shape.

"He likes you."

"Nah, I had bacon."

"He had a pretty traumatic experience recently, and he's cried every time a man delivered room service. I had to ask for women to bring the food. But he didn't cry when you showed up. He asked for your help and he fell asleep on you."

A tight ball of emotion sat in Jack's gut like a stone. It scared him, and excited him too. He turned to look at Eli before she could see the raw feelings in his eyes. "Then I guess he likes me. How about that?"

The day was wonderful. After a little bit of wrangling to get a car seat and fit it into Jack's Mustang, they'd set off for the Eastern Shore of Maryland. Gina had never been there before, and she slowly fell in love with the quiet landscape far beyond the reach of the Beltway. It was green and beautiful, punctuated with tributaries of shimmering water that flowed into the huge Chesapeake. They'd crossed the Bay Bridge earlier, its tall spans giving her a glorious view of the bay and Annapolis behind them as they'd driven toward the Eastern Shore.

Once there, Jack had taken them to Waterman's Cove, a small, quaint town with old shops and plenty of restaurants along the bay. They'd eaten at a place called Cindy's Crab Shack where the decor was plain and homey and the food was plentiful and yummy.

Gina had worn her hair in a ponytail, and she'd put on a Baltimore Orioles cap with the bill pulled low to help hide her face. She'd worn a pair of sunglasses, naturally. She'd finished the outfit with jeans, a pair of Converse instead of her trademark heels, and a loose T-shirt that she half tucked in. She was slouchy and casual, and the farther they went from the city, the happier she was.

Eli was well-behaved and currently preoccupied with a learning toy she'd given him. They were strolling along the waterfront and Jack was pushing his stroller. He'd insisted on leaving the cane in the car, so they were taking it slow and easy. The sun shone down on the water, and boats bobbed gently in the harbor. It was the kind of place that felt natural and free, and Gina's heart was light as they ambled down the boardwalk.

She slanted her gaze at Jack, and her heart turned over the same as always. He was so damn handsome, so strong and self-contained. He didn't need anyone. He was a rock unto himself. Women stared at him as they passed. What wasn't to like? Tall, golden, hard-bodied man pushing a baby. It was enough to make ovaries everywhere explode.

If they only knew what he was capable of in bed.

"I like it here," she said after a few quiet minutes. "It's peaceful."

He nodded. "Yep, not a mob in sight. Though don't take the cap off. Pretty sure that would change even here if they knew who you were."

She sighed. "It's been a long time since I could be anonymous."

He stopped and leaned against the railing, his back to the water. And then he opened his arms and she went into them. They stood there for a long moment, just holding each other. His cheek was against the top of her head, and his hands lay lightly against the small of her back.

Then he straightened and pressed his mouth to hers. Gina sighed, leaning into the kiss, but he broke it before she wanted him to. She clutched her fingers into his shirt and stood there staring at the logo on it as if it contained the secrets to the universe. So many emotions rolling through her. It was like she'd swallowed a hurricane. Parts of her were chaotic and dangerous, and other parts were calm and sure.

A car came up the street. The top was down and the

radio blared. Gina's words echoed back to her from a song and she turned to look as the girls drove by, singing and laughing.

"That's why I do it."

"It makes you happy to see them happy. Singing your songs, dancing to the beat."

"Yes." She squeezed her shoulders up around her ears for a second as the heat of happiness and, yeah, even embarrassment, flowed through her. "Those songs are pieces of my life. Makes it seem like it wasn't in vain if someone gets joy or finds comfort in my words."

He ran a finger along her jaw, frowning. "You deal in joy. I deal in death. We're polar opposites, babe."

Her heart thumped. "You deal in justice."

"Yeah."

She didn't like the darkness in his tone, or the look in his blue eyes. Faraway, like he was somewhere else instead of with her. Times like this, she felt as if she could never understand him.

"Why don't we head back? Cassie should be at the hotel by now."

She'd called her nanny this morning and arranged the flight because she could no longer put off her obligations. She'd thought about asking the firm for another nanny, but Cassie was a good kid, and Gina knew what it was like to need someone to believe in you. So long as she made sure that a bodyguard was with Cassie and Eli at all times while she was working, everything would be fine. Not only that, but Eli was used to Cassie. She'd been a part of his life for ten months, and he didn't need someone new when there'd been so many upheavals in his life recently.

The thought of leaving Eli and Cassie for even a minute made her stomach churn, but she had to let life return to normal. Stavros was dead and though there would always be crackpots, that couldn't stop her from living. She had a nanny because she needed help—and she had to use that help or quit working and become a recluse. If she did that, then Stavros won. She wasn't going to let that happen.

She was also having her assistant find a real estate agent so she could get a house in DC. Though maybe she could have one here. She looked at the peaceful surroundings and pictured how wrecked that would all be if she moved in.

In Europe, she could live in a house on a cliff overlooking the Med and no one would pay her much attention. Here, things were different. She sighed her disappointment.

"Something bothering you?" Jack asked.

She shrugged. "No, just thinking about how peaceful this is and how much I've enjoyed this outing."

He squeezed her hand. "There'll be more."

Her heart lurched. "Will there?"

He pulled her hand up to his mouth and kissed it. "I think so, yeah."

She felt warm inside as they headed back toward where he'd left his car at the restaurant. It was only a short walk.

"Goddamn," he said softly as they turned a corner.

Gina's stomach fell. There was a small crowd of people gathered around the car. The girls that had driven by with the radio blasting her song were also there, their car parked nearby and still thumping out the beat of another dance tune that had gone to number one.

"I'm sorry," she said. "I shouldn't have taken off the glasses in the restaurant."

"You can't fucking eat in the dark, Gina. It's not your fault."

Their waitress had seemed more interested in Jack than in her, but when Gina thought about the looks the woman had kept slanting at her, they took on a whole different meaning now. She'd thought the woman was jealous of her good fortune to have a man like Jack.

"Maybe we should call a taxi. I can send someone back for your car—"

"No." His voice was a whip in the air. "We drove here together, we're driving out together like normal fucking people."

"They don't mean any harm, Jack. It's the price of my success. I owe them."

"You don't owe them anything but the happiness they get when they listen to your songs."

She put her hand on his arm. "It's okay. We'll get through it. I'll sign a few autographs and we'll go."

"You take the stroller. I can't protect you if I can't reach my weapon."

She blinked. "You're armed?"

She didn't know why she thought he'd left the gun in the car, but of course he wouldn't have. He looked down at her like she'd lost her mind. "It's what I fucking do, Gina."

"Right then." She swallowed. "Just don't shoot anyone, okay?"

His teeth ground together. "Not if I can help it."

She only half thought he was kidding. The crowd spotted them as they moved again and people began to scream. A couple of them rushed over and Jack stepped out in front of her and Eli, looking perfectly menacing.

"Back off, girls."

The girls stopped, eyes wide. "Is it you? Are you really her?" one of them said, peering around Jack.

"I am," Gina said. "But you have to be calm about this, okay?"

The girls hugged each other and jumped up and down. The rest of the crowd had moved over to stand behind them. Everyone looked expectant.

"Hey, y'all," Gina said. "We were just out here enjoying your beautiful town today. But it's getting late and my baby is tired, so we need to get going."

"Will you sign my shirt?" someone asked.

"Do you have a pen?" When the girl nodded, Gina looked at Jack. He'd gone into protector mode, and he looked utterly cool and frightening. "Will you take Eli so I can do this?"

He came to stand behind the stroller while she walked out in front. She knew he didn't like it, but she wasn't about to start being rude to fans.

She signed autographs and posed for phone pics for twenty minutes before Jack called a halt to the impromptu session. The crowd stepped back as he took her and Eli to the car and put them inside. She smiled and waved at everyone while Jack strapped Eli into his car seat and put the stroller in the trunk.

Then he was inside at the wheel, face tight as he turned the key and the engine roared to life. He backed out of the parking lot, then gunned the engine, and they shot down the road.

Gina let out her breath and sank into the seat.

"You okay?"

"Yes," she said, lifting her hands in front of her face. They shook, and that wasn't like her. She wasn't afraid of her fans. But since Stavros had orchestrated a kidnapping and made her terrified for her baby's life—and then hers and Jack's—she'd been on edge.

"Goddamn, Gina, you're shaking."

"I'll be fine. I will." She gulped down her fear and looked at him. "They got you on their cell phones, you know. We'll be on Twitter by now."

He reached out and took one of her hands, threaded his fingers through hers and drew it into his lap. "It was bound to happen sometime."

"But you weren't ready for that yet." A different kind of panic flared to life inside her. He wasn't even accustomed to her life yet, and already he was about to be a news story. What if he freaked out and decided it was too much hassle to be with her?

He squeezed her hand. "Don't worry about it."

She didn't let go again until they reached the city.

TWENTY-FIVE

WHEN THEY GOT BACK TO the city, the nanny was at the hotel. Jack had a visceral reaction to the idea of handing Eli over to anyone else, but he told himself he was overreacting. She'd seemed a little spooked at meeting him, but thankfully Gina hadn't told her the truth of his relationship to Eli. He was glad, because after their trip to Waterman's Cove he was convinced it was something that was going to need to be handled delicately.

The media would mob her if they found out. And him. He didn't think Mendez would appreciate that at all. It was bad enough they'd gotten pictures of him, but he'd been wearing sunglasses at least. He wasn't anyone famous, so he wasn't immediately identifiable. The girls would tweet pictures of Gina, and he might appear in the background. He'd told Gina not to worry and he meant it.

But that didn't mean he thought the issue would go away. If he stayed with her, it would only get worse.

Though Eli knew the nanny well, he still cried for a few minutes while she soothed him and rocked him. Jack wanted to take him back, but Gina gave him a look that said to give it a second. He could see the uncertainty in her eyes, but he followed her lead, even though it twisted him up inside to listen to Eli cry. But finally Eli settled down and Cassie took him to his room for a nap.

"How long has she worked for you?"

Gina looked up from where she'd been checking her messages, her eyes a little wide. "About ten months. She came highly recommended from the firm, and I needed someone to help with Eli when I was recording or touring. The previous nanny got married and she wanted to concentrate on starting her own family, so I had to find someone new. Why?"

Jack shook his head. "I just wondered."

Gina smiled as if to reassure him. "Eli loves her. He's just tired after a day in the sun and fresh air. It's past his nap time, and he gets cranky."

He frowned. "I don't know anything about kids."

Gina stood and came over to put a hand on his cheek. His skin tingled at her touch and instant desire leapt to life in his groin.

"You'll learn. I like that you care about him so much."

He took her hand and kissed her palm. "I do care. About both of you."

She was a good woman, and a good mom to their son. Watching her today had only cemented that opinion of her. She did what she thought best for her son, and he knew that included bringing him into their lives too. She hadn't called him a year ago, but not out of spite. He knew that.

Her eyes softened. "I'm glad. I care about you, too."

She hadn't said she loved him again. He told himself it wasn't fair to expect her to say it when he didn't know what to say back. But he found that he still wanted to hear it.

"I need to go home," he said quietly.

Her expression fell. "I thought you might stay with us tonight."

"I need to get some clothes, babe." He let his gaze wander over their luxurious surroundings. "Not sure I have anything that fits the decor though, I gotta say."

Watching those fans go insane over her earlier had really highlighted the differences in their lives. She was a superstar. He was a grunt. How did you deal with something like that on a regular basis?

"That's okay. I like you best when you wear nothing anyway."

He laughed. "That might be a little more difficult with the nanny around."

"Just stay in the bedroom. And don't wear anything at all while you're in there. In fact, if you could sprawl on the bed and look decadent, that would be just fine."

He was starting to get hard. "I'll do my best." He kissed her until she went limp in his arms. He was no longer *starting* to get hard; he was all the way there. He looked at the door to Eli's room, but there was something about taking Gina to bed with the nanny here that didn't inspire him. "Why don't you come with me for a couple of hours?"

She turned her head toward the bedroom where Eli and Cassie had disappeared. "I want to, but I don't think I should leave them."

"We'll be back before he wakes up, I promise." He frowned. "Wait, how long do kids nap?"

She laughed. "It depends, but he'll be out for about

two hours."

"See? Perfect. He'll never know you're gone. Besides, I'd love to do a famous pop star in my own bed."

She arched an eyebrow. "And I'd love to do a hotshot sniper in his secret lair."

He ran his hands up her arms. He definitely wanted to be with her, but he didn't want her to be worried about Eli. "It's fine if you don't want to go with me, Gina."

She looked conflicted. "I have to get back to normal. Eli is safe. There's no threat anymore and Cassie's with him. Darren is also here—I don't think he's as good a shot as you, but you have to admit he's bigger and meaner-looking."

Jack snorted. "He looks like a frigging Abrams tank. Wonder what he eats for breakfast?"

"Whatever it is, I definitely don't want any."

Jack let his gaze drop to her breasts. "No, probably don't need any growth here."

"And I thought you'd say the bigger, the better."

"I've got something that's better when it's bigger. Want to see it?"

Her eyes sparkled. "I definitely do."

"Then come with me and I'll show you the minute we arrive."

She lifted one eyebrow. "The minute?"

"The second minute. Don't want to scandalize the neighbors."

She looked torn. And then she nodded. "All right, I'll come."

Jack's apartment was tucked away in a suburb of Maryland, close to the base where his job was. It was still daylight when they got there, but Gina wore her sunglasses and hat and wasn't taking them off for anyone. Until they got into his apartment and he pulled the hat and glasses off while crushing his mouth down on hers.

Gina moaned as his tongue slid into her mouth. They started ripping at each other's clothing as soon as the door closed, discarding garments as he walked her to some unknown destination. When she was completely naked, he picked her up and sat her down on what turned out to be a breakfast bar.

Gina gripped the edges tight, arching her back as he devoured her breasts, licked a trail down her belly, and thrust his tongue into her pussy.

"Jack!" Her voice was a high-pitched squeak as he spread her wide and teased her clitoris with his tongue. Then he thrust two fingers inside her and worked them slowly in and out.

She came much too quickly, his name a harsh cry as her orgasm ripped through her. Then he picked her up and she wrapped her legs around him. He lowered her onto his cock, supporting her with both hands. When she was fully impaled on him, he lifted her up and then plunged into her again.

Gina cried out at the intensity of the feelings roaring through her. Her body was on fire. Her nipples were tight little points that ached for his mouth, and her pussy gripped him tight as he lifted her and thrust into her again and again.

"So fucking hot, babe," he said. "Can't get enough of you."

"You can have me, Jack," she gasped. "As much as you want."

He carried her over to the couch, still impaled deep inside her, and then lowered her to the cushions. Their mouths met and he put a hand under her ass, lifting her so he could pump deep inside her over and over. She came again, her vision going black for a moment as her body detonated.

He was there with her, following her over the edge of the precipice, his groans mingling with hers as they came. When it was over, she wrapped her arms around him and held him tight while he tongued the hollow of her throat.

"That was nuclear," he said after a long minute, shifting so his full weight wasn't crushing her into the cushions.

She toyed with the damp hair at his brow. "I love when you do those things to me. It's never felt like this with anyone but you."

Her heart beat hard saying that to him, but she wouldn't hide her feelings or be careful what she said anymore. She couldn't. She wanted him in her life.

"That's sweet of you to say," he told her before tonguing her nipple.

"It's not sweet," she said. "I love you, Jack."

His head lifted, his eyes so hot and blue. "I care about you, Gina. More than I'm comfortable with, if I'm being honest. But I need to figure out what that means."

She traced his lips with her finger. "I know."

His brows arrowed down as he studied her. "You're pretty remarkable, and not because you're Gina fucking Domenico. I want you to know that."

His praise filled her with warmth. "When I'm with you, I'm just Gina Robertson from Nowheresville, USA. I don't even know who Gina Domenico is at times like this."

"Yeah, but the rest of the world won't forget."

He was still buried inside her, still hard. And her body zinged with sparks whenever he moved. "I don't want to think about that life when you're inside me, okay? I just want to think about you."

"Guess I should give you something else to think about then."

"Maybe you should."

This time he drew it out between them, making love to her leisurely and thoroughly. Gina was spent when they finished, her body boneless and so relaxed she didn't think she could move from this couch for the rest of the night.

But they had to, and when he stood and pulled her up with him, she followed. He led her into the bathroom and started the shower. It was a small room, but sparse and neat. They showered together, but they were too satiated to actually have sex again. He dried her off and went to collect her clothes for her as she followed him into the living room wearing nothing but a towel.

For the first time, she paid attention to the apartment. It was small but neat and almost bare. There was a couch, a chair, a table, and a television in the living room. In the dining room, there was a small table and four chairs. Every surface was clean. There were no dishes in the sink, no garbage on the counters. Nothing that even indicated he lived here.

He was still naked as he came back with her clothing and laid it on the couch for her to sort through and put on.

"Are you a neat freak, Jack?"

He followed her gaze, and then he laughed softly. "Yeah, I guess maybe I am. I don't like clutter."

"Mmm, guess we'll need to look for a modern-contemporary house then. With lots of closets, because I definitely have clothes."

He frowned a little but didn't comment, and her heart skipped. Dammit. She sighed and spread her hands in apology.

"You already know how I feel. And, yes, I want you to move in with us. But I won't push it."

He raked a hand through his wet hair. "It's complicated, babe."

"Which part?"

"All of it."

She wrapped her arms around herself. She knew he had to be thinking about the mob of fans earlier, among other things. "I know that, but are you going to stay out of our lives because I can't change who I am? Walk away from your son because his mother lives in a spotlight?"

His lips tightened. "I didn't say that."

She reached for her pile of clothing and found her panties. She knew she needed to be patient, but after everything they'd just done, after the way he made her feel, it hurt that he was still so noncommittal. "Forget I said anything. It was a mistake. I'll buy a house with gothic touches and gold-leafed toilets and you'll just have to live with it if you decide we're worth the trouble."

He caught her arms and gripped them tight, forcing her to look at him. "You're worth a lot of trouble, Gina."

She searched his gaze, her throat closing up. And then he spoke again, and her stomach fell to the floor.

"But I'm not sure I am."

"That's ridiculous," she gasped. "Without you, I wouldn't be here. Eli wouldn't be here. You're worth a lot of trouble to me."

His grip on her tightened for a second. And then his hands slid down her arms as he shook his head. "Is that all it is? The fact I saved you? Anyone would have done it. It just happened to be me."

"Do you really think that's the only reason?"

"What else could it be?"

"Why did Hayley love you?"

He stared at her for a long minute. "I don't know. Because we grew up together, maybe. Because I was her first."

"You aren't giving either of us enough credit." She stepped into his space, put her hands on his cheeks. "We can make this work, Jack. You just have to be willing to try."

He gave her a quick kiss and then set her away from him to grab his jeans. "We won't solve this tonight so let's stop talking about it."

"We have to talk about it sometime."

He straightened and her mouth went dry at the sight of his hipbones. He hadn't zipped his jeans yet and the fly hung open, exposing his flat belly and the taut line of muscle there.

"Yeah, but not tonight. Let's just enjoy each other, all right?"

She nodded stupidly. But her heart hurt when he turned away and shrugged into his shirt. She had everything she could ever want because she'd worked hard to make it happen. But you couldn't make a man love you, no matter what you did. He had to do that on his own.

And she was very afraid he might decide she wasn't worth the trouble after all.

TWENTY-SIX

THE RIDE BACK TO THE hotel was silent. Jack turned into the drive and stopped before he reached the valet stand and the uniformed man standing there. He'd been thinking the whole way back, the words building inside him until he thought he might burst. He didn't know why he'd said that to her about not being worth the trouble, but the truth was he'd been thinking about her life, about how she had everything, and he'd wondered what in the hell a woman like her could see in him.

Hell, he'd often wondered what Hayley saw in him that made her willing to put up with the life they shared. God knows he hadn't been there when she'd needed him most. Maybe because he was so used to not having anyone be there for him when he'd been growing up that he hadn't thought it was a problem to be gone so much. He'd just assumed she would be there whenever he was home.

"I've never had anyone in my life I could trust to be there for me, except for Hayley," he said, not looking at her. "My own parents couldn't even be bothered to go to my shooting tournaments. When Hayley died, they were on a cruise. Do you think they cut their vacation short to come back for her funeral? No, they didn't."

"Oh, Jack—"

"Hayley was the only one I could count on, and look what happened to her." And there it was, that fear that he'd lose his way again if he opened himself up.

"There's your team."

He squeezed the wheel. "Yes, and I trust them with my life. But if I got reassigned tomorrow, I'd learn to trust my new team just as much. It's not the same thing."

She unclipped her seat belt and moved as close to him as she could get with the hump between the seats. Her arms went around his neck, one hand on his cheek until she turned him to face her. "I'm not leaving you, Jack. Not on purpose anyway. You think this isn't scary for me? Everyone I've ever cared about has either left or been using me for money. And since I live in this bubble created by fame and fortune, I can never be sure that anyone who gets close to me is interested in the real me or in the money."

His heart squeezed tight. "I'm not interested in your money, Gina."

"You think I don't know that? You haven't asked me for anything, and you yelled at Barry."

"He was being a prick."

"Barry's a teddy bear most of the time. But no one who wanted in good with me would even consider tangling with him. You not only yelled at him, you practically accused him of kidnapping Eli."

"If you need to rest, I'm yelling at him. And there was a reason to be suspicious."

"I know. On all of it."

"You know this is only scratching the surface, right? If I moved in with you, and you got pissed because I was in your space, then what? I'm going to get angry when you're onstage in something bordering indecent and a thousand assholes are drooling over you. You understand that, right?"

"I think it's sweet."

"You think it's sweet now. You won't think it's so sweet in a year."

She sighed. "Jack, we'll adjust. It's what couples do. You'll learn to accept that I know what's best for my career and you'll frown, but you won't make me change my shows."

He put a hand on her throat, skimmed his thumb over the hollow. "And what about my job? I'm a soldier. I'll disappear, often on very short notice, and you'll have no idea where I am or when I'm coming back. And then there's always the chance I won't come back at all. Do you really want to live with that?"

He could feel the bob of her throat as she swallowed. "Evie lives with it. Olivia and Georgie do too. Lucky goes with the team, but even she lives with it. I'm as strong as they are, and if that's what it takes, then that's what I'll do. I'll live with it."

It was so tempting. For a moment, he actually believed her. Because Gina was strong and she could do anything she put her mind to. But then he leaned his head back on the seat as reality crashed down on him. There were other issues at stake, too. "Who am I fucking kidding? If I choose you, I've lost HOT. The attention that comes with you is too much. Mendez won't like it. Hell, he's probably already seen the pics from today."

259

She didn't speak and when he turned to look at her, there were tears on her cheeks. His heart twisted.

"Me or your job? Wow."

"You see why this is so fucking hard? I want it all, and I don't see how I can have it."

She let him go and turned to face straight ahead. "I get it, Jack. You can have me and Eli in your life, all the time, or you can have a *job*."

He heard the hurt in her voice and he understood it. But dammit, it wasn't as easy as she thought it was. HOT was his life. The guys were his family. If he lost them, then what? Yeah, he could be reassigned, but that wasn't the same as leaving altogether. "Is what you do just a job? Would you choose between being Gina Domenico and being with me?"

"That's not what we're talking about."

"No, but would you?"

"If I had to."

"That's a lie."

She whirled on him. "How do you fucking know? You don't, because that's not what's at issue here! I can give you everything you could ever want, Jack. You won't have to work if you don't want to. Or you can work. I don't care."

Now he was just getting pissed. Because she was belittling his career as if it weren't important. "You know, I may not make a million dollars, but what I do is pretty fucking important. It makes the world a safer place while people like you benefit from all that freedom and safety that people like me provide."

"Then work for me. Be my bodyguard. I'll pay you a million dollars if it'll make you happy."

He blinked at her. And then the fury started rolling through him again. He was trying to figure this out and she was pushing too hard. "You don't fucking get it."

She shoved the door open, her lip trembling, and he felt like an asshole even though he had a right to be angry.

"Oh, I get it just fine. You say you need time, but the truth is you care more about killing people than you do about me and Eli."

"Gina—"

"No!" She scrambled out of the car and slammed the door.

Gina ran into the lobby of the hotel, pushing past the doorman and ignoring Jack as he yelled after her. She was furious with herself and furious with Jack. She shouldn't have said that, but she'd been so angry and hurt that she'd lashed out. And now she was crying, working herself into an emotional mess. She just wanted to get upstairs and see Eli.

Jack would follow, and then when they'd both calmed down, they could talk about it like adults. No, it wasn't fair to ask him to leave his job. She knew that. But when he said he wanted it all and just didn't know how to have it, she felt like he'd stabbed her in the heart.

If he loved her, it would be an easy choice. But he didn't. She didn't doubt he felt something—lust proba- bly—but love clearly wasn't it. And she wanted love. She *deserved* love. She'd had enough of lust and she wanted more.

She took the elevator up and emerged on her floor. Fishing the keycard from her purse, she walked up to the door and swiped it over the lock. The suite was quiet when she went inside and she stopped, frowning. There was no sign of Darren. He could be in the bathroom, of course, so she told herself not to panic just yet.

Eli's door was shut, and she expected that Cassie was in there with him. It was eight o'clock, so he should be going to bed. Still, she wanted to see him. She went over and knocked softly on the door. When there was no answer, she opened it carefully.

The room was empty and her heart began to thrum. She whirled around and headed for her room. It was empty too. She went into the bathroom to check, even though there was no noise—and stopped when she saw the body on the floor. Her heart shot into her throat as her stomach twisted into a knot.

Darren lay on the floor, his eyes wide open, a bullet hole in the center of his forehead. Gina's legs turned to liquid. She stumbled, turning, trying to get back out of the bathroom and to the front door. She had to find Jack. He was the only one who could help her.

"Eli," she cried, pressing her hand to her mouth. "Oh God, Eli."

It couldn't be happening again. It just couldn't. Stavros was dead. His compound had blown sky-high. She found her legs and ran for the door, praying Jack was on his way up.

Oh God, oh God, oh God!

She ran into the hall and bolted toward the elevator.

When she reached it, she started jamming the Down button. It seemed like it took forever, but the doors finally slid open. She jumped inside and pressed the Ground Floor button with shaking fingers. Her vision blurred with tears and her voice choked out in sobs that she gulped down.

"Keep it together, dammit," she hissed to herself.

The elevator took its sweet time—and then it stopped one floor down and Gina jammed the button again. But the doors slid open anyway.

A man with a gun stood there. She squeaked and lunged for the Close Door button, but his arm shot into the space and then he followed, wedging the doors open almost brutally.

Gina grabbed the railing for support and kicked out, trying to hit him in the balls. He successfully dodged the blow—and then he leveled the gun at her heart.

"Fight me again and your lover dies. Keep fighting and your child dies too."

Her heart raced hard and black spots appeared in her vision. She blinked them away and focused on breathing. Her hands were clammy where they gripped the brass railing.

"I'll pay ransom. Just tell me how much. But you have to l…let them go."

The man laughed. "You're barking up the wrong tree. I suggest you discuss the arrangements with your husband, Mrs. Metaxas."

TWENTY-SEVEN

"MY DARLING WIFE," STAVROS SAID as Gina entered the room of the private house where he was currently lounging on a couch and looking like the proverbial satisfied cat. He was wearing a tuxedo and smoking a cigar. She was so stunned to see him that she could hardly process it. "I'm so glad you could join me."

The man behind Gina gave her a little push and she went forward, folding her arms around herself in a useless protective gesture.

"You're supposed to be dead."

He spread his hands wide. "And yet I am not, as you can see."

"Your compound exploded. You were in it."

"Ah yes." He took a puff of the cigar. "Fortunately, I had a hardened shelter built in the basement for just such emergencies. I would have been here sooner had we not needed to dig ourselves out of the collapsed rubble. Your people caused much damage in their zeal."

She lifted her chin. "Where are my son and his nanny? And what have you done with my bodyguard?"

Stavros snorted. "Your bodyguard? I think you mean your lover, Gina *mou*." He shook his head and tsked. "I am very disappointed in you. Me not even cold in my grave and you took a lover."

"What do you want from me?"

Stavros stood and jerked his head at the man, who then turned and left, closing the door behind him. Gina's heart pounded hard, but she swallowed and told herself to keep her wits about her. They were still in DC. She'd been driven to this palatial estate in the northwest of the city. And then she'd been made to sit in a room with Stavros's thug guarding her for two, maybe three hours, until she'd been brought into this room.

A chill snaked down her spine and she shivered. Eli, Jack, and Cassie were still missing. Or Eli and Cassie were, anyway. Perhaps the man had lied and Jack had gotten away. She prayed it was so, because then he would come for her.

Or maybe he wouldn't. She'd accused him of killing people, as if he were the criminal instead of one of the good guys.

"I want my wife to be faithful. Is that so much to ask?"

She wanted to object that she wasn't his wife, but she didn't want to antagonize him. She had to think fast on her feet, but the trouble was that he terrified her and she had no idea what would set him off next. She made her voice soft.

"Where are they, Stavros?"

He shrugged as he went over to the window, jamming his hands in his pockets as he looked out onto the lawn. Lights lit the perimeter in a soft glow. She had no doubt there were guards stationed along that perimeter.

"The boy is fine. His nanny has been most helpful, by the way." He turned back to her, a smile curling one corner of his mouth. The kind of smile that said he was ridiculously pleased with himself. "It took me a very long time to insert her into your life. A very long time."

Gina's stomach turned to stone. "I… I don't understand."

"Dear Cassie is a Metaxas, my love. Did you not ever see it?"

She felt faint. "I… No, I didn't."

"Her mother is a cousin… I forget how far removed." He waved a hand. "This does not matter. She is a Metaxas, and the family comes first. Cassie knows this quite well."

"You sent her to me so you could kidnap my baby?" Betrayal was a hard pill to swallow. She'd liked Cassie, trusted her, felt *sorry* for her. She'd brought Cassie back into her life today to take care of her most precious possession. She'd brought the spider into her home.

Gina reeled. She realized now that Cassie must have handed Eli over and then made up a story about being cornered. If she walked into this room, Gina would launch herself at the woman's throat.

"I sent her to watch you, Gina. Until I was ready to claim Athenasios's child. The kidnapping was rather inspired, don't you think?" His eyes hardened. "And you deserved to suffer for what you'd done. It was the least you deserved."

Gina shook her head, biting down on the inside of her cheek to keep tears from falling. "I didn't do anything, Stavros."

"You kept the child a secret. You never would have

told the truth." His voice grew louder, his tone more adamant. "My mother does not deserve this. She lost her eldest son, her beloved boy, and she *will* have her grandchild."

Gina bowed her head, trembling all over. She had to appease him. He was unbalanced, and fighting only made him angry. "Of course she will, Stavros."

He stalked over and gripped her chin hard, forcing her to look at him. His fingers bit into her skin. "Who were those people who took you away from me on St. Margarethe and destroyed my property?" His dark eyes were black and fathomless.

"M...mercenaries. I hired mercenaries because I wasn't certain you didn't mean to kill me."

His grip didn't soften. "I should kill you, Gina *mou.* I may yet. But not before I've had my fill of you."

Her insides turned to liquid. He was going to rape her, and she was going to have to pretend to enjoy it if she wanted her baby.

And Jack. Dear God, Jack. Would she ever see him again? Would she ever get to apologize for the things she'd said?

"I'll do anything you want."

"Of course you will, my love." He let her go and reached for his zipper. "Right now, you can suck my cock. After that, perhaps I'll allow you to see the boy."

Her heart plummeted and her stomach churned with bile. She thought she would be sick. Tears sprang into her eyes until her vision went blurry. Cold, iron-hard fury scoured through her. Men who thought they had the right to demand sexual favors, who used their power to do so, made her want things that would otherwise horrify her.

Their penises sliced off their bodies, for instance. Their balls shoved into their mouths. Their gruesome deaths.

"I won't be your whore," she choked out.

He laughed. "Oh, I think you will." He reached into his jacket pocket and pulled out a cell phone. Then he turned it to her and pushed a button. There was a lock screen, of course, but it was one she'd seen before.

Jack.

"I have his phone, which means I have him. If you don't do as I wish, he will be the first to die." He put the phone back into his pocket and laughed as he reached into his trousers. "Up to you, my lovely wife, what happens to him now…"

Jack's leg hurt like a son of a bitch. That was the first thing he noticed. The second was that his head hurt too. He blinked, but his surroundings were dark. The last thing he remembered was tossing his keys to the valet so he could take off after Gina. He'd headed for the elevator, the doors had opened—and someone had hit him.

He listened, trying to make sense of where he was. There was the smell of oil and diesel, and… yes, a bobbing sensation. He was in a boat, in the engine room perhaps, or somewhere below the waterline. He lay on his side, curled up on a hard floor. He pushed himself upright carefully. His head swam a bit, but he took his time. Nausea swirled in his gut and he lifted a hand—well how about that? He wasn't tied up. Stupid sons of bitches.

He gently probed his head. There was a knot at the back where someone had hit him pretty hard. He wondered how they'd gotten him out of the hotel without anyone noticing. Then he decided it didn't matter.

What mattered was Gina. She'd been upset and she'd taken off. Had someone grabbed her too? Was she somewhere on this boat as well? Or was it just him they were after, and she was safe and well in her room with Eli and Cassie?

The feeling of utter despair that claimed him when he thought of Gina and Eli in danger made his stomach turn over again. He couldn't lose them.

He groped his pockets, but his cell phone was gone. That was unfortunate since his team could track him that way once they figured out he was in trouble. Though he was on leave for a few days, he was still required to check in on a regular basis. When he didn't, they'd start looking.

Finding him was another matter. He had to get out of here just as soon as he could stand.

When his stomach didn't churn as much as it had been, he pushed to his feet. His hand shot out and encountered a wall when he stumbled. He stood there for a long moment, swallowing the nausea and listening for sound.

There was nothing—and then the engine spooled up and water churned against the hull. They were moving. But where?

He figured he'd been out for an hour, maybe more. Logically, he was on the Potomac or the Chesapeake. His money was on the Potomac. The Washington Harbor was close to the hotel, and it made the most sense.

He groped his way around the room, feeling the

walls. There were boxes in one corner, and shelves along another. He found the door finally, and he tugged on the handle. It was locked.

He made his way along the opposite wall, feeling for anything he could use as a weapon. When his fingers closed around a net, he clutched it, pulling it toward him. It was long and heavy, and he shook it out until he could find the edge. He tugged it with him as he continued to explore. There was nothing else, but he found the door again and sank back against the wall to wait. He held the net against him, his fingers curled around the edges. After a while he wanted to go to sleep, but he knew he couldn't, so he pushed upright again and made himself stand on one leg and then the other. Anything to keep alert.

He didn't know how long he waited, but eventually the engine cut to a dull idle. His senses ticked up then, because if anyone were coming for him, now would be the time. He waited for long minutes until he almost thought he was wrong—and then a key turned in the lock and his body tensed.

A light flicked on, blinding him, but he blinked against it and prepared to spring when the door opened. His eyes watered and the light stabbed into his brain, making his head pound even worse. But he had one chance to get out of here. One chance to find Gina and Eli.

The door scraped open on rusty hinges—and Jack lunged, flinging the net over the body that came through. A man roared as he went down and the gun in his hand discharged. The arm holding the gun was still free of the net and Jack grabbed the weapon, twisting it out of the man's grip before landing a blow to his head that made him go limp.

If there was another man behind this one, Jack was done for since his gut churned and his head swam and he needed a minute to focus. But no one else came, and Jack shoved the body into the room before turning off the light and closing the door. The key was still in the lock, so he twisted it and pulled it free, locking the man inside. Then he crept down the dimly lit passageway, listening for sounds of other people.

The boat was old and big, appeared to be a fishing boat of some kind, quite possibly for taking massive groups of tourists out at once. He revised his estimate of the Potomac and decided he was on the Chesapeake. His kidnappers must have drugged him, which meant he'd been out longer than an hour.

Fear rolled through him. If Gina had been the target—and he was pretty certain she had—she could be anywhere by now. But he wasn't giving up. He would find her, and he'd kill the motherfuckers who thought they could take her away from him.

He went up a set of stairs and listened for movement. All was silent, but he smelled cigarette smoke. He checked the weapon—a nine mil with a nearly full clip—and prepared to burst through the door.

After counting to ten in his head, he kicked the door open and emerged topside. Two men whirled, hands reaching for weapons, and Jack fired, taking them down before they had a chance to draw. He battled his nausea and a sense of dread as he checked the rest of the boat. It *was* a fishing boat, and he was the only passenger aside from the guards. One man was locked in the hold and these two were dead. He bent over and sucked in a breath, blinking back the agony of a blinding headache.

A check of the GPS indicated they were on the Chesapeake, southeast of Annapolis. The depth readings here were 174 feet. He had no doubt what they'd intended to do with him. The net, some concrete blocks maybe, and goodnight, sweet prince.

He throttled up the engine and steered for the nearest harbor. A quick check of one of the bodies landed him a cell phone. He checked the other, just in case they had his, but that was a no-go. Fortunately, the phone numbers he needed were imprinted on his brain. He punched in the numbers one-handed and pushed the throttle higher.

"Girard," came the answer on the other end.

"Hey there, Richie," he yelled over the roar of the wind and the engine's chugging. "Got a situation here."

"What, another one? Where the hell are you?"

"Yes, sir, another one. And I'm on the Chesapeake, making for harbor. Two dead, one captured."

"Son of a bitch. All right, I'll round up the posse. Give me your coordinates and we'll get it cleaned up."

TWENTY-EIGHT

GINA WAS PARALYZED. SHE KNEW she needed to drop to her knees and do what Stavros wanted, but she was frozen. He stood there with his hand in his trousers, stroking himself, and she hated him so much in that moment that she wished she could kill him with her bare hands.

"Gina *mou,* I'm waiting," he said none too gently.

She pulled in a breath, and then another, willing herself to comply. To be the biddable woman he wanted until she could ensure her child's safety. And Jack's, though she didn't know that Stavros would keep his word. For all she knew, Jack was already dead. Her heart cried out at that thought.

"I need more than a phone," she cried. "I need to see Eli. And I need proof that Jack is still alive."

Stavros's face turned dark with rage. He lashed out and grabbed her hair, twisting his hand into the heavy mass and jerking her forward. Gina screamed.

"You'll do as I fucking say! You're mine, Gina! *Mine*! And you will obey me when I command you."

Gina's hands went around his. "You're hurting me."

273

"I've changed my mind," he hissed in her ear, tugging her toward the couch. "I want to be inside you. I want us to make a baby brother for Athenasios."

Her stomach turned upside down. He meant Eli, but he'd said his brother's name. He wasn't sane...

"Stavros, please, not like this—"

There was a knock on the door that made her jump. Stavros seemed to ignore it entirely, but it came again, louder this time. "Mr. Metaxas. You have a call."

"Take a message."

"The caller says it's important, sir. Regarding the deal."

Stavros stilled. And then he shoved her away and Gina huddled into her corner of the couch, shaking with fear and anger. Stavros zipped up and stood over her for a long moment, his eyes as mad as ever. "When I come back, you *will* be happy to receive me."

He turned and strode from the room and Gina deflated. Then she shot up and hurried over to the desk sitting against one wall. She yanked open drawers, looking for a weapon of some kind. There was a silver letter opener, and she grasped it in shaking hands before shoving it beneath her T-shirt and into the waistband of her jeans. Thank God she'd worn a loose shirt today.

The door swung open again and she shot over to the window, pretending to be looking outside. It wasn't Stavros who'd entered, but the man who'd taken her from the hotel.

"I suggest you remove whatever you stashed in your pants and drop it, Mrs. Metaxas."

"I... I don't know what you mean."

"Sure you do. And if you don't drop it, then I'm going to come over and take it off you."

She lifted her chin. "I don't think my husband will like it if you touch me."

He snorted. "Like it? Actually, it'll turn him on. Mr. Metaxas is quite generous with his ladies."

The leer on his face made her reach for the letter opener. She dropped it on the ground and backed away, arms around her body.

He leaned down and picked it up. "You're gonna be a fun one, I can already tell."

"Fuck you."

"If you're lucky." He winked and went over to sit on the couch, letter opener twisting in his fingers like a toy.

Gina huddled into one corner of the window and turned her face toward the glass. "Jack," she mouthed silently. "Please come and get us one more time."

But she feared it was a hopeless plea. Because Jack was most certainly already dead.

Mendez looked absolutely furious. His face was mottled with rage and his eyes flashed fire. "Goddammit," he roared at someone on the other end of the phone, "you can't keep information from us like that. We should have been told."

Jack's gaze was focused on the colonel. They were all focused on the colonel. HOT had arrived at the dock in full force, ready to take charge of the situation and clean up the mess. It was dark and muggy and mostly silent, except for Mendez. Jack had taken the boat into one of the inlets, to a private dock where he'd been instructed to meet his team. They'd swarmed over the boat, along with a few support personnel, and collected the bodies and the lone survivor.

The guy was happy to talk. He'd been hired by a man with an accent who'd told him to make Jack disappear. These guys had decided that disposing of him in the deepest part of the Chesapeake made the most sense, and if he never came up again, that was fine with them.

Iceman had given him some painkillers, and he'd suited up while they waited for Mendez to get off the phone. When the colonel finally turned to them, he was still spitting mad.

"Metaxas is alive. And he's in DC. He was at a congressional fundraiser tonight, of all things, and he's currently renting a house in the northwest of the city. Just fucking business as usual and no one thought we needed to know."

There was an iron ball in Jack's belly. Metaxas wasn't dead. Jesus. "Does he have Gina?"

He was very afraid he knew the answer to that question. And it made him sick.

"She's not at the hotel, and neither is her nanny or baby. I'd say the answer is yes."

Jack saw black spots. He sucked in a deep breath, willing himself not to pass out. No fucking way was he going down for the count. He had to find Gina and Eli and bring them home.

"Hey, got a ping on Hawk's phone," came a voice from the van. They all rushed over to find Billy the Kid sitting at the console, tapping fast at his computer.

"Northwest DC…"

A few seconds later, he rattled off the coordinates.

"Go," Mendez said. "I'll take care of it on this end."

"What are the orders, sir?" Matt asked.

"Rescue the hostages. Lethal force authorized." His gaze lit on Jack, but he didn't say anything. They exchanged a look, and then Mendez was turning away and barking orders at the support staff.

The guys all piled into the van and Flash gunned the engine. It was about forty miles to where they needed to be, but they couldn't risk inserting by helicopter. Metaxas would hear them coming and he'd be ready.

"How'd he fucking get out of there alive?" Brandy asked. "The place blew to kingdom come. Nobody could have survived that."

"He must have had a bunker. Goddammit," Jack said, slapping the side of the van.

"It wasn't on the schematics we got from Intel," Matt said. "He must have added it over the last couple of years."

That didn't make Jack feel any better. He hit the side of the van again. Brandy reached over and squeezed his shoulder.

"We'll get them back, Hawk."

"Yeah," he said, because he couldn't envision a future where they didn't.

This would be a delicate operation because they were in the middle of a city, but it wasn't anything they hadn't trained for. Matt went over the battle plan, and once they were all in agreement, it was quiet. Just the roar of the engine and the rattle of their gear as they sped up the road.

After what seemed like forever, they were heading up the quiet, tree-lined streets of Northwest DC. This was where the rich people lived, where diplomats, government officials, and captains of industry bought houses behind ironwork fences and automatic gates.

There was security in a neighborhood like this, but it was amateur hour in comparison to HOT. Flash brought the van to a rolling stop at the designated drop zone and they piled from the van and fanned out, guns drawn and ready.

The lights around the perimeter of the house blinked out, and Jack knew that Billy had hacked into the system.

The team poured over the fence and onto the grounds. Jack wanted to bolt for the house and keep going until he found Gina and Eli, but he knew that wouldn't be wise. If they were still alive, he'd endanger them if he did anything like that. No, he needed his cool. Now was not the time to have it desert him.

But goddammit, his heart pounded as his mind raced with thoughts of what Gina might be going through in there. Metaxas was obsessed with her, and he'd had her captive for hours now. Had he hurt her? Raped her?

Jack's stomach twisted. Brandy was beside him as they came up against two security guards. The men had their backs turned and were talking and smoking. Jack and Brandy each took a man and delivered a knockout blow. No shooting until necessary. This wasn't a foreign op, and these men weren't part of a terrorist cell. They could be Metaxas's own men, or they could be hired security from a local company.

The lights were still on in the house, but Iceman and Knight Rider would take care of that soon enough. Jack and Brandy drew up closer to the house—and Jack went utterly still. He gave Brandy a signal, and his teammate nodded.

Gina was looking out a window, but Eli wasn't with her. Jack's heart twisted with relief and frustration. He wanted to charge up there and get her, but they had to take this easy and do it right. He had no idea who was in that room with her.

"Visual on Gina," Jack said into the mic. "No sign of Eli or Metaxas."

"Copy."

"Hold steady, boys and girls," Iceman said. "Power going in just a few moments…"

They were some of the longest moments of Jack's life.

The lights had gone out on the perimeter of the grounds a few minutes ago. The second it happened, the man sitting on the couch stood up and stared out the window like a terrier sniffing out a rat. Gina's heart thumped as hope swelled.

But nothing else happened and the man grunted something about timers before walking over to the door. Stavros came back inside the room then, his brows drawn low. He'd been gone for a long time. Whatever news he'd gotten hadn't been good, judging by the look on his face.

"We're leaving," he said. "Get the others."

"Yes, boss," the man said before disappearing through the door.

"Wh…where are we going?"

"Home to Greece. I have business there."

"Let me go, Stavros," she begged. "Please just give me Eli and let me go. You'll never get away with this— people know who I am, and I can't just disappear—"

He came over and grabbed the back of her head, crushing his mouth down on hers, his teeth clashing with hers as his tongue plunged into her mouth. It was vile. He tasted like cigars and alcohol and her gorge rose swiftly. She pushed against his chest and finally he stepped away.

Then he laughed.

"You are my wife now. I have the papers to prove it, and no one will question me."

"The ceremony wasn't completed."

"The papers say it was. It's a nice, long ride to Greece. And you're going to spend it naked, Gina *mou.*"

He wrapped his hand around her wrist and jerked her toward the door. His man was on the other side, waiting. Cassie was there, holding Eli, and Gina rushed forward to snatch her baby from Cassie's arms.

"You bitch," she spat as Eli put his arms around her neck and hugged her tight. "I trusted you!"

Cassie glared at her. "He's a Metaxas. You have no right to withhold him from the family."

Gina was trembling all over. But she had her baby, and she held him tight, her hand on the back of his head. She wasn't letting him go again. Cassie reached for Eli, but Gina stepped back, bumping into the big man as she did so. She didn't care. The man's hands went to her arms, steadying her.

Stavros said something in Greek. Cassie answered, her eyes flashing, and Gina wondered that she'd not realized before how much her nanny despised her. Ten months, and she'd never known. The look Cassie gave her was filled with hatred. It shocked her.

"You sent those threats to me, didn't you?" She thought back to Cassie's schedule and realized that the letters always arrived after her nanny took a long weekend. How difficult would it have been for her to mail them from wherever she'd traveled to?

"You had no idea. It was fun watching you after you got them."

"You said you wanted me dead. I've never done anything to you."

Cassie sneered. "No, you just thought you were the most perfect princess. So entitled, so rich and beautiful. You always get your way, Gina, but I wanted you to know you weren't any better than the rest of us. You weren't going to get away with keeping Eli from his family."

"Go check on the car," Stavros ordered, and Cassie turned and walked away while Gina's stomach churned. She'd had no idea her nanny hated her so much. All that time, that poisonous woman was caring for Eli, and she'd had no clue. She gripped her baby tighter.

Please, God. Please let us get out of here.

The man holding Gina pushed her forward. She took two steps—and the interior lights went out, plunging them into utter darkness.

Stavros yelled. Someone grabbed her and pushed her back inside the room she'd just come from. A second later, there was a light. The big man had turned on the light app on his phone. Stavros pulled a gun from inside his jacket. The other man already had his weapon out. There was no noise but the sound of Gina's heart filling her ears with its relentless pounding.

"We're too late," Stavros grated. "They're coming."

Gina prayed it was Jack and his team coming for her. He had to be alive. Had to be, or she didn't know what she would do.

There was a crunch outside the door. Stavros whipped her back against his body, his gun pressing into her temple. She held Eli's head down against her shoulder, determined to protect him even if Stavros shot her. She wouldn't let her baby die. There was no way she would let that happen.

Everything was so silent and still. The big man crept toward the door, sliding up against the wall to hide himself from whomever came through. There was a tall plant near the door, and he would be completely hidden if he stayed behind it. Except that he didn't shut down his light. That was the one thing he didn't do, and it gave her hope. If Jack knew where to target, he could save her. She knew he could.

And then the light went out and the room was plunged into darkness once more.

TWENTY-NINE

JACK RUSHED DOWN THE HALLWAY on silent feet, flashlight sweeping the territory in front of him, Sig in his hand and ready to fire. He knew the room Gina had been in. He'd studied the schematic of the house on the way over, as they all had, and he'd counted the windows. It was the library and he knew exactly how many steps it would take to get there. She'd stepped away from the window before the lights went out, but even if she'd been moved, they wouldn't have gotten far.

He and Brandy reached the door. They looked at each other, and then Brandy kicked the door in. It swung open on silent hinges and crashed into something. But Jack's attention was on the man standing in the center of the room. He had a gun to Gina's head. Gina was holding Eli, who'd started to scream.

Metaxas ducked his head behind Gina's, but he didn't remove the gun from her temple. Fucking coward.

Gina kept cutting her eyes to the left, to the left, and Jack got that someone was there. Brandy got it too. They had to time this just right or Gina was dead. In that moment, watching her standing there with a gun to her head and tears falling down her cheeks, he knew that losing her would destroy him.

He couldn't go through it again. Losing Hayley had nearly killed him, but this time he'd be done for. He'd been lucky enough to be loved by two incredible women in his life. And he loved them both with all the passion he had in him. Hayley was gone, but Gina was here. And he wasn't letting her go.

"I'll kill her if you don't drop the guns."

"If you kill her," Jack said, his voice deadly calm, "I'm killing you. No second chances, Metaxas. Keeping her alive is your only hope."

"If I can't have her, you aren't getting her either," Stavros said. And then he laughed, the sound so unbalanced that it sent a chill down Jack's spine.

Gina was trembling, but her mouth was set in a determined line. Eli was crying louder now, and she kept him pressed to her, his head on her shoulder. But she wouldn't be able to do it for much longer. He would start struggling, and if she moved, Metaxas's finger might slip on the trigger.

Jack had to take the shot. It was risky, because Metaxas was hiding behind Gina, but he had to peek around her head from time to time to see them. And that's when Jack had to fire, in that split second that Metaxas was visible. If this were a distance shot, he'd have to fire before Metaxas moved. But it wasn't, and the bullet would travel faster than the man could duck.

"We can make a deal, Stavros," Jack said. "Take it easy and listen to what I have to say."

The man snorted. "I'm not dealing with you. I have

friends here, powerful friends, and you're going to regret this—"

Stavros moved, his head barely peeking around Gina's—

And Jack took the shot. Over Gina's shoulder, so close to her neck she would have powder burns, so close that if she moved at all, the bullet would hit her too.

But she didn't, and Metaxas dropped. At the same time, Brandy pivoted into the room and fired at the man who'd been hiding. He fell with a thump and Jack lowered the light so Gina wouldn't be blinded by it as he rushed into the room to take her and Eli into his arms.

She was cold and shivering, and Eli was sobbing. But he couldn't let them go. He buried his head against her neck.

"I'm sorry, babe, so sorry I had to do that."

"I… I…" She sucked in a breath and he steered her over to the couch and sat her down on it. She shifted Eli and he lay down on the cushions and threw a fit.

Richie, Big Mac, and Iceman came into the room, guns drawn.

"Hostages rescued. Target neutralized," Matt said into his mic.

Mendez would get that report in short order. The lights flickered and popped back on, and Jack moved to shield Gina from seeing Stavros on the floor, his head lying in a pool of blood.

Gina looked up, her eyes glassy. "You came for me. I knew you would."

Jack sank down on one knee and slid his hand against her cheek, cupping her beautiful face. Her skin was soft, and his was callused. But she didn't flinch. "I'll always come for you, babe. Always."

"I know you will."

He'd almost lost her. "But do you know why?"

Her gaze dropped from his. Her body was still trembling, but he knew she was trying hard to regulate it. "No." Her voice was barely a whisper.

Maybe he shouldn't say this now, with the guys here and two dead men on the floor, but he couldn't hold it back any longer. He'd almost lost her, and that changed a man's perspective. "Because I love you, Gina. I love *you*. Even if you lose all your money and grow a wart on your nose, I love you. And I love Eli, too. You got that?"

Her head snapped up, her eyes wide. "Do you really mean it?"

It killed him that she could even ask, but he knew why she did. She'd given him every chance and he'd told her he didn't know how he felt. Well, that was bullshit. He knew exactly how he felt.

"Yeah, I mean it. In fact, I'm refusing to marry you until you make me sign a prenup. I get nothing if I don't love you forever."

"You want to marry me? I thought you were still mad at me." And then she tilted her head to look at him sideways, her forehead scrunching up. "Jack, did you get hit on the head?"

Someone snorted, and he turned to glare at them. He was putting his heart on the line here, and they were all watching. Nosy bastards.

"Well, as a matter of fact, I did," he said, fingering the knot on his head. "But that's not the reason I want to marry you. I want to marry you because you and Eli belong with me. Because I love you both and I'm not letting you go ever again. Yeah, I was pissed, but I'm over it. The future is the important thing here, not the past. I wasn't ready, but now I am. For you. For Eli. For us."

Eli burrowed into her side, sniffling as his fit petered out, and she put her arm around him, running it up and down his little back. She was perfect. Eli was perfect. He'd gotten so lucky when he'd rescued her the first time. So damn lucky.

A single tear spilled down Gina's cheek as she put her free hand on his wrist where he was still cupping her face. She leaned forward and pressed her mouth lightly to his. "I love you too, Jack. And you can have everything you want, but I refuse to make you sign an agreement. We'll just have to trust each other, okay?"

"Gina, I don't want anyone ever saying—"

She put a finger over his lips. "Shh. I trust you, Jack. Always."

"And I trust you," he said when she finally let him speak.

"Then kiss me to seal the deal."

When the guys took Gina outside, she saw they had Cassie with a group of men they'd disarmed and made kneel with their hands over their heads. Cassie didn't look up as they passed by, but Gina trembled with fury. She'd trusted Cassie, liked her, but Cassie was a Metaxas and she'd lied, threatened Gina, and stole her baby.

Gina's blood pulsed hotly through her veins. She wanted to punch something, preferably Cassie. She ground to a halt and stood there breathing hard.

"Babe?"

She looked up at Jack. He was watching her carefully, his eyes vivid blue against the greasepaint on his face.

"I can't let her get away with this."

"She won't."

Eli held on to Gina's neck tightly.

"Not good enough." She turned and marched over to where Cassie knelt. "Eli is *not* a Metaxas. You wasted your time because he belongs to that man right there." She nodded toward Jack. "Three years ago, he saved my life... and Eli is the result. You were just too stupid to see it. Remember that when you're in prison—you did it for *nothing.*"

Cassie looked up, fear and uncertainty in her eyes. Gina almost took a step back, the transformation was so shocking. "He made me do it, Gina. I had to or he would have hurt me. Hurt my family. Please, please don't do this to me. I'm sorry. I would have never hurt Eli. I love him."

Gina lashed out and slapped the other woman hard across the face, causing Cassie's head to snap back and her eyes to blaze with fresh hatred. "How dare you? You can't manipulate me anymore, so don't even try. I trusted you, but never again. You can rot in prison for all I care."

She turned and went back to Jack, who was frowning. Cassie started screaming, calling Gina every name she could think of, but Gina didn't turn around again. She was done feeling sorry for Cassie.

Jack put his hand on her back, his touch comforting and firm. She needed that right now. He didn't say anything, just ushered her away from the scene. Once again, he was there for her, giving her precisely what she needed.

When the door had burst open, she hadn't been able to see who it was because of the bright light shining on her, but she'd known in her gut that it was Jack.

And she'd been right. He'd dropped Stavros with deadly accuracy, though for as long as she lived she was never going to forget the hot whoosh of that bullet as it passed by her cheek. He'd shot Stavros, and he'd freed her and Eli. She loved him so much.

"There's going to be paperwork and reports tonight," he said when they stopped by the van that had arrived. "I don't know how long it will take."

"I want to go with you, Jack."

"You can't, babe. But you can go stay with Evie, if that's okay. After that, I'll take you back to the hotel."

She shook her head. "I'll go to Evie's, but then I want to go home with you. Your home, Jack."

"You know it's not much to look at."

"Home is where you are. Don't you get that by now?"

His smile made her heart break. "Yeah, I get it."

She hefted Eli up. He was getting heavier the longer she held him.

"Let me take him." Jack took their son, and Eli put his head on his father's shoulder as if being held by a grease-painted, dark-clothed man bristling with weaponry and high-tech military equipment was a normal, everyday occurrence.

"I'm sorry for what I said earlier," Gina told him. "Before I ran away."

"It's already forgotten, Gina. I was a dick to you, and you were hurt." He blew out a breath. "But I'll make it clear here and now that there is no choice but you. If I have to give something up, it's not going to be you."

She stepped in and slid her arm around him. "I don't want you to give anything up. I want you to be happy."

"So long as I have you, that's enough."

They were soon separated. Mendez arrived and sent a HOT support member to take Gina and Eli to Matt and Evie's place. Evie hugged her, and they took Eli to the guest bed and placed him there. Then, because Gina was too keyed up to sleep, they went back into the kitchen and shared some wine and girl talk. Gina liked the other woman so much. She'd never felt comfortable sharing things with other women, but she found herself telling Evie things that surprised her.

Hours later, when Gina had fallen asleep beside Eli, Jack came and got her. He took her and a sleeping Eli back to his apartment, where he carried Eli inside and laid him on the couch. Gina tucked a blanket around him and sank onto the floor to push his golden curls off his face. When she looked up at Jack, he was watching them both with such an intense expression on his face that her heart melted.

"I want you very much right now," he said, "but if you want to take him to bed with us, we will."

She stood and put her hand on his cheek. "I never want to let him out of my sight again, quite honestly. I don't know what I would have done if I'd lost him."

Jack kissed her forehead. "You don't have to worry about that. He's safe. You're both safe. No one is coming for you ever again."

"I know." She looked down at Eli. He'd flopped onto his back and was completely out. Her heart filled with love. And with the certainty that Jack was right. They were safe here with him, and no one would harm them. She put her hand into Jack's and he led her into his room.

He undressed her carefully, kissing his way over her body, his fingers following his mouth and making her ache and tremble and want. By the time he was inside her, his body rocking into hers slowly and deliciously, she was a mess of emotion and desire.

"Jack," she gasped as he moved. "I love you so much, so much…"

"Yes," he said, his mouth on her throat, "need you… love you… only you…"

She sobbed when she came, and he buried his mouth against her neck, groaning her name as he followed her over the edge.

She was almost shy when he levered off her and pulled her against him. They'd done this before, and yet it was so new and raw now, and she kept waiting for it to hurt somehow.

"I'm leaving HOT," he said quietly after a few moments, and she pushed herself up to stare down at him, not quite certain she'd heard him right.

"What? Why?"

"It won't happen immediately. I'm still enlisted, and I have a few months to go yet. But I'm not re-upping. I got a better offer."

She blinked. "I… okay. Where?"

He frowned. "Don't tell me you forgot. A million dollars to guard a delicious pop star? How could a guy say no, especially when the perks are so good?"

"Oh, that offer."

"Aw, fuck, am I too late? Did you fill the position already?"

She couldn't help but laugh. "No, of course not. But are you sure, Jack? Really sure?" Because if he was unhappy leaving his team for her, she wouldn't be able to stand it.

"I love what I do, but nothing says I can't start my own security firm. Maybe I will." He shrugged. "Sometimes the military is a bit confining. If I ran my own team, I could do things my way."

She sank down on him again, pillowing her head against his chest. "Is that something you've thought of?"

He twisted a finger in her hair. "Hell, I think we've all thought of it. Mendez worked long and hard to get us where we are now, but even here we have limitations. Oh, the funding is top-notch, but the red tape can sometimes be pretty tangled."

"Who would you get to join you?"

"Some of the guys would come on board, I think. I'd find others."

"But you have a while to think about it."

"Yeah."

She found herself tracing her fingers over the ink on his side, following the loops and dips of Hayley's name.

"Does that bother you?" he asked after a few moments and she realized that he knew what she was doing.

"No." She could say that truthfully now. It *had* bothered her, but now that she knew he loved her, it didn't. Because Hayley was a part of him, and she accepted that. She tilted her head back to look up at him. "Would you think I was crazy if I said I sometimes think she sent you to me?"

He was quiet when he spoke. "No, I wouldn't."

She bent and kissed the name on his skin. "I thought she was keeping you from loving me, but I don't think that anymore."

"I was scared, babe. Still am, but you're worth the risk."

She crawled up his body until she could press her lips to his. "So are you."

His fingers tangled in her hair, his tongue plunging into her mouth. It didn't take long for them to get hot again, and then she sank down on him and rode him until their bodies were slick with sweat and the pleasure was so intense she didn't ever want it to end.

"Goddamn," he said when it was over and she collapsed against him. "I think I died and went to heaven."

"Mmm, not yet," she said. "Soon, though, if we keep this up."

"Yeah, but what a way to go."

"I think that's going to be the title of my next song."

"What is?"

"What a way to go. I'll extol the virtues of your penis, of course, and then the whole world will be singing about you."

He snorted. "Sounds like a hit."

"It will be."

He pushed her hair back and looked at her, his brows drawn low. "You're kidding, right?"

"Maybe I'm not. The world should know about your penis, Jack. It's my solemn duty as an artist to make art when I'm inspired."

He stared at her for a full minute. And then he laughed. "It's going to be interesting with you, isn't it?"

"Oh, yeah," she said, grinning. "You just wait and

see…"

EPILOGUE

Two months later…
Eastern Shore, Maryland

JACK KISSED HIS BRIDE WHILE everyone clapped and cheered. He didn't want to let her go, but they were pulled apart when everyone rushed forward to congratulate them. He caught Gina's eyes over the crowd and nearly laughed at her shrug. Yeah, he wanted to be alone with her, but they'd invited their friends—Mendez and the team, and Barry and his boyfriend—and they couldn't disappear.

He let his gaze wander over the grounds of the house they'd bought. It was close to Waterman's Cove, but not too close, and of course it was big and expensive. Which really meant that Gina had bought it, but that didn't bother him in the least since she'd refused to buy a thing until he'd agreed it was perfect.

Which he would have done several houses ago if he'd known that's what she was waiting for. But, really, this one *was* perfect, so maybe it was a good thing he hadn't caught on.

Eli had been the ring bearer, and he'd done a good job of it. He was sitting in the grass, staining his white shorts and playing with the tiny dog Barry had carried in with a big pink bow around its neck. Jack had glared and told Barry he was taking the dog back out again when he left. Barry had shrugged, and Gina'd laughed.

Jesus, he was going to be walking a tiny dog on a pink leash before this was all over with. Someone handed Jack a beer and he took it. He didn't want to think about walking a pocket dog right now.

"Man, you are one lucky dude," Flash said.

Brandy nodded. "If only I'd taken the route through the forest that night. I could be the one with a sugar mama!"

Jack punched him in the arm, but it wasn't a serious blow. "You wouldn't have stood a chance with her, so forget it."

A few feet away, the women were laughing and talking. The rest of the guys walked over to where Jack and the others stood. Even Mendez had let down the formality for a change, though none would dare to call him anything but sir.

It had been a helluva couple of months since they'd rescued Gina and killed Stavros. Mendez had been pissed that night because he'd put out a call to all the intelligence services for information on Metaxas after the mission to rescue Eli. If Metaxas was alive, they should have known about it. But someone up the chain had countermanded that order, and he'd only learned about Metaxas being alive and in DC that night. It had almost been too late, and Jack was still fucking pissed that someone had put Gina in danger like that.

If he ever found out who it was, he'd consider putting a bullet in their brain as well. But so far, the identity of that person remained hidden behind red tape. It had put a damper on Mendez's attitude for a while now. Stavros Metaxas had been an arms dealer, but he'd hidden that business behind a legitimate shipping business, just as his brother had done. And he'd made friends in Washington, though right now no one was admitting to that friendship. And why would they? The man had been in the midst of a red-hot deal to sell arms to terrorists.

"There's intel from Qu'rim," Mendez said, and everyone perked up. "Someone's pulling the strings in the Freedom Force again."

"Fuck," Kev said, shooting a glance toward his wife, who was laughing with the other women. After all Lucky had gone through to put an end to those fuckers, Jack didn't blame him. "Y'all should have let me kill the motherfucker when we had the chance."

"It's not Al Ahmad. He's on a rock with no comm in or out that's not monitored. It's someone else." Mendez took a sip of his beer. "Nothing major yet, but I think we aren't quite done with them after all."

"Shit," Iceman said. The rest of the guys grumbled their agreement.

"At least we stopped Metaxas from selling arms to them."

"Yeah, but someone else will do it. It's only a matter of time."

"Saw your face on the cover of the *Enquirer*," Flash said. "You've reached new heights of fame, man."

Jack shifted his stance. Yeah, that was the part of being with Gina he didn't like, but he was dealing with it. The fact that the hottest pop star in the world was seeing a regular guy was big news and the media couldn't get enough. For now, Mendez kept him shielded. As soon as he crossed the security barrier of the base, he was outside the media's grasp, which certainly made things much easier. They knew he worked for the government, but they had no idea what he did. And they weren't going to find out.

Gina had announced to the world that Eli was his child. He'd hated that violation of their privacy, but it was necessary in case any other members of the Metaxas family had ideas about Eli's parentage. He'd called his parents before it happened and told them personally. His father had congratulated him. His mother cried. They'd come to visit Eli, and Jack had watched as the busy people he'd grown up with turned into the kind of grandparents who acted like the kid was the most fascinating thing in the world.

Which he was, but Jack hadn't expected his parents to care. It was oddly touching that they did. No, his relationship with them wouldn't ever be perfect, but he was learning to accept that.

The guys drank their beers and looked at the women. Mendez had taken him aside earlier and told him he didn't have any news on Gina's sister, but he wasn't finished working his contacts yet. Maybe one day Jack would be able to give her some good news. He hoped so with all his heart. She'd made friends with the fiancées and wives of the other guys, but he knew she would love to find her sister too.

After a while, Jack felt a tug on his trousers. He looked down to find a pint-sized toddler standing there, one little arm held skyward.

"Daddy," Eli said. "Up, Daddy."

Jack bent and scooped his son up, love rushing through him, warming him all over. God, he was a lucky man. Gina's eyes met his again, and he tipped his beer in a salute. She blew him a kiss.

"Who is the luckiest man on earth right this minute, buddy?" Jack asked Eli.

"Me!" Eli crowed.

"Yeah, okay, I can accept that. But I'm next in line."

He carried his son over to his wife and put his arm around her. She hugged him back and Jack sighed. He had something to show her later. He'd gone just this morning and had her name and Eli's inked on his skin near his heart. He hoped she liked it.

"Is it everything you thought it would be?" he asked her.

She looked up. "Which part?"

"You. Me. Marriage."

She laughed. "We've been married for half an hour."

"Yeah, and it's been perfect, hasn't it?"

"Oh yes. Every moment with you is perfect, Jack."

"Because you make me better, Gina. That's all there is to it."

Eli wriggled as the puppy galloped by and Jack set him down.

Gina sighed. "He's dirty."

"Mmm, I'm dirty too."

She laughed. "Tell me something I didn't know."

"I'd rather show you."

"Think we can sneak off for a few minutes?"

"A few minutes? Babe, don't you know I need hours

with you?"

She squeezed him tight. "Good thing you've got forever then."

He dipped his head to kiss her as hot emotion flooded
him. "I do, don't I?"

ACKNOWLEDGMENTS

AS ALWAYS, THERE ARE PEOPLE to thank. I couldn't do this series without Mr. Harris, who keeps me as straight as possible on military stuff (though I take liberties as necessary for the story). I've said it before and I'll say it again: a real military Special Operations team wouldn't have as much freedom as my guys have. But my world, my rules, right?

Gretchen Stull has proven to be not only the World's Most Wonderful Assistant, but also an amazing (and lightning fast) beta-reader.

With the very first cover in this series, Frauke Spanuth created an outstanding brand that readers know immediately, and she quite possibly outdid herself this time. I don't know how she finds the perfect photos, but she always does. And then she makes magic!

Jean Hovey and Stephanie Jones, aka Alicia Hunter Pace, are always there for brainstorming and general listening when I need to complain or whine. They also enjoy a good hockey game, which thrills Mr. Harris to no end.

Anne Victory is not only a great copy editor, but she's also become a friend. She cracks me up with her witty remarks peppered throughout the manuscript. If there are editing mistakes in this book, it's very likely because I failed to change something she told me to change. It happens.

Thanks to wonderful friends and indie authors Kathleen Brooks, Ruth Cardello, Melody Anne, and Sandra Marton, who encourage me on this path and who are always there to answer questions or just hang out when we're at conferences together. You ladies make everything so fun!

As always, thanks to my readers. You make writing this series a blast! I hope you love Jack and Gina as much as I do—and stay tuned, because there's another story coming soon…

ABOUT THE AUTHOR

USA Today bestselling author Lynn Raye Harris lives in Alabama with her handsome former-military husband and two crazy cats. Lynn has written nearly twenty novels for Harlequin and been nominated for several awards, including the Romance Writers of America's Golden Heart award and the National Readers Choice award. Lynn loves hearing from her readers.

Connect with me online:
Facebook: https://www.facebook.com/AuthorLynnRayeHarris
Twitter: https://twitter.com/LynnRayeHarris
Website: http://www.LynnRayeHarris.com
Email: lynn@lynnrayeharris.com

Join my Hostile Operations Team Readers and Fans Group on Facebook:
https://www.facebook.com/groups/HOTReadersAndFans/